Taking a
CHANCE

Sprats To Catch Mackerels

Lesley M Francis

Matador
9 Priory Business Park,
Wistow Road, Kibworth Beauchamp,
Leicestershire. LE8 0RX
Tel: 0116 279 2299
Email: books@troubador.co.uk
Web: www.troubador.co.uk/matador
Twitter: @matadorbooks

ISBN 978 1785890 215

British Library Cataloguing in Publication Data.
A catalogue record for this book is available from the British Library.

Printed and bound by CPI Group (UK) Ltd, Croydon, CR0 4YY
Typeset in 11pt Minion Pro by Troubador Publishing Ltd, Leicester, UK

Matador is an imprint of Troubador Publishing Ltd

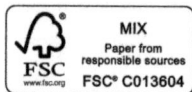

For Pat

Overture

*Trust her to die happy! Just lying there in bed – all tranquil –
not a care in the world – smiling sweetly too like she's taking
a refreshing nap. Listening to the heavenly choir no doubt!
And another thing, that's a real smile… Well, anyway, it's not
the usual allure-free rictus she pins on – the one that's about
as soothing as a 'Jolly Roger' suddenly hoisted on the only
lifeboat responding to your Mayday call.*

*You'll have to excuse me. Not the moment for levity, is it?
But along the way I seem to have developed an overwhelming
urge to joke in the face of shock or fear. Shouting back at
the devil I call it – giving as good as I get. That kinda thing.
Softens the blow a tad I find.*

*Now let's have a closer look-see. Her eyes are closed,
mouth slightly open. Yes – all soft, eager surrender. And trace
of exultation too? Yeah, definitely… more than a trace at that.
Well, she never did have any shame.*

*Always thought she'd outlive us all – go on for ever like
she was immortal! Well, how wrong can you be? Stone cold
dead – and no return of any kind.*

*Me? I'm doing nothing but gaze at her – and what's more,
she can't get mad at me for doing it. So now I won't end up
saying the wrong thing as usual; upset the apple cart, let slip
the dogs of war, catch the tiger by its tail. It's the same old tiger
all right – but with a different tale this time. Can't catch me!*

*Seriously though, is it because her face is immobile? I
mean, years ago I was used to seeing her looking beautiful, but*

never quite like this! What's the word here? Transcendental? Yeah, that's it! That's the one. Makes me feel, well, reverential – like I'm in the presence something almost holy. It's also like being held in the unreality of one of those soothing dream sequences when you don't particularly want to wake up. Know what I mean?

Mind you, try to recall relaxing in the presence of this particular celestial being, or even approaching it, without fear-restricted breathing and that primal urge to flee, then I run smack into a hard place. So no, apart from a few treasured occasions, that just about sums up my normal reaction.

Normal? Is "normal" a word I should be looking for here? Normal and Ada? I don't think so! And I should know – none better. Spent a lifetime trying to anticipate her delinquent moves, guess what horror of embarrassment lay in ambush – waiting to spring on the unwary. And I always was – unwary, I mean – 'spite of the warnings of bitter experience.

Well, that's all over now. That's why, for the very first time unchecked, I'm at liberty to study my mother's face.

And I'll tell you something else – I'm just plain hopping mad at her! Why was it always so easy for her to manipulate me? I wouldn't say I was particularly dim, but she's managed it right to the end. Always had to have her own way – and big stupid me – ever ready to accommodate!

Well, I didn't ought to stand here all day gaping at her. Time to face reality I guess.

Naa. Slow down an itty-bit. Who wants reality just yet? Why not ignore it a bit longer, eh? After all, she spent her whole life doing just that, so why shouldn't I – just this once? I'm in no rush for reality anyway. Not me! Only too well acquainted with the pain that particular thug brings to a party.

Seems like hours since I let myself in here. What's the

time? Nope, it's only just past eight. Five minutes – that's all it's taken!

This is first of my twice-daily visits – thankless fixtures in my life when I attempt to bring order into the chaos that was hers. Was? My God! That's going to take some getting used to… although it's funny how easy it slips off the tongue… Hmm, yes, well, least said about that, the better.

Bring order to her chaos did I say? What a joke! What a sad, sick joke! She'd always recreate havoc soon as I left – probably out of spite. Don't really know. Never going to now. Yeah, but I can make an educated guess can't I?

Not that I care very much anyway – never have. To grab a cliché off the peg, she might have been a monster, but she was my monster. Makes all the difference, doesn't it? Well, doesn't it? Mother and daughter. Only survivors of our little family. Never had any sisters – brothers long dead – father too. So, with perversity that defies all logic, I've clung to her. Blood of my blood, bone of my bone.

Yes, I know! Could have left when I was young. Should have done really, you know, embraced my own fate – left her to… whatever. Instead I became a workhorse. Always carrying the weight of her life – in tandem with my own where possible – but always my life for hers. And I wouldn't be minding so much if it was just my life she messed up.

All our birthdays, anniversaries, high days, holidays – waiting for the usual frantic phone call – mixture of alarm, pathos and arrogant command. 'My electricity has all gone out! I can't even make a cup of tea! You'll have to come and sort it out for me! I can do absolutely nothing… don't even know where to start.'

'Calm down, Mother – I expect it's something quite simple. We'll be with you as soon as possible. We're having a party. It's Geoff's birthday… he's forty. We've got friends round.'

'What does he want with birthday parties at his age? In any case, how on earth can it be something simple? Everything's off, I say! Just get here. And don't tell me to calm down either! Who do you think you're talking to?'

Blow out the candles, my darling, no point wishing for anything different. No point upsetting myself either now – it's too late for that – and really, I can't say I've any lasting regrets. Couldn't have lived with myself if I'd… No – no! I'd do it all again. But different! Huh! Wouldn't we all?

Right – that's it! Dream-time over! I'm getting angry – and it's just so much wasted emotion. Why's her death such a shock anyway? Not as though it's unexpected. She's been poorly for ages. No need to go all of a wotsit. There must be something to do round here – there always is! Let's have a deco.

Blimey – it looks odd. Tidy!

Few stray cups to clear and wash up. That's it. Put everything in it's place. Hang the wiping-up cloth on its hook. Carpet to vacuum? Mmm? Maybe not… there's no mess – not even round her chair! So – just her tablets to put away then. No need to lock the medicine cupboard this time. Right, that's yer lot!

Now. Let's have a look at her. What can we do? Mmm. Tuck in the bedding, plump up the pillows – make her more comfy. Brush back those wisps of hair from her face. Brrr! My God, she's dead all right! Her make-up's on the dressing table – just where she left it. She'd hate to be seen without it. S'pose she ought to look her best for the doctor. Don't fancy touching her again, though! Besides, I'm not the artist she was.

CHICKEN!

Oh, all right then! Do my best. Bit of lippy – perhaps some blush. Eye shadow? Ugh! Cold. Still, got to make her drop-dead gorgeous – if you'll pardon the expression. I mean to say, can't let her down now, can I? After all, it's her last act! Time to take a bow, Mother.

Now. What's the time? Just gone half past. Got calls to make.

'Hello, this is Mrs Phillips' daughter – could you ask Dr Chapman to come round when he has a moment. I can't wake her up. Thanks.'

'Hello, Mandy, it's Imogen – I'm with Mother. Won't be in today I'm afraid – tell Maggie for me. Thanks.'

Surgery and office – both know my situation. There are no questions.

Oh, well, may as well make myself comfy while I wait. Mmm, lov-er-ly soft chair! My, it's nice here by the window in the sunshine.

Y'know, it's occurred to me I must be unique! Well, fairly singular anyway. No one else I know has actually welcomed the advance of senility in an elderly relative.

All that confusion – short-term memory loss – strange inexplicable behaviour. Just part of the landscape, isn't it?

There's sympathy and understanding for an identifiable, recognisable condition. There's comparing experiences, 'Ah yes, our poor old dad… did just the same – nearly drove us all mad!' Bonding with similarly afflicted relatives – supporting each other in nonplussed camaraderie. Part of a group. Accepted – acceptable – anonymous… Wonderful!

Oh, yes! Ada's condition towards the end of her life was understandable all right – and acceptable too. But during a lifetime of eccentric behaviour she stabbed and killed her husband, my father, with the seven-inch blade of a kitchen knife – and let me tell you, there's not much group empathy to be gotten out of that little lot!

Official records claim logical mitigation for such seeming violence. Oh, yes, perfectly logical!

Official records be damned! You want the truth? It's so bizarre, so outlandish, as to be beyond the wildest imagination, so don't try guessing! At first, only Ada knew her precious secret – lived and died thinking she was alone and safe with it. Well, she was always safe, but gradually I managed to piece together all the weird and disparate details – and so, God help me, I also held the macabre key.

That knowledge took me right up Shit Creek, then left me all on my own in a leaky canoe – without an exit strategy!

I'm getting mad again! Take deep breaths. Calm – calm. That's better. Now where was I before I got carried away? Oh, yes, I remember…

Mother's great mystery.

May as well say it outright. Ada had a secret lover! Yep, one glance exchanged with Charlie Elrington well over thirty years ago, and she was lost – suspended in time and space.

Coincidentally, that moment, which stayed with her in vivid immediacy for the rest of her life, also banished over fifteen years of marriage, home, husband and two young children. They dwindled into insignificance as he became the only love of her life. Not even the over-abundance of her self-love, came anywhere near.

In a way I can just about understand her falling for that lovely man, in spite of my dad being what he was – handsome, intelligent, sweet-natured – and in addition, a man with a lifetime's ambition to pander to her every whim. But the consistent, obsessive quality of her ruthless self-serving – where on earth did that come from? It's always had me completely baffled – I mean, no one's born that way, are they? So at what stage in her development did it begin?

ACT ONE

One

'That's a truculent little madam – and bad tempered too! You mark my words, you're going to have your work cut out as she gets older. I never met a child more determined to have its own way. And flighty with it!'

Ada's grandmother and namesake glared at the eighteen-month-old, who glared right on back – eyeball to eyeball.

'I tried to get her father's fountain pen off her – she'll be covered in ink before we know anything. She's just hit me with it – look, there's a dark red mark on my hand now! Naughty – and wilful, that's what she is!'

'Oh, Grannie – how can you say such dreadful things? There, darling, Mummy's got a sweetie; I'll swap it for Daddy's pen. There's a good ickle girly-whirly!'

Granny's blood pressure soared. Stratospheric – outer space – missed lunar landing – Jupiter here I come!

'Things have changed since my day – and not for the better. Girly-whirly indeed! You and Arthur must be more firm with her – let her know who's in charge. The pair of you are just spoiling her. I tell you, she'll bring us all to grief if you don't watch out!'

Hastily gathering her belongings, the old lady swept off to the sanity of her own home where she promptly suffered a stroke and snuffed it – as if to prove a point.

Granny's only legacy for ickle Ada was a lifetime's retribution in the name she would grow up despising as old fashioned and unrefined.

Hard to dispute Grannie's verdict either – stubborn, self-willed, given to aggression if all else failed. And let's not forget 'flighty with it'. Even those for whom ickle Ada was the pivot of existence found it hard to avoid this particular 'F' word – industriously inventing an ever-lengthening stream of excuses for hurtful, careless behaviour.

They had long since given up hope of such a blessing and as both parents were over forty, both in gainful employment (she teaching, he in the higher ranks of the Inland Revenue), they enjoyed that gratuitous compensation for childlessness – a heavily pregnant bank balance. Consequently, when their precious, late lamb arrived, every indulgence was lavished on the child. They became her willing slaves as she grew up indolent, frivolous – a wilful, scatter-brained dreamer – she who must be obeyed!

Accustomed to inspiring love in her world of adults, she rapidly discovered charm could effortlessly win the day. Honed to warm perfection, it became her favoured means to an end. She found all reservations regarding reprehensible conduct soon dispelled as the world became her plaything. Growing older, she never for one moment questioned this gift, using it shamelessly to gain any objective – however extraneous – just for the hell of it!

When Henry Phillips met her in the autumn of 1938 she was nearly twenty-three years old, lovely, fascinating – but, for some obscure reason starting to feel mildly apprehensive about her shelf life – bored to death with a seemingly endless line of admirers anyway. Immediately, he was helplessly floundering under her spell. And Ada? Well, she made up her mind to razzle-dazzle the poor sap, seizing the opportunity to break free from a love-stifled home life – try something new – something exciting – something unpredictable.

Once in love, he continued to worship at her altar until the day he died. Ada just fell in love with free-falling. The future – her future – suddenly exciting, was wrapped in nebulous, fairy-tale romance!

Only her mother had reservations. 'Are you absolutely sure about him, my sweet?'

'He's the most good-looking man I've ever seen, Mummy. So romantic… '

'Yes, darling, but do you love him?'

Ada laughed. 'Well, if you can tell me how it feels to love, maybe I could answer that.'

'Do you think you could spend the rest of your life with him then?

'Of course I can. I couldn't bear to be without him!'

'Then there's nothing more to say, is there?'

Cosseted, over-protected Ada – the average four-year-old more worldly-wise – her ignorance-based over-self-confidence failed to recognise that pleasurable frisson generated by his company emanated from her own inadequacy. Instead she experienced pleasing novelty, appealing to the inner girly-whirly. Made her go weak at the knees!

In addition to his physical attractions he was, although only three years older, light years ahead in experience – and he led such an exciting life! Even better, it was a life that could easily accommodate her – that is, with the help of her parents' ever-open moneybags!

A young man busy establishing himself as a violinist of some considerable talent, he opened up a whole new world of experience to ickle Ada as she accompanied him to concerts in London and the provinces.

Should he take lead, she would loudly point him out to her neighbours as her exclusive property, 'He's my fiancé you know! Isn't he just brilliant?' Sharing his limelight to a chorus of indignant but unheeded shushing.

After the performance, late parties, with many a romantic rendezvous tête-à-tête in exclusive restaurants that cost him more than he could afford.

'Marry me?'

The following May, she became his wife and the new couple set up home in a village just north of Oxford in the house that was her parents' wedding present.

Two

'I'm going to enlist. Army. Got to do my bit.'

'But, darling, what's the rush? We don't know if there's going to be a war.'

'Oh, yes, we do! I may as well go now rather than wait to be called up. This way I'll have a bit more choice – maybe train as an officer.'

'What about us? We've only been married for a few weeks.'

'I know, my love. I wouldn't go if I didn't feel I must, but it probably won't last long – not like last time.'

* * *

During the next six years or so their meetings were loving and sexually explosive – friendliest of fire resulting in two notable victories.

The first, Robin, arrived in the bleak of February 1940, fruit of a joyfully uninhibited honeymoon that deliciously shocked Henry – barely satisfying a gratefully liberated Ada. The girl, result of unexpected leave, was called Imogen after the daughter of Henry's favourite composer Gustav Holst ('People don't realise, he wrote so much more than *The Planets* suite!') had the good grace to make an entrance favoured by clemency of mid-May two years later.

There's a fondly perceived, but impossible human

condition called *'the perfect mother'* – given Ada's own coddled childhood, she would always lack the selflessness to aspire to such a title.

Even failed to make second billing in the more populous category featuring mums stumbling through maternity's script, desperately trying to get their lines right. Fact is, after both initial productions, she went on to become a complete flop.

Without her husband, poor Ada simply had no idea how to react to these small strangers. A puzzle without a key? Rather than endure unnecessary headaches, she simply lost interest.

Whilst she did manage a species of lukewarm partiality for the girl, on her first-born she lavished a stone-cold nothing. From the start he could do no right – never please. As a result he developed into a diffident, hyper-sensitive child that simply withdrew from human interaction until he found his own sweet sanctuary – an exclusivity that left her stranded on the outside, unaware of lost riches.

With a father absent, he was left, an abandoned infant on the barren hillside of wilful maternal neglect, having to utilise all his resources of stoicism. The expenditure left him vulnerable and where he *did* love, unable to cope with loss or rejection.

It created an estrangement that deprived Ada of her share of filial devotion. Worse still, loss was compounded as affection for her girl child proved to be so much wasted emotion. Doting on her brother, Imogen transferred the mother's share of allegiance to him, giving him all her unconditional love and loyalty, toddling in his wake, anticipating his every need and, much to his chagrin, demanding his rights for him. 'Give it to him. He needs it. He'th a *good* boy!'

At first a matter of infant instinct, as she grew it became conscious determination to protect him from Ada: defend his golden creation of imagination from their mother's desecrating impact. As reward, she was occasionally allowed inside his world to share its unvarnished, untarnished joys. Only on very rare occasions did she spare her mother a backward glance, whilst Robin simply ignored this woman – who should have been his closest friend and confidant.

Three

'Now you listen to me – in case you haven't noticed, we've got two small children, so just tell me how we're supposed to survive financially whilst you re-establish yourself? It'll probably take years. Might never happen.'

Ada was glaring at Henry, voice low, harsh with anger. Never having experienced anything like it from her before, he suddenly understood the future might not be the 'roses all the way' he'd fondly anticipated.

Stuttering, he managed, 'W-well, I was thinking—'

'NO! That's just the trouble – you're *not* thinking. I don't want to hear another word on the subject. You'll have to think again, won't you, dear?' This last word, spoken with a bright smile containing neither sweetness nor humour, chilled him more than her preceding words.

Whilst the Second World War was busy grumbling its way into history and Hollywood celluloid, newly demobilised Henry was coming face to face with the forgotten reality of Civvy Street; reality within which it seemed he would probably have to reinvent himself.

During rare moments when his mind hadn't been filled to overflowing with the misery of the war-torn Europe he'd been sent to help liberate, he had nursed a dream. The dream had been escape – beguiling haven amid the aftermath of moral incontinence with its stench of decomposing humanity and smouldering civilisation – a soothing duality combining his longing for music with the peace of home life. It never occurred to him he couldn't have both!

Throughout the altercation, Ada's unflinching eyes had closely watched her husband's face, gauging every expression. In contrast, his gaze had wandered wildly round the room, seeking any object that might offer sympathy. Ada's cohorts merely stared back in unflinching self-satisfaction. Serenely unaware of any irony, she told him, 'It's about time you thought of others…'

He was weakening!

Go for the kill! Pathos mixed with a little self-pity. 'And what about us? We've been so long without you – I can't bear to think of you leaving us again.'

Had his full attention now! Eyes fixed on her face, he moved towards her.

'My own sweet darling – I'll never leave you again – I promise!'

GOTCHA!

Ever after Henry would recall this encounter with his wife as a 'discussion'. Such civilised definition would pre-suppose an element of accommodation. Love would forever blind him to the fact that there never had been any question of compromise – just termination of his music dream with Ada dotting the 'i's and crossing the 't's.

In one short, decisive engagement he willingly jettisoned half his dreams; dreams of making music he'd heard sweet singing above the chaotic rhythm of battle – music that had told him he would survive. And, so effective was Ada's camouflage, he'd failed to sight any real enemy.

Six years out of the profession. Six years! Insurmountable!

Somehow, within the confusion of emotion that had been his first three hours of home life, the artist that had fought so long for freedom of expression, died a swift, silent, unmourned, unsung death.

'I'll just pop round to see Mother – she must know I've arrived. She'll be wondering where I am.'

'So? She knows where you are. She'll be along soon. Don't go, darling. Don't upset the children. Come on, you two, give Daddy a nice big kiss.' The last thing Ada wanted! His wretched mother exerting influence – spoiling things. But the children hid under the dining table – obstinate – refusing to be *her* ally. What was all this? Who was this *huge* brown adult with the nice smile? *Kiss*? Like with Grandma?

'No, I think I'll go. No need to rush things with them.' He lifted the edge of the tablecloth and winked at the two startled refugees. 'I won't be long.'

As he marched up the street, Ada glared at the two children, who edged further under the table. Then smiling to herself, dismissing annoyance, she sauntered out of the room. Knew she'd won. Could afford to be generous in victory. Time to turn down the bedclothes, choose a nice revealing nightdress. Soon bring him to heel!

The table sighed relief.

* * *

His decision to see his mother so soon stemmed not only from filial devotion (of which there was no shortage) but also contained an uncomfortable element of cowardice. A decision about his career had been reached. He feared her opposition – wanted her understanding – the sooner the better!

He had nothing to fear. After initial joyful greetings – followed by his hurried admission – the old lady threw up her hands in a gesture of contented submission. Just a mother, grateful as mothers are for the safe return of a child from danger.

The prop and dedicated helpmeet of youthful endeavour, who had patiently nurtured his talent (inheritance from a long-dead, still-mourned father) regarded him with tears of pure joy. 'My darling boy – I don't care what you do. You're home! That's all that matters to me.'

As he set off for home he sighed as anti-climax seized the pit of his stomach creating perverse regret, which he immediately condemned as weakness.

He raised his chin as his shoulders went back in reaction. *Bloody rot! Six years! Forget it! Too much. Too much to ask!* He would have needed solid support from Ada. He couldn't blame her. Not him! Poor darling had suffered enough – alone here among the dangers of the home front.

Bombs! Doesn't bear thinking about – and two babies to look after! No, no. My place is here. Thank God there's still a 'here' to come back to. By the time Captain Phillips saw his street in the distance he was marching – and the song in his heart was *Home Sweet Home* as he began to anticipate the delights of his marriage bed after long years of celibacy.

Waiting for his return, knowing the fiddle was now history, Ada remembered with heartfelt regret those carefree times before his wretched enlistment (unable to appreciate any perspective but her own, she always considered this action of her husband's the epitome of selfishness) when she had been free to follow his career, attend performances, share his travel, share his busy life.

Gone! Vanished under a welter of domesticity. More precisely CHILDREN!

'My beautiful angels!' she would gush in company. Privately, their very existence precluded anything worthwhile. She valued them accordingly.

Because of her children, Ada had managed to avoid female war work (the mere idea made her shudder). Now she was trapped in her own charade! But if he'd gone his merry way she would have been abandoned in a domestic backwater to which she was obviously unsuited. Paradoxically, Henry's absence might well have benefited the marriage, after all it had preserved Ada's affections to date! Instead, having secured him to her, she would suffer a resultant claustrophobia of togetherness – that led to festering dissatisfaction and ultimate tragedy.

Henry's love for his woman included blissful ignorance of most problems as *he* enjoyed a life that was pretty damn perfect! He wallowed in the joy of her eager, free-handed sexuality at night, becoming reacquainted with his children in the comparative composure of daytime domesticity.

Maybe occasionally, very occasionally – just a fleeting melancholy deep in his eyes? Surely more emotion than anticipated by the composer?

Four

Even the wilfully blind could hardly avoid Ada's shortcomings as mother.

'You know, Mum, I do believe she could neglect the children without realising what she was doing. Good job I decided to stay, I'm thinking. She's delicate, you know – can't really manage them on her own.'

His mother, who knew Ada much better than he did, wisely contented herself with platitude. 'Oh, I'm sure she loves them – in her own way.'

'Yes, you're right, Mum! I'm just worrying about nothing. Of course, she'd never let them come to harm.'

Typical Henry, faced with Ada's quirky, eccentric take on motherhood unknowingly followed the example of his children, simply accepting it as normal – initial alarm swiftly giving way to indulgent sanction, coupled with his own increased parental devotion by way of unconscious compensation.

This accommodation rapidly became family lore as, unused to so much attention, the children reciprocated with unconditional love.

Initially, Henry had exchanged military mentality and uniform for the tweedy, pipe-smoking persona beloved of his class when relaxing. Then he took a long slow look at the English countryside, identifying flaws it had developed – coincidentally deciding his own future career.

Land girls of the war years had vanished without

trace and consequently farmers were experiencing wearying effects that a shortage of manpower has on a labour-intensive industry.

Two wars in one lifetime had caused the mind of many a pastoral boss-man to focus with interest on possible benefits from modern technology.

'What's needed is a machine that does the work of two or more labourers,' Henry told a baffled Ada. 'Why, it would pay for itself in saved wages within a year!'

'You don't say… What's that got to do with us?'

'Just you wait and see! Farmers are a pragmatic old lot. Most of them know they have to adapt – those that don't will just go to the wall.'

'That's as maybe, but I repeat, what's that got to do with us? You're not thinking of becoming a farmer are you? I don't think it would suit you, and I definitely don't see myself as a farmer's wife!'

'A farmer! Me, a farmer? You must be joking. No, I see myself more as catering for their needs – machinery, seeds, fertilizer – that kind of thing.'

* * *

What happened to Henry after this conversation could only be regarded as metamorphosis. Abandoning rediscovered comfort of old cords which now somehow just made him feel sloppy, he opted instead for the tailored elegance in dark grey suits, spotless white shirts and subdued ties.

'Surely you're not going to wear those clothes to work, Henry – you'll be filthy in no time. How about smart cavalry twill trousers and maybe a good corduroy for your jacket?'

'No. This is the way I want it. I don't intend to get down

and dirty in the warehouse. My job will be in the office – drumming up custom. In any case, you know me – know how I love the incongruous!'

'I had noticed. Two or three times every night – and I lose count at weekends – yes, I've definitely noticed!'

He ran an exploratory hand up her thigh as they sat together on the bed half naked, discussing his sartorial plans. She giggled playfully. 'Not now, darling. Surely last night was enough for any man.'

'It's your fault for being so damned irresistible. I can't help it if I always want you. Morning or night – I'm not fussy. In any case it takes two and I never see much resistance! Come on – just a short one, eh? Before Ella gets here. Make a nice start to the day.'

'Well, you're seeing resistance now! Besides you don't know the meaning of the word short – there's nothing short about you! It's time you had breakfast and were gone!'

'I'm all fired up and raring to go – and so are you!' He softly laughed as his hand began to explore among the silk of her panties.

Swiftly she stood up and moved away from him still smiling, aroused but determined. 'No chance! My period's due today, might have started already after all that action last night. Go on, go and make some money for us.'

'Ah well, if you say so – but all I can say is you're missing a fine opportunity here.'

* * *

In a short time his farm-supply business, started in a small way with a bank loan, became an institution in the district. His instinct proving both correct and lucrative.

It's a rare combination – artist and pragmatist – but

maybe because of this duality in his temperament he proved to be far and away a better businessman than anyone could have anticipated.

Thanks to energy and hard work, together with the loyalty he inspired in his staff, within five years there was nothing similar in the area to realistically compete with Phillips' Farm Supplies.

A casual glance at the Henry Phillips of these years would gather the immediate impression of a man 'at home' with himself. Charismatic, impeccably dressed, six feet tall, middle build – the epitome of a successful entrepreneur.

Should curiosity be tickled, further perusal would discover that his dark-brown hair had receded slightly at the temples; this had occurred in his late twenties on the battlefields of North Africa, since when it had loitered as though awaiting further orders.

His eyes were a dark hazel, often sparkling with a smile that was as ready as the wit for which he was famous; wit that could occasionally turn acerbic if imposed upon, to become the only signal of his displeasure. He had never been known to lose his temper.

His nose had once pointed straight ahead in shapely decision, but had suffered a slight change of direction during a brief, youthful flirtation with rugby football – a dalliance which build sanctioned, but temperament resisted. Happily, the result bestowed a rugged attraction to a face that might otherwise have been considered somewhat feminine in its beauty.

However, anyone given the task of describing this man in any detail would rapidly fall headlong over the word 'crisp'. Immobile, his appearance just about avoided the suggestion – although it would have to be acknowledged that his shirts were always crisply white, his hair cut in the short-back-and-sidesy crispness beloved of a generation of men that had come of age in an enthusiastic military milieu. Certainly, his moustache had a distinctly martial crispness. Oh, and the handkerchief in the top jacket pocket of his well-tailored suit was glowing white, and, you've guessed it… starchy crisp.

However, it was as soon as he moved or spoke that that crispness of manner became unavoidable, fully revealing the military precision that had become his very essence – a man who did nothing without intention.

His walking pace was measured but always brisk and he wore highly polished, black leather shoes that had steel insets round the back and outside edge of the heel – ostensibly for extra wear, but really because he liked the crisp sound as he walked – which made him comfortably aware of his own entity. No mistaking his approach. No soft-shoe shuffle for *this* man. Gestures restrained, speech patterns and choice of words all deliberate – nothing was wasted or superfluous, no more, no less than was needed. I present Henry Phillips.

He grew red roses. Only red. It was something of a passion – the perfect red rose. Pruned in autumn and spring, fed the choicest of manure, sprayed against pests, every leaf carefully scrutinised for the dreaded black spot. Come the summer he would joyfully cut selected blooms to present with a flourish to his other passion – his wife.

'There you are, my love. These are for you!'

'Which one are you calling your love – me or the roses?'

'Ah, you know quite well which is my dearest love.'

'Do I?'

Occasionally, he would perversely sacrifice one of his darling buds, taking the masterpiece from its frame – slender, artist's hands gloved against the downside of devotion. Tenderly placed in his buttonhole it became embodiment of one love, emblem of the other.

Five

Henry's business premises were located at the end of Wharf Lane in a group of airy buildings surrounding a large courtyard, all abandoned with the demise of canal transport.

The canal remained, although business in the area had turned a disdainful back. Now, for want of bona fide employment, it had become the place where Henry's male workforce went to sit on empty crates, feed ducks lunchtime sandwiches and themselves roll-ups, tea and smutty jokes.

Every day a succession of elderly vehicles clattered down the lane; a ramshackle collection of assorted farm transport. Mud-coated Land Rovers of more affluent customers hobnobbed with a redundant army of superannuated jeeps abandoned in '46 and then conscripted to fulfil a more arduous peace-time role – and tractors of every age and condition.

Interspersed with the motorised vehicles plodded a motley procession of dispirited cob horses, some pulling large flat carts (still a major form of farm haulage); often as not, just the tired old nag carrying the weight of a master who lavished much encouragement round its ears – thence to wait, tied to some convenient hitching-post in sad parody of a favoured image of the American Wild West.

Men who could assess a bargain on the hoof and next week's weather in one glance gravitated to this point of business in a steady stream. Attired in boots, battered tweeds and corduroy, they carried with them relics of their occupation as talismen against an ill wind: bits of straying straw or hay, skeins of fraying string – to come in useful some time; copious amounts of mud to frustrate the courageous efforts of receptionist Brenda Cosgrove to run a clean ship – inevitably leaving her all at sea; small, odd-shaped pieces of metal – essential component for only they knew what mechanism; and always, just a few ears of grain from the last harvest.

They also brought a defining aroma: organic matter of an indefinite source neutralised by acres of fresh air to eliminate any offensive component. An integral element, it emanated from them in much the same manner as a High Court judge exudes authority – but without the ominous portent.

Pragmatism apart, in appearance and inclination Henry Phillips was a complete contrast to his customers, who liked him in spite of the divergence – or maybe a little because of it. Certainly no local farmer ever contemplated going elsewhere – they knew a fair deal when they met one! But they were not above a sly dig.

'Won't shake hands on it, Henry. Don't want to get yer fancy duds all messed up. What would the lady wife have to say if you bowled up home looking an' smelling like you'd rolled in the pigsty?'

'Ha, ha. Straight down the divorce court for me!'

Henry never resented their comments, he felt relaxed and comfortable with them. A blackbird amongst grouse – not exactly birds of a feather, but carrying plumage of reciprocal mutuality that contained much respect.

He sincerely enjoyed the company of his customers, knew all their families intimately, liked the language they used, understood and spoke it (with a distinctly foreign accent) and drank with them, enjoying the bar-room conversation and jokes. Knew all their histories, could quite accurately predict their futures – and coincidentally, who on that basis would be good for future business.

This business wasn't something he'd just settled for. He loved it, did it well; as a consequence he was fulfilled and happy, justifiably proud of his achievements – in a modest, almost reluctant manner.

Chief among these achievements were what he considered a good marriage and perfect family life. Between ourselves, if asked to choose between home and work, the grouse would have been rapidly put to flight; but since the two were mutually dependent, happily no such alternative was ever an issue.

Complexity in the man allowed him concurrent fulfilment in a bucolic, essentially male, farmyard-informed work life within which the dowdy Brenda represented her sex with such neutrality as to be discounted, and the antithesis of a beautiful, sophisticated, excessively feminine wife; contrast between the two providing the piquancy vital to his existence.

After the day's work he needed his delicate hot-house flower – needed her like a drug. His hopeless addiction – essential fix.

Coincidentally, Brenda's helpless love for Henry transmuting over the years of her moon-calf dedication, now also included his wife in the redundancy of its embrace. The inevitable realisation that her feelings for the husband would forever remain unrequited had resulted in gradual assembly of a gloriously complicated vicarious relationship – to include both husband and wife – until she was successfully in love with the *idea* of Henry and Ada as a couple. Happy at last! Blessedly so – as long as they were. Taking regular long walks in a delirium of vague joy – walks that always included slowly passing the end of their drive on the chance of glimpsing either of them.

Six

'If we take it, everything's got to be done to the highest specifications. Half measures would be false economy. You'll just have to trust me on this.'

Rapt in customary admiration, Henry smiled indulgent acquiescence.

'Well, the children are growing fast – we need more room. This place has plenty of that! Just think what a super party we could throw for Robin's birthday – a real whoopity doo-da.'

'Don't be silly, Henry. His birthday's too soon. It'll take a good six months to do all the work and then we'll be looking at furnishings after that. I would say it will be at least nine months before it's ready.

'Anything you say, darling. You're the boss.'

She had moved on. Like any good executive she had no time to listen to inane mouthing from an inconsequential subordinate.

They were viewing the large country house Ada had selected as her new setting. Informed by her assured proprietorial demeanour, Henry merely followed the vanguard – accompanied by a growing certainty! Not that he was dismayed – he could afford it. Besides, there was definite potential. He loved the way it was set right back from the road with a commanding sweep of drive and beauty in a huge weeping ash (gift of Victorian horticultural enthusiasm) growing in regal splendour in the middle of what would once again be peerless lawn.

'Magnificent – just the job! It's a bit of a mess inside, though. Still, probably be able to get the price down – big, old places like this don't sell so well these days. It'll have to be in your name, though.'

He misread her look of greedy incredulity saying in hasty reassurance. 'No need to worry your head about it, darling – merely for tax purposes… '

'Brookfields', a venerable Georgian mansion, had suffered grievously from numerous modernising improvements – culminating in several years of total neglect. This time the poor old house was systematically stripped of anything post-eighteenth century that failed to please, to be replaced to Ada's stringent specifications.

And Henry was right – his wife did have superb taste. The house was restored to its natural glory; all fittings and furnishings in complete sympathy with the building – and of the very finest quality. As a final touch she hired landscape gardeners to transform overgrown grounds to verdant beauty. And who would be so crass as to query expenditure?

Never before had Ada's life been so enjoyable! Spending money – such sweet pleasure! Deeeep in debt, Henry considered it a small price to pay just to see her so happy.

Whilst Henry and his children simply *moved in* to their new home, she would talk of having 'taken up residence'.

'Expense? That's your concern,' she informed her consort. 'And don't make the mistake of thinking moving in heralds a period of economy because it doesn't.'

'Well, money is a bit tight at present. We just opened at Thornton. The business is stretched as far as it will go… '

'Like I said – that's your concern. You'll just have to sort it out, won't you?'

Seven

Self-adornment had always been priority but after the move it became an all-consuming passion; clothes, make-up, perfume, jewellery – all of the very best quality. No half measures here either.

Her normal routine was to be in bed before he finished in the en suite bathroom. Tonight though, she lay naked on the bed chatting to him through the open door.

'You wouldn't believe how busy it was in town today. Oh, that reminds me… I meant to tell you, I saw the most fabulous handbag in Bertram's.'

Walking into the bedroom, his eyes registered lust as he saw her. 'Oh, yes? Well, you must get it then.'

'Don't you want to know how much it is?'

Hardly able to restrain himself, he murmured, 'Not particularly,' and then walked swiftly to his dressing table. Wrenching open a draw he took out a condom.

As he fumbled to open the packet, she said, 'You don't need to bother with that tonight. We're quite safe.'

He got onto his side of the bed and started to stroke her breasts as she chatted on about her trip to town. Unable to restrain himself further he moved towards her, but she briefly held him off. 'You know, it's just occurred to me, darling – don't you think it would be much better if I had my own account with my own cheque book? It would save having to bother you every time I need something.'

'Good idea, darling. I'll get on to the bank first thing tomorrow.'

Her arms circled his neck. 'Your such a darling man. Come to wife-y.'

Sometimes the list seemed endless. Then he would voice disquiet, but she always had an answer. 'You surely don't begrudge me a little extravagance once in a while? Don't I please you any more, darling?'

So it continued. Meals out at the finest restaurants. Extravagant shopping sprees to the best shops in London and Paris. Frequent cinema visits to view films that held her entranced in ecstatic wonder. Oh, and international holidays to kick-start the post-war tourist industry.

'Culture? Don't be stupid, Henry! Sun and sea!'

'What about the children? They'd love the beach.'

'The children will love staying with Granny. Besides, just think of all those lovely warm nights. You know how I am in hot weather! You'd better pack plenty of French letters – I'll need several epistles a day... not to mention night-time!'

In the next bedroom, Imogen stirred in her sleep as her mother's laughter rang out – followed by, 'Oh, Henry, not again!'

Should she be even mildly thwarted, things got very uncomfortable for the rest of the family. Sullen in sulks, electric storm would break in violent rage. Afterwards, a prostrate Ada would take to her bed – to continue epic abandon in comfort.

'Don't disturb your mother, she's got one of her headaches.'

She also got her way as he would tap gently on the bedroom door. 'If that's what you want, darling, you must have it – no need to make yourself ill. Come on down, we'll listen to some music – something nice and soothing, make you feel better.'

Usually, his attempts at reconciliation were ignored – but noted. Some time later she would emerge smiling as though nothing had happened.

Certainly he never tired of giving her benefit of the doubt; doubt made ever more questionable by an Ada seeming to beg his poor opinion, petulantly throwing down the gauntlet he never would pick up.

The perfect wife who'd given him the perfect family and a perfect home. The perfect wife who alone was capable of making a coward of him – a fact to which he was wilfully blind.

Eight

Unless otherwise provoked, Ada's role in the quotidian pageant at Brookfields was that of omnipresent household goddess. A fragrant presence displaying little interest in devotionalists – beyond her own concerns.

'What's that you're reading, Imogen? Oh, jolly good. Carry on.'

'Why aren't you ready, Henry? Must you keep me waiting?'

Irrevocably deaf to their prayers and oblivious of their needs, she wafted around the stage, single-mindedly intent on her exclusive *modus agendi*.

There exists a theory that since we are all born into a pagan state, piety should be nurtured as we learn to love or fear the deity. Ada's great mistake was to neglect both hypothesis and remedy, preferring to delegate the task of indoctrination to those with more energy.

It was a style of mothering that naturally failed to influence her young infidels. Lacking what they considered to be rational prompts elsewhere, they early learned to humour their father's worship whilst circumnavigating the deity, playing infant roles without a mother's influence to inform the canon.

She did maintain limited interest in the girl – despite what she considered an unaccountable lack of encouragement, but if she noticed Robin at all, she preferred not to acknowledge the fact, early evolving a system of communication that spared her the necessity of the direct approach.

'Imogen, come in for tea – tell your brother to wipe his feet, he's been in the mud.' Or, 'Henry, you really must tell your son not to slam the doors. Makes my nerves so bad.'

Imogen would invariably ignore such instructions as excess to requirements and Henry's wry, humorous glance of admonition to his son with an added 'Shush' fulfilled his part in the equation.

Her husband's state of favour all depended on how well business was doing. Given favourable circumstances, customary glacial politeness could turn to warm invitation. 'Why don't you slip away, darling. I'm sure they can manage without you for a while.'

That should keep him on his toes!

Charm? This woman could charm for Africa. No mere 'birds from the trees' touch – more like 'lions from the kill', that kinda thing.

Moments of intimacy apart, this ability was rarely employed at home. Outside, she was justifiably famous for it – calculated sham remaining forever covert since it was also utterly convincing, earning her respect, devotion even, from a wide range of potentially useful society.

'You never know,' she would inform her husband, 'if and when you might need someone… never neglect *anyone*! That's my advice. Remember – sprats to catch mackerels, Henry, sprats to catch mackerels!'

Henry would smile with uncomfortable indulgence, 'You're *shameless*!'

Made her laugh that did. Brittle, tinkling, soft-ruffled wind chimes – high pitched and musical.

Imogen hated that laugh. On a sleep-disturbed night, she sometimes heard it together with the soft murmur of her father's voice from her parents' adjoining bedroom. For some reason it made her feel uncomfortable. *Daddy must be telling her jokes. Why doesn't she laugh at them during the day?*

Henry had qualms, but not so urgent as to interfere with business instincts! After all, this beguiling gift of Ada's achieved pre-eminence as an aid to commerce, making her his most valuable business ally with many a lucrative deal concluded in the warm glow of enchantment created by her undoubted skills as hostess.

No detail was too small as she made minute study of the lives and inclinations of guests. With greatest care she catered for *all* tastes – just like a practiced whore, but without the distasteful necessity of a stranger's sexual proximity.

Should a visitor eschew ostentation, simplicity and restraint ruled. At the other extreme, no expensive sparkle spared. Success always rewarded these efforts, helping create a flourishing business – eventually extending into neighbouring areas with seven additional branches.

By contrast, her attention to any domestic issue was hard to gain – and of the shortest duration.

Nine

'It'll be good for them – help build their characters.'

Ada favoured boarding-school education for her precious angels – preferably in an establishment that would keep them both term-time *and* vacation – in the style of unwanted Victorian orphans.

There was amused cynicism in her face as she looked at him. Fully aware what his reaction would be, she still thought it worth the try. Besides – such fun to tease!

Predictable outrage, Henry's response almost a bark. 'No way! For God's sake, what an idea! Junior school here is perfectly adequate for now and the grammar is second to none.'

'But what if they fail their eleven plus?'

'They won't – they're both bright as buttons.'

Ada made one last attempt, 'I do wish you wouldn't be guided by sentimentality – I know you don't want to be parted from them, neither do I, but the people round here are so coarse. Do you really want your children infected with head lice and bad language? Besides, we'll have a lot more time alone together… no interruptions! Won't that be nice?'

She was aware she had broached probably the only subject on which he would consistently attempt to oppose her view. The thought of a Jane Eyre or David Copperfield in *his* family was an affront to his fatherhood which he simply couldn't contemplate.

In his indignation, he failed to register the blatant sexual invitation in her last remark as he spluttered, 'W-well, we'll face all these problems as and when – as and when.'

'You mean, *I'll* have to face them! You're not here when they get home.'

Henry wasn't for budging. Ada had noted his lack of attention. Her offer ignored? Momentarily the lapse angered her. Then it amused. Normally a few words like that would have her sexually insatiable husband on the boil, but she looked at stubborn rebellion etched on his face and paused to consider her options.

Truly engaged she would have put up more of a fight – made him sweat for victory, dangled the sexual angle with increased allure – caught his attention. She always knew how to catch his attention! Still, she'd let him think he'd won this time.

Her mind drifted back to the time he first came home. Knowing how regular she was – that her period was due imminently, she had allowed his full, sustained, unfettered access to her body for two nights. Most enjoyable! Well, it had been a long wait for both of them.

To her consternation he'd made it quite clear he wanted another baby.

When her bleed happened so quickly he was dismayed, but his response had been typically sweet, blaming himself.

'I'm so sorry, darling – maybe I was too rough. Perhaps next time, eh? Don't be downhearted. I know you're keen. I suppose I'm especially so because I've missed both your pregnancies. I would love to see you swell with my baby. I bet it's the most beautiful sight. You'll look gorgeous!'

She hadn't tried to hide her dismay. 'Pregnancy doesn't suit me, my love. I felt dreadful all throughout both times –

and the agony at the end! Please, please don't make me go through all that again.'

'But it would be different this time. I would be here to look after you.'

'Yes, but you can't give birth for me can you?'

She'd made him wait well over two weeks.

'Isn't that bleed of yours ever going to end, surely it shouldn't last so long? We've got a lot of lost time to catch up. Babies to make, eh?'

'I know, darling, it does seen to be taking a time. I can hardly wait for you either. Come here, let's have a kiss and a cuddle.'

'Kiss and cuddle! My God, what d'you think I'm made of – stone?'

Then one evening she'd walked in from the bathroom completely naked – to sit trembling on the bed. 'I'm ready for you now.'

She'd watched him fumble with the rest of his clothing. As he'd walked naked towards her, after one intent glance of awe-filled lust she had demurely averted her eyes, then with shaking hand held out an unwrapped condom – a child with a last sweetie for its closest friend.

'Just try it, darling, just for me. Please! I'm absolutely terrified of getting pregnant again.'

He'd halted, speechless with dismay.

Looking up at him, her face had registered nothing but bashful concern as she'd pleaded, 'Please, please, my love. You do want me to enjoy it too don't you? I never will if I think I'm going to be pregnant again. Here let me help you with that.'

Finally laying back, she'd stretched out her arms. 'Come here, my lover. Just for me, eh? Just try it. I bet you'll enjoy it once you're used to it.'

As his silence was finally broken, his voice had been hoarse amid her soft moaning. 'Just so long as we can do this often.'

When she'd eventually answered it had been frenzied cry. 'As often as you want, my love. As often as you want!' He'd forgotten all about babies.

As they'd subsided she'd rubbed her hands down his back then pulled his buttocks in towards her. 'That was utterly phenomenal. Thank you, my darling man, thank you so much. Was it nice for you too, did you enjoy it?

'Nice? Good God, it was sublime.'

She'd reached under her pillow and laughing pulled six more packets of condoms, tossing them in the air with a flick of her wrist.

As they landed on the bed he'd looked at them greedily, then scrambled to his feet laughing. 'Don't you move a muscle, you clever little woman you. I'm just going to the bathroom, I'll be back in two ticks. Get one of those things ready for me – we'll do it properly this time.'

In his absence the next day, she became aware that victory had been too easy. Not only had it become anti-climax overnight, there was also a certain element of contempt in the mix.

She'd told herself that had he been more of a man, more assertive, demanding, she would certainly have been pregnant this morning. It might have been nice to have a baby with him. After all, that's what marriage was all about, wasn't it? Well, some of it anyway. It seemed that every woman she saw was heavy with child – women whose husbands had also returned. Real men! Men who would never tolerate any kind of barrier to long-awaited fulfilment.

At that time, arousal was always easy for her. As her hands ran over her flat belly, imagining it rounded, imaging his desire growing as it got bigger, her nipples hardened. Two pregnancies had not only left her breasts shapely but also added a mature fullness. At the homecoming, Henry had been joyously amazed. 'Wow – just look at that! What *have* you been doing to them?' They both enjoyed her breasts!

Then suddenly she'd envisaged them bloated, milk oozing from nipples once again sore and ugly. And another thing, if she were unprotected he had only to look in her general direction to hit the bulls-eye – look what had happened the last two times! And knowing his sexual appetite, she could well be in that condition for the next ten years or so. Time after time!

No, no. It was better this way – and in any case, when it was a safe time of the month she could occasionally let him have it in the buff, so to speak. Be a nice treat for him – for them both, if she were really honest about it. And he would be *so* grateful – that was always useful.

All the same, she'd wished he was more assertive with her. A lot more assertive!

Since that time she had increasingly come to enjoy her domination in their sex life. A bed had been made up for him in an adjoining room where he was sent when he became too much of a nuisance. She had long since discarded the grateful little woman routine, liked him to do all the supplication – permanent penitent missionary. Indeed, she often idly wondered just how much humiliation he was prepared to endure before he received his reward for good behaviour.

The event-filled delay allowed her to become sufficiently aroused whilst he forgot all that reverential 'with my body, I thee worship' guff and took her with satisfying, maddened violence.

How delightful it would be now to withhold the goodies till she had gained his total capitulation! She'd done it many times before. Yes, she knew how to get his full attention all right!

Now, reminiscence brought a slow, lascivious smile to her averted face. But as boredom prevailed, she knew she wouldn't bother – not on this subject anyway. Coldly, she looked him full in the face. *Yes, he'll pay for this!*

Exaggeratedly yawning she returned to perusal of the inevitable glossy that had never left her hands during the altercation. The children's education? Per-lease! 'I didn't bargain on all this hoo-ha. We'll do what you want, as usual. It was just a suggestion, but, *of course*, you know best.'

Ada's increasing insouciance saddened Henry but he learned to accept it. This, then, was *the* price. Well, it was worth it!

But his acceptance favoured no one. As the years rolled on she became increasingly remote – to the point where, apart from conventional communication, very few subjects of mutual interest existed. The silence between them contained his mute adoration – together with her withdrawn cerebral and emotional presence.

Sex became evermore infrequent – and violent when it did happen. Her need for excitement had become evermore extreme, but that excitement was essential to the consent that was prerequisite for her slavish husband,

His attempts to please her in any way invariably irritated, but this base obsequiousness filled her with utter contempt.

In spite of everything, he still managed to convince himself that life was pretty near perfect! Well, we all know how easy it is to rationalise a situation when choice is not an option – OH, YES, WE DO!

Ten

Absences from Brookfields were only ever occasioned by a penchant for motherhood; so, with the aid of a daily cleaner, Ella Adkins was Ada's devoted housekeeper-cum-basic cook-cum-you-name-it.

Pregnancy never interfered with loyalty to her adopted family; even confinement occasioned minimum disruption. With older ones in her mother's care, the latest addition would accompany its mother – to be fed and changed in between other chores.

The Brookfields children were accustomed to watching and waiting as baby suckled at its mother's breasts. 'I think he's finished that side, Ella – hurry, he might cry otherwise. Don't forget, it's my turn to hold him when he's finished.'

Henry, the only one to be mildly embarrassed, turning in the doorway with a 'Pardon me. Are those two bothering you, Ella?' would be mildly rebuked.

'Of course not! They're helping me – aren't you, my loves?'

Homely, comforting, caring, she somehow managed to combine work with an over-abundance of love, which included Ada and Henry – but more especially, their children. These two she regarded as an extension of her own large family – bonus of devotion. Concern for their well-being went far beyond wages – would have endured with or without payment.

Towards her ever-open arms they toddled, drawn by the magnet of unfailing maternal hospitality.

'Look, Ella – look what I've made for you!'

'Oh, thank you, my lovie. Isn't that clever?'

Or just a sobbing wail, 'Ell-ll-ll-aaa!'

'Never you mind, darling – there, kiss it better! Come and see what I've just taken out of the oven… '

With infallible infant instinct, they nestled in her warmth with never a thought of rejection. In Henry's absence *she* was their lodestar – applauding witness of small triumphs and joys, comfort in overwhelming vicissitudes of childhood.

It was Ella's children who became their first playmates – rolling, racing, tumbling in joyous abandon in the large council house and garden that was a *real* home – with a *real* mother.

But Ella would be callously disregarded the moment Henry arrived. What this man lacked naturally in maternal ease, he more than compensated for in the profundity of his love. With them he lost his 'business' persona, becoming cuddly – malleable as a well-loved soft toy. *They* brought him to his knees as no adversary or act of piety could have done. Down on the floor he became one of them; wilfully loosing his adult status to become utterly absorbed in the latest game – sometimes as initiator, more generally as punch-bag and fall-guy.

A passing Ada would regard the scrum with scorn tinged with a wistful envy.

'Don't be so rough with them – it'll all end in tears. And mind your trousers! Couldn't you have changed *before* you decided to roll all over the floor?'

As the children grew, Ella continued to provide a background of tender protecting fellowship, but it was Henry's support that became the keystone in a plethora of ideas and enthusiasms spawned by lively imaginations.

And he never failed them – suggesting modifications or new angles, broadening minds, widening perceptions.

'What's it look like upside down?'

'Ooooh, yes! Why didn't we think of that, Imi?'

'Shouldn't we consider putting the whole thing on wheels? I've got two sets of castors in the shed. Come on!'

'I love you, Daddy.' The little girl would nestle against him in the purity of childhood adoration.

'Watch out! She's after something!' Ada's amused warning would go unacknowledged by a moist-eyed Henry, who only intensified the embrace, sending his wife from the room on a surge of irritation.

Henry was also a keen amateur chef – fortuitous, since Ada's take on preparing for a meal rarely advanced beyond deciding which outfit to wear, or (of less interest) which outside caterers to employ. Everyday meals that devolved to her responsibility ('Surely Ella doesn't need yet another day off!') inclined towards the decidedly lacklustre or the 'help yourselves' kind of arrangement – much preferred by her family.

'The best meals are always the ones you do in a hurry from scratch – come on, you two, let's see what we can rustle up. To the kitchen!'

Being 'like Daddy' became the summit of ambition. He could play the violin – so would they! Failure! Other instruments? Maternal displeasure. 'Can't you stop them, Henry? This house is untenable with all that caterwauling going on.'

With his usual tact, Henry jokingly altered the focus of miserable failure. 'There's them what plays and them what listens! No, seriously though, there's no point having one without the other. But you should always remember – whilst the audience may be as important as the artist, only the music is vital.'

Peace resumed as practice ceased. 'You want music? Come with me. Come and listen. I've just got a new recording of the Beethoven's sixth. Come on, Imi, come and listen for the cuckoo.'

Eleven

Lazing in armchair comfort on a summer afternoon, suspended in amber fastness of meaningless melancholy and nameless longings, Ada Phillips dreamily stroked the silky head of the small child lolling against her legs.

Normally sturdily independent, five-year-old Imogen was momentarily engrossed in an intensity of attention that absorbed all her strength. She was closely inspecting the brightly lacquered nails of her mother's left hand as it lay on the silk expanse of lap just in front of her face.

Idly, Ada's thoughts wandered. *This is nice – just the two of us. The little one is just like a pixie. A real cutie.* She almost lifted the child onto her lap to cuddle. Instead her left hand remained motionless as the other wandered aimless through the thick satin of the child's hair, gently twisting some of it between two fingers, enjoying the slippery sensuality.

Discontent, only ever slightly submerged, surfaced with mild irritation as she let her caressing hand fall. *Not even the slightest wave – never mind curls!* With a soft sigh of regret she told the oblivious child, 'You're never going to be a Shirley Temple!'

Lost in fervent contemplation, by now almost consumed with longing, Imogen failed to notice her mother's slight movement or words. Oooo… her lusting thoughts – *boiled sweeties! Just one lick – just one!* A salivating, extended tongue approached forbidden fruit…

For the first time Ada became aware to the child's steadfast fixation – and dribble it was creating. Unnerved, she abruptly stood, agitatedly wiping the front of her skirt as she moved towards the door, almost shouting. 'Run along now. Find something to play with. Find Ella.'

Her sudden action caused abrupt descent. Trance shattered – breath and epicurean desire blasted to oblivion. Recovered breath was exhaled in a sustained wail of loud anguish followed by heartbroken, mucus-producing sobs.

Concern caused a momentary check on Mother's flight – concern extinguished by the vision of Imogen's snotty face. Hands firmly pressed to her ears she sailed on through the doorway calling, 'Ella! Imogen wants you.'

Twelve

Taking their cue from Ada's method of communication with her son, the children rarely spoke directly to her – in fact, with careful, instinctive avoidance, whole days could pass without any outright contact.

As the mother became almost an irrelevance, there grew an affinity between brother and sister that might occasionally admit a favoured few – but would always exclude the alien being that wafted by their world on a cloud of expensive French fragrance, uttered a few invariably irritated and largely unheard words, then floated off again – thistledown on a summer breeze, leaving a fading aroma to betray recent presence. Fading into careless oblivion. Gone.

The fortress, created initially as defence to simply exclude Ada, gradually evolved to become a place of security – protection from unwelcome intrusion. Considering her indifference, this reaction might seem excessive, but bitter experience highlighted the impossibility of negotiating existence without contagion.

Imogen had little difficulty avoiding invariably bungled attempts at intimacy. However, without warning, Ada would turn on flamboyant, public displays of motherly affection involving both children.

'What do you think of my Robin – isn't he growing tall? Takes after his father. And what about my pretty little darling Imogen? They're such good children – such a blessing to their father and me!'

Bad enough! But occasionally, performance would take place in front of school friends. Impotent, they could only vow to fight another day as injustice added extra scourge; both were convinced the audience, comprehending deception, convicted them of complicity.

Hapless infants reduced to mere stoic endurance as 'her darlings' were required to respond fulsomely to unwanted caresses – play happy families for the audience. With the full glare of a spotlight on them, their parts were invariably performed with smirking alacrity – or displease, incurring later, unhappy results to complete the desecration of motherhood.

'You can both go to your rooms, I'm going to lock you in, so you needn't think of getting back together. There's too much of this collusion – I won't have it. DO YOU HEAR ME? And there'll be no tea for either of you!'

Thus they early learned all about the hard, cold insincerity hidden within over-sentimentality. Worm in the core – 'roach in the doughnut.

Abuse of a child, be it physical, mental, or emotional, wraps the victim in noisome, adamantine coils of guilt-ridden silence. In later years people would remember the apparent warmth of Ada's mother-love – considering it her only redeeming feature. 'Well, at least it was *something*!'

The straight-faced daughter never contradicted anyone – preferring they keep the fiction – unwilling to reveal her mother as total villain – still not entirely convinced of her own innocence anyway.

Their children were perfect! Henry was saddened his wife failed to share the conviction. Her attitude baffled him – and Ada also had her moments of perplexity.

'You do realise, darling, we've got two beautiful, intelligent children – they're such a credit to us. How come you don't see it?'

'That's all very well for you to say, but you don't have to deal with all the playing up during the day. You only see them evenings and weekends. They're good as gold then all right – butter wouldn't melt… I can't think what I've done to deserve such treatment.'

It was an exchange they often had.

'I just don't understand their behaviour… It's almost as though they hate me.'

'Now you're being silly! They love you. We all love you.'

'If you say so, dear.'

Obsessed as she was with appearance, how come she failed to appreciate what was so obvious to, not just her husband, but everyone else?

To begin to unravel enigma, it's essential to become detective – probe intimacies of the early days of their marriage with forensic thoroughness.

All right, not *that* thorough! BEHAVE!

Thirteen

It may be recalled that shortly after marriage, considering it duty to his country, Ada's lovely new husband enlisted. What may not be fully realised is that she took his action as personal betrayal. This feted, over-privileged, over-indulged hot-house flower became, overnight, as 'twere, well and truly abandoned. Sleek, new express train mistakenly shunted into a remote siding to moulder; thoroughbred racehorse finding itself at the local gymkhana receiving a yellow rosette for third place instead of the winner's enclosure at Cheltenham. That kinda thing.

Unescorted treats? Ada favoured an attentive male companion – with deeeep pockets! Besides, in pre-war Britain, unaccompanied women were birds of suspicious plumage. Marriage had reduced the rota to one, and now German nationalism completed the process.

As though this deprivation wasn't sufficient, her mother upped and died all unexpected like – thus demonstrating terrible timing and a distinct lack of consideration.

Leaning heavily on his fragile child as they teetered precariously over a be-coffined grave like two sombre drunks, the bereaved husband moaned, 'I just can't bear it.'

It wasn't rhetorical. He visited his bank, wrote his child a note, then held a solitary wake. Painkillers – lots of 'em – washed down by enough scotch to kill all pain by itself anyway – an act of self-indulgence that left Ada feeling more indignant than bereaved, even though, following his last instructions, the stash of crisp, white five-pound notes she discovered in his desk was a comfort – and enough to bury him ten times over.

At the end of an embarkation leave hijacked by funereal considerations she waved a tearful farewell to Henry, only to discover he'd left her pregnant! Alone, alone, all, all alone with just nausea and gloomy apprehension, a heavy albatross hanging round her neck.[1]

Abandoned by all she'd previously relied upon, like so many seemingly weak people, Ada demonstrated amazing resources, rapidly reaching the conclusion she couldn't be expected to do housework in *this* state!

As new wife, she'd been eager to demonstrate home-making skills existing only in an imagination fired by the enthusiasm of novelty – ardour that tarnished as quickly as silver wedding gifts.

A speedily discovered antipathy towards housework had merely created an unsuccessful quest for renunciation. Doing it badly only resulted in her husband's policy of gentle encouragement as she tentatively menaced dust with feathers on a stick. Just another of her endearing little ways he thought. 'You'll master it given time, my love.'

In those halcyon days the klutz had a lot to learn…

When Ada had raised the domestic help question he'd dismissed it lightly, 'We can't afford anyone just yet, darling. When our ship comes in, eh?'

In addition to the cash already in her possession, as her parents' only beneficiary she became wealthily independent, but it must be noted here and now that at no point in their later life did she consider sharing this bounty with her husband – or anyone else for that matter.

Regretted absence now assumed the character of fortuitous convenience as with the acumen of a long-established city broker she salted her windfall away in diverse safe but lucrative areas of the market economy (never again to see light of day until it caused happy amazement in her beneficiaries half a century later). *Her* ship had nicely docked – thank you so very much!

Although Henry could hardly be unaware of his wife's wealth, the subject was subsequently never raised between them. On the eventual return of the breadwinner, not even interest on the accounts was ever used again. Like the little peach of emerald hue – it grew and grew!

Meanwhile. Abandoned, pregnant but affluent, Ada felt fully justified in her decision. To hell with endearing little ways!

Her luck, always good, became phenomenal as fifteen-year-old Ella Mullis left school and answered her advertisement.

Country born and bred, Ella was strong as any man, but that's where masculinity ceased – hips and bosom having already developed a life of their own that was over-generously female. Good natured and obliging, she was what used to be described by employers of domestic labour as one of life's natural treasures.

'Don't you worry about a thing Mrs Phillips – you just put your feet up. Leave it all to me. What do you fancy for lunch?'

To begin with, Ella was the 'daily'– arriving promptly at seven in the morning, using her own key to avoid disturbing the expectant one. Supposed to leave at five after preparing a tasty supper to tempt the jaded appetite, departure was invariably delayed by give or give an hour or three.

'Why don't you move in with me here? There's plenty of room and I could do with somebody to look after me in the evenings.'

'Oh, Mrs Phillips! What a smashing idea. It's not good for you to be on your own in your condition you know.'

The new arrangement, so exactly suiting respective personalities, delighted both women. Ella was a compulsive giver. Ada's unfailing Instinct was to take – flippantly stifling a lazy conscience with the reasoning that if the girl obviously found joy in the gift of her present life, it would be wrong to deny such pleasure. Besides, Ella inspired affection – even Ada responded to her benevolence with a muted reciprocation which made her uncharacteristically clingy.

Ah, but there's a downside to increased leisure. Our Ada now had ample time to regard the growing burden of her distending body, experiencing concurrent growth of fear and disgust. What was happening? Why did her tummy ripple? She'd understood there was pain! How much pain?

The questioning was beyond sad; tragedy lay in the fact there was no one to enlighten ignorance or calm fears. No mother. No best friend (Ada wasn't a best-friendsy kinda gal anyway). In fact, no experienced female confidant at all – and her childhood doctor had long since retired.

Someone from school days? No – all just jealous cows. Her new doctor?

'Don't you worry about a thing, Mrs Phillips.' But she did worry. She also shrank from disclosing total ignorance to a newly qualified male stranger who would soon depart for the theatre of war anyway.

Anyone? Anyone? NO ONE!

Temporary anger surged. Pointless, irrational, fury spiting, fear-fuelled hatred drowned the memory of all who had abandoned her to lonely, hideous anticipation. Deliberate conspiracy!

As fear regained supremacy, she clung all the harder to

Ella – knowing the girl was hopelessly inexperienced, but unable to escape class-bound isolation that prevented her seeking advice from Ella's mum – who would willingly have answered every question!

Fourteen

Since mankind is such a smart-arse, eventually a way will be discovered to conquer Daddy Time – make him go back or sideways switchback style, or maybe simply merge into a parallel state.

How-ev-er, back in Ada's world, the stubborn old bastard is still in charge; doing his usual efficient thing – landing her in the hell-on-earth of a hospital delivery room run by destiny's nuns.

And by the way, hell is white. Not black or red. No flames, no smoke – just an eye-searing brilliant white – where the damned cast no shadow. Tiled in shade-free totality from floor to well-lit ceiling, the walls of this infernal, inner chamber are unrelieved even by the black-out of a window.

Instead, a ghastly glitterati of chromium-plated paraphernalia leers and winks knowingly at any imminently expectant mother who, as yet, clings to apprehensive ignorance.

Those women who have passed this way before know *exactly* to what use this shimmering array will be put. The knowledge is not comforting…

No hint of colour brightens brilliant gloom. No magazines or books (germ-laden!). No friendly ticking clock, no radio. Nothing to distract from ever-increasing surges of white agony. In these pre-epidural glory days, such suffering is all part of the fun – to cease with baby's entrance, whilst concentrating the mind on just that outcome with unerring enthusiasm.

Ada lies helpless in this special hell as day follows night and then unseen shadows fall on yet another day. Hour after hour, alone in a world of terror – and steadily increasing pain.

'Baby seems to be in no hurry.' The face of a white-clad sister glowing with carbolic cleanliness and saintly disapproval materialising at her side clearly blames 'Mother' for the delay. Somewhere – in another life – the apparition has informed her, 'I'm your midwife. I'm here to help you.'

'Help? Help! HELP!'

Midwife is her official function. Real mission? Ensure *labour* lives up to its name – hard and painful as humanly endurable – without incurring irksome involvement/interference from a doctor. Agonising, demeaning, exhausting but uncomplicated. The ultimate issue! A fine line certainly, but one the good sister usually walks with unerring accuracy.

In her small world she is omnipotent, dispensing penance that would make an inquisitor blanch. These harlots wouldn't be here unless they had turned their backs on *her* God to indulge filthy, carnal lusts. No marriage vow mitigates *the* mortal sin. For this Holy Terror, screams of her writhing victims induce wild excesses of joy, their agonies achieve her orgasms.

Not someone a girl should go looking for in her hour of need...

'It's no good. You need the doctor. Let's hope I can wake him.'

No amount of midwifely 'help' has even begun to produce the desired effect, and now she's going to have to do that which is most undesirable. Time to wipe her hands of this slut anyway... *What does a respectable married woman want with painted nails? And that hair! Bleached! She's sorry now all right. Well, she's going to be even more sorry – serve her right.*

'I've got to get him – you need more help.'

'Help... yes... yes. Help, oh, please... HELP!'

Ada's hell transmutes as a grubby, old, unshaven man, materialising from the whiteness breaths alcoholic fumes over her as personal malediction – curse on her and her wretched, unwanted, unwilling child. Chrome-influenced, pain alters, becomes urgent, more intense. More, more... until, satisfied she's now broken, it reluctantly fades, altering screams to a whimper.

A booming noise emerges from the white liquorous fug. Voice of doom. 'Oh, by the way,' it says, slurring its words, 'you've got a boy.'

Somehow Ada hears – fails to realise she's being addressed. All part of hell – boom, boom. All right, boom if you must, but please, please, no more pain!

Exertions over, our grubby old man stands back to survey his handiwork with a grunt of satisfaction. Rubbing his hand against the bristles on his chin in reflexive, comforting sibilance he murmurs, 'Just a couple of stitches... that's it. She'll heal.'

A glance of insipid enquiry at the unhearing, white-draped exclusion zone busying itself with newly arrived soul informs him his presence is excess to requirements. Just like his country, no one here needs *him* now.

Displaying an enthusiasm hitherto absent he shuffles out of the door and out of Ada's life. Within minutes, reunited with the source of all joy so unceremoniously dashed from his lips, he soon forgets they had ever been parted!

Brethren, let us hope and pray, in all piety, that the esteemed doctor has found time to wash his hands, for at no stage of the proceedings has he worn gloves.

Ada's descent into hell has been so protracted she's entirely forgotten the reason for her presence there at all. So when a small white bundle with a contrasting glimpse of puckered mauve flesh at one end is presented for her inspection, she's baffled. The bundle immediately screams its hatred, making her flinch away as though from a vicious, madly barking dog.

Realisation slowly percolates through incomprehension, past disbelief, ignoring disinclination as an irrelevance, through to a revolting reality. *This* is why she's here!

Aware now of a uniformly expectant expression on faces surrounding the bundle, she obediently mumbles, 'Very nice,' glancing apprehensively at the puckered mauve end. 'Very nice,' she reiterates with more assertion, like she'd been shown the mirrored back of a new hairdo – only displaying considerably less enthusiasm.

Expectant expressions persist. The bundle moves in for the kill. Unable to move further away she simply stares, hypnotised by its hideousness. Failing to realise she's expected to hold it, she makes no move to do so. Instead, turning wearily to face the neat, now comforting comprehensibility of white tiles she weeps. Sobbing self-pity, overwhelming self-pity – gently sweetened by relief as pain recedes – along with infant tumult. Out of the room – down the corridor. Away. Away.

Fifteen

A lifetime later Ada wakes to lay quietly relishing the crisp, cocooning comfort of her immaculate bed, dreamily watching the quietly bustling ward, enjoying the restful peace surrounding her tranquil renaissance.

Witnessing her long awaited return to life, the good sisters smile knowingly at each other. 'Ah, bless her, she's looking for baby – go and fetch him before she starts to fret. Might quieten him down too… anything's possible!'

Still screaming, the bundle materialises anew. Ada shudders as caterwauling approaches. *Dear God, no!* She's forgotten all about this!

The bundle is now resplendent in baby-boy blue – a colour that does absolutely *nothing* for a complexion deepened, if anything, to an even angrier shade of mauve.

It is at this point that Ada's aversion alters as she feels the first stirrings of deep maternal loathing.

And the feeling grows as hours pass. She's being systematically robbed! Hasn't this awful thing robbed her of her girlish figure? Because of it, wasn't her hair, that beautiful halo of gold falling out by the handful leaving a few bedraggled wisps of derision? Another robbery!

Worse – much worse – it's robbed her of all self-awareness and with it has gone self-confidence, which she now discovers to be the source of her famed serenity. Gone, all gone. That happy equanimity – refuge from the more unpleasant aspects of life. Vanished! Parents, husband?

All have deserted her, but this is by far the heaviest blow! Unprotected by it, she becomes aware of new fear. The bundle's permanently wailing, open mouth has a peculiar, trembling, wedge shape that reveals gums and flattened tongue, more terrifying than foam flecked fangs of a rabid dog. The only respite is to let it satisfy its endlessly recurrent hunger – a process that not only robs her of the beauty of her breasts, but of her very autonomy.

She fakes a muted enthusiasm for the bathing routine, hides disgust whilst removing the filled nappy, cleaning genitalia and behind. But all the time her awareness concentrates on the total depredation she is experiencing – and the warmth of her phobia becomes a furnace.

Asked for a name for the birth certificate, it's so easy. 'Robin' in two separate syllables. Pressed for a second name to soften the blow she merely reiterates Rob-in.

Come the day of departure, she would love to leave the Robin bundle behind. But no – it has to accompany her.

Alone, she's forced to contend with unremitting wailing – which only ceases when *it* is fastened with vice-like grip to the inflamed chafe of her breasts. *Her* breasts! Traitors, in league with *it* – weeping constantly in *its* absence. Just these milk-laden impostors and the bundle – no room for her anywhere in the equation.

Perhaps if she could make friends with the newcomer – things might improve? Overcoming aversion, she makes tentative overtures of assumed affection. The bundle's having none of it – meets 'em with raging scorn... and hell has no fury like a mother scorned! Regret makes rapid exit as the trumpet call of maternal loathing increases by default.

Relief is at hand! Ella has been taking instruction from her mum. Now armed with bottles of milk, piles of warm nappies and oodles of eager love, she advances confidently on mother and child – to be greeted with relief by both.

'Oh, isn't he beautiful?'

'I thought you'd like him… '

'I'll take him in the other room, give you a chance of a proper sleep.'

'That would be just marvellous, I'm so very tired.'

'Do you want anything before I go?'

'No just some peaceful sleep.'

'Okay. If you want anything, just call.'

'Thank you, Ella. Oh, I know, there is just one thing more. Get a doctor from somewhere will you? He'll have to stop my milk since you're taking over.'

'Okay. Will my doctor do – or have you got anyone in mind?'

'No, your doctor will be fine. Thank you, Ella.'

Sixteen

Our precociously competent teenager loves babies with a passion. Would prefer motherhood for herself but lacks understanding parents – or, since she makes no secret of her need, a boyfriend willing, despite surging teenage testosterone levels to risk a shotgun up the jacksy. Sex? Yes, yes, yes! Any time, any place. Fatherhood? No, thanks! Thus Ella, having eagerly awaited this surrogacy, now pours forth all her pent-up maternal instincts and eager fecundity like a balm over baby Robin's forlorn helplessness.

Ada, listening as wailing abruptly ceases, deduces blatant disloyalty. Like a fool she's allowed that noise to distress her! Cessation endorses all negative emotions, justifying renunciation of an unwanted role as pangs of convention-induced guilt are negated in a surge of indignant justification.

With joyful solipsism she gratefully resumes habits of her former, self-contained life – within a separate existence that also obeys rules of conventional respectability. In the home that Ella and the now contented bundle share with a liberated but irreproachable mother, there exists only cheerful but distant harmony.

'We're just off down the shops. Nearly out of tea. Can I get you anything?'

'No, thanks. Wrap up warm the pair of you. It's cold out there. Don't keep the door open too long – lets all the warmth out.' The recumbent Ada holds out her hands to the blazing fire, sighing contentment. Ella, with Robin cosy in his pram, wonders if there might be some cheese at the shop. Make a nice little treat on toast for Mrs Phillips.

It is universally understood that, provided the lady is running the show, everyone who comes within her influence succumbs to the spell, so Ella loves Ada.

Too young for the kind of inward, intellectual debate that might question a mother's cool attitude to her child, Ella is easy conquest. Since that's in her interest, Ada makes every effort to keep it that way – treating the girl as a younger, much valued member of the family.

When a further hurried, passionate visit from her soldier husband results in another pregnancy, Ada feels much more confident.

'I'm going to have another baby,' she tells Ella.

'How lovely! Robin will need a little playmate.'

Ignoring the girl's reply, Ada carries on – thinking aloud. 'I'll be confined in the comfort of my own home this time… the best doctor and midwife money can buy… I'll have no more of what I had to endure last time, thank you very much! And surely no second child will cause as much agony?'

'My mum says the first is always the worst. Didn't they look after you very well when you had Robin?'

Merely concluding her thought process, Ada says brightly, 'And this time I'll have you with me too!'

'Of course you will – you just try and keep me away!'

Taking Ella's hand she smiles sweetly, 'Yes, this time I'll have you.'

Possibly because of her more relaxed attitude and the fact that a quirk of campaign strategy results in brief embarkation leave for Henry at the critical moment, relaxed confinement is over so rapidly she barely registers labour pangs. Certainly, with an attentive husband to shower flowers, gifts and heartfelt praise, she feels sincerely proud of her achievement.

Later, in the leisure of his absence she begins to brood. *Twice! Twice he's done it – then calmly gone, leaving me to carry the burden and face the horror all by myself. He didn't know he'd be around for the girl's birth. For all he knew (or cared!) it might well have been just like the other one.* Ada shudders. *Admittedly, this time the pain was less – but there again, pain is pain. No. Made up my mind, never going to happen again. All his fault. Just like an animal – never taking any precautions. No thought of anything like that, just wants his way. Well, I can't stop the pregnancies – it's up to him, but he'll have no choice in future. He won't come near me unless I am protected!*

And just look at the way he drooled over his wretched infants – why, he spent more time with them and Ella than he did with me. Left me on my own most of the time – and just because he couldn't have my body as usual. Well, at least he hasn't left me pregnant this time!

Ada has begun to perceive herself neglected – abused even. A slow-burning, irreversible resentment takes root.

* * *

So. Post-natal depression or full-blown puerperal psychosis? Take yer pick – but please be warned that later in life she became capable of psychotic delusions on a catastrophic scale.

Within either explanation lurk just two tragic certainties. Her first-born became an impostor in her life; an unwanted foundling, resented imposition – to be merely tolerated –

whilst his over-privileged, over-indulged mother failed to receive desperately needed help and understanding. By the time such help was considered, it was far and away too late for either mother or child.

Seventeen

Awed, subdued. Whispered, foreign word. 'Ella, what's school?'

'Oooo, it's a lovely place.'

'What, better than this?'

'Nowhere's as nice as home, darling!'

'So why does Wobin have to go there every day? He should be here with us.' Infant misery overflows.

Three years married, Ella Adkins, her ample female charms increased by a second pregnancy sits down and lifts the infant to her lap. 'Don't you cry, my lovie. School's where the big children go. Here – where's my hankie… wipe those pretty eyes… now blow… there, that's better.'

She's lost him! Away! All day! Worse – veneration of the returning hero suffuses evenings and weekends in diffident daunting.

'Don't fret so, darling. You'll soon be going with him – then what am I going to do all day without you?' Smiling down at the small, doleful face nestling against her swelling, with sad-serious voice she continues. 'Who's going to help me make gingerbread men then?'

Temporarily distracted by concern for a friend, the child's arms reach up to draw Ella's face down for a kiss to console both.

Come the day, Imogen enters a new world of duality with her brother.

Partly the creation of family circumstance but also

resulting from inclination, they happily share their lives with friends whilst at school; away from it, together they are totality.

Good looks, intelligence and ready wit ensure popularity's fete among a loyal clique of admiring friends who never waver in allegiance – in spite of unwritten law forbidding social intimacy outside the schoolyard.

The foolhardy who venture to call at Brookfields never do so twice. Not only a remote situation (more than a mile from the village) but given their class-ridden society, Ada's 'residence' is just too daunting. Besides, the lady of the house has an infallible formula. For an interminable thirty seconds or so she stares silently down at the brave soul shuffling nervously on the doorstep in front of her, then walks away calling, 'Imogen, tell your brother there are *people* here to see him – and to go outside with them. We don't want the door open losing all the heat.'

Neither does Ada encourage 'visiting' in the village. Birthday invitations always regretfully declined; none ever issued. Natural resentment in rebuffed parents soon melts away – soothed by a mixture of charm and blatant blame-shifting. 'I just can't get them to mix – they're such an insular pair. Even refuse to have parties of their own, can you believe?'

Later, with other similarly offended mothers, the verdict is forgone conclusion. 'How such a lovely lady like her comes to have such a stuck-up pair of brats is beyond me! I feel really sorry for her.'

Walk away from the playground – disappear into exclusivity – enigmatic behaviour seasoning prestige with a flavour of the mysterious – somehow ensuring devotion that fails to germinate resentment. Far from being suspicious outsiders, they are the essential element of any school playground activity: 'What does Robin say?' 'Ask Imogen – she'll know what to do.' 'We can't start without them!'

Children roam the land – protected only by the armour of childhood artlessness. Vulnerability providing their only security, they wander the length and breadth of assured safety that is post-war Britain.

Naïve unto negligence, most fifties' parents decline to interest themselves in the activity of older children. Proximity can easily engender irritability. 'Get out from under my feet. Don't you dare bring mud home – and don't make such a racket – you'll wake the baby. Go on, get outta here. Hop it!'

'The war's over at last, isn't it? Good old England's *safe*! We *fought* to make these blasted kids safe. Noisy little buggers – always hanging round. Time for us to relax – enjoy life for a change. Child molesters? What are they for Gawd's sake? Peedoerfiles? Don't talk Greek!'

The prevailing attitude is classless, even if expressed in different language. That suits our two to perfection. Supervision? Intolerable!

With a secure system of espionage in place (within which awareness of the different farming season's activities is essential) all should be safe. Discovery can bring disaster… 'Clear orf outta there or I'll tell yer parents… And don't think I don't know who y'are!'

Childhood days of glittering gold and silver; days of sunshine, frost or snow passing in joyful parade to which rain merely brings an extra dimension of splashy splendour. An endless, seamless procession – all different – identical. Mellow days of pastel, blending in mellifluous, coagulating hues – dreamy oil floating on life's surface. Or maybe brassy days – hallelujah days – days of excitement and anticipation. Days that can barely contain themselves as the trumpets of enthusiasm blare confidently and cymbals of adventure clash strident harmony.

Prolix? Who's prolix? Oh, all right, have it your own way. They enjoy an ideal childhood. That concise enough for you? ONWARDS!

Eighteen

Now these two children of fortune have a truly special place – magnet that draws them back time and again. 'Tis a landmark in the area – known locally as 'The Dutch Barn'. Emphasis might well be considered comic in a countryside dotted with similar constructions but for the fact it's distinguished by being much bigger than the rest.

About eighty feet in length by thirty wide and forty or so at its highest point, it stands in isolated splendour at the top of the hill at one end of a long, narrow field on Burton's Farm – a position to cause much rancour among hardworked farm labourers faced with a long hill of mud to climb before the day's graft can begin. An enormous black beetle with nowhere else to run, it glowers defiance from a hill down which rainwater oozes to form a small lake around the gate at the base – 'What kind of a silly bugger would go an' built it *there*?'

For such an imposing building it's deceptively simple in construction. Consisting of a framework of iron girders shaped like the first Roman numeral and held together by enormous iron bolts, the structure holds aloft a black, rounded, Nissen-style roof of pitch-covered corrugated iron; the same material clads the two long sides and back of the building to within three feet or so of the ground.

They regard it as *theirs*. No hated monster this, but the hallowed cathedral of two small, but all-powerful gods.

To mere mortals, it shelters oblong bales of straw common in the countryside of that pre-polythene era. Unknowing, faithful toil of mortals provide protection from prying eyes and shelter from the cold of winter for the resident Lordly Ones.

Every good home must have furniture (even gods need a table and somewhere comfortable to sit or lay when relaxing). Bales provide for all needs as summer's sweet warmth cheers winter bleak.

Harvest toil completed, gate finally closed, new labourers take warning from experience as someone nods at the baked ruts of cart tracks with ominous foreboding.

'You reckon that was hard enough? Let me tell you, it's not so bad takin' it up there this time o' year, but jus' you wait till we needs to get some out nex' Jan'ry! Yonder's a bloody quagmire then.'

Winter permanence of this lake – such a focus of detestation among farm labour, concurrently provides good defence to those up aloft by making access noisily difficult. A moat no less, with security further enhanced since the field containing the barn at its farthest end is otherwise surrounded by dense blackthorn hedging bristling with angry thorns – impenetrable to all but occasional wildlife – and diminutive deities.

Concealed in snug paradise, immortals receive ample warning of approaching menace. Snug and smug, calmly watching as struggling humanity flounders through floods, up the soggy, slippy slope – loudly cursing the weather, the field, its gateway, but most of all, a heaven that decrees the labour of lowly status, and then rains on it to add insult to inequality.

High among uppermost bales, impassive watchers survey entertainment below, watching the pageant with benign curiosity – close encounters providing enlightenment to children raised within the linguistic confines of bourgeois society. Forbidden delights of ribald, fragmentarily understood language. Alien language of a strange parallel world. Exciting. Alarming. Delicious. Fascinating.

Further entertainment! Someone below passes wind. A good, loudly satisfying fart. The louder the better. An emission of *real* force, to ricochet off walls and roof – increasing in velocity on its journey.

Only true gods, invincible, all powerful ones, can resist the explosion of childish mirth. Instead? Childhood's plague – the joyful agony of stifled giggles.

Discarded lengths of substantial rope litter the floor, some of it knotted onto roof supports – original usage lost in the mists of agricultural history. Now, they have become swings – requiring but a small leap of imagination to transform into jungle lianas – swinging Tarzan-like, from tree to tree.

'We've got to save that missionary from the pot!'

'It's okay, I've got him – look out for that lion!'

Till, in a change of mood, world-famous trapeze artists – wowing a breathless audience with audacious skill.

'Look, Imi. Bet you can't do this!'

'Bet I can!'

Paradise holds further joys. Quiet days spent cocooned in fragrant warmth with comics, iced buns fresh from the bakery and fizzy lemonade. To make heaven complete it should be raining – heavier the better – drumming in loud impotence on the iron roof to emphasise cosiness of sanctuary.

Here I go again! All right, all right. For those with no poetry in their souls, cosy as you can get without being tucked up in a nice warm bed.

Nineteen

Precious moments of complete tranquillity can flow un-bidden, at any time into any life, no matter how arid. With considerable luck and a good following wind they'll be recognised for what they are and savoured as possibly unrepeatable joys. Evanescent treasures to be stored against a time of want, they are moments especially delightful combined with the virtue of being well earned.

This particular afternoon, on the day of her mother's death, is one such time of bounty for Imogen – earned with the toil of a lifetime.

The poor cow deserves a treat, so we won't begrudge her, eh?

Closing her eyes, she basks in the sunshine, ensconced in a chair conveniently placed by the window to allow perfect viewing of the outside world. Obviously, it's not just any old chair, and just as merely looking at her mother without censure is a first, so also is daring to relax in its vicinity – never mind take a seat!

Her daring makes her giggle as with undisciplined relish she settles into opulent upholstery.

Thus enthroned in secure comfort, Ada has watched the world go by her window. Year on year. Patient. Confident. Waiting for her visitor. 'He'll be here any day now you know.'

Under the influence of unaccustomed relaxation, Imogen's thoughts have already willingly slipped back to her childhood to recall a clear image of Ada when that lady first saw Charles Elrington.

The daughter's eyes are moist with the sweetness of fond reminiscence, but vision is unwavering. Her prospect of the distant past is unobscured by nostalgia's ultra-efficient palimpsest with its concatenate seduction of wishful thinking to distort truth and call sober hindsight an inebriate liar.

Ah, the splendour of life before the world started to go bad!

Yes, but understand, Imogen's youth ended in abrupt brutality; there never has been opportunity for nostalgia's enchantment, consequently her recall is pragmatic as the woman herself. Even so, she's happy this far – safe and secure in the world of recollection she wanders – inviolate – in Ada's chair in the sun.

Denouement of her mother's earthly existence has made it possible for Imogen to focus on the 'glory days' – that sunshine time before insidious, grey-cloud old age first shrouded lustre, then effected a total eclipse. Now divest of all obscuring elements she recalls with delighted amazement that her mother had indeed been a beautiful woman and the sight had been joyfully dazzling.

Twenty

Ada and the 1950s – like she'd never existed before! Think Monroe, Gardner and Mansfield if you must, but ultimately discard them all – in favour of our girl!

As permanent, compulsive fecundity in Mother Nature responded to Father Time's unquenchable lusts (a mating of prodigious passion that defied both age and gravity) the pair created the fifties. On the birth of their love-child they looked about them to adopt a perfect playmate for the new infant – and found Ada.

After her renaissance, Ada was profoundly relieved to find the miserable austerity of the forties with its dearth of life's little luxuries now fading from existence.

Bombs had held no personal fear – nor pity for others; widowhood's distinct prospect created little more than fleeting concern. But, the awful deprivation created by clothing rationing with consequent lack of choice caused untold grief – filling her mind to the exclusion of all other considerations.

The war nonsense finally over ('What has Poland got to do with us anyway?') she had discovered the aftermath of hostilities merely increased distress.

Others might celebrate – her conflict continued. In fact, privation intensified – worsened by the unfulfilled promise of better to come. '*Make do and mend*? Make do – well, I've got no choice, have I? But *mend*? Please!' Like babies and their soiled nappies, that was for others to cope with – waved disdainfully away by a well-manicured hand.

Ah, but during the *next* ten years, Ada began to glow in radiant serenity, pervasive as a full moon in velvet warmth of a cloudless midsummer night's sky. Just everything conducive to her complete satisfaction.

She was beautiful, money was plentiful; she had love, respect, adoration and a more than satisfying sex life. People seemed to fall over themselves to make sure she always got her own way. Every whim catered for!

It need not concern us overly, but it'll probably be no surprise to learn that towards the decade's ending Nature and Time sort of 'fell out'. Nothing permanent, you understand, but a definite souring of relations – and nasty enough while it lasted! Nature claimed she'd been raped, Time decided he'd been cheated – misled by packaging – demanded his money back! Near the extinction of the fifties came a grand reunion. Anticipation of the coming decade promising excitement to rejuvenate and rekindle even the oldest of passions.

Once fully reconciled, both parents lost interest in their adopted child, proceeding to abuse her with increasing virulence. Finally bored, they abandoned her to the slow, creeping embrace of an old pal – tall guy, black hood, scythe over his shoulder.

How-ev-er, it should be noted that Ada remained blissfully unaware of her forlorn, unloved condition during the remainder of her life. When clouds appeared in *her* sky, she simply went to play hide and seek among them with all the other stars.

Back in the safety of *her* decade, at no time did Ada question the self-evident principle that men existed only to protect and provide for women.

Should that principle be questioned Ada would laugh. 'Sexual equality? Ha ha, sounds like some nasty, outlandish perversion! Work? Contribute financially to the home? Don't be ridiculous!'

She was aware that *some* married women worked – working-class women. Women who lived in that other world – crossing the great divide to serve her in shops or do her housework. 'Heaven knows they're paid well enough for what little they do… '

She had chosen her husband with great care – knew just how to keep him too! By so doing, she avoided such farce.

Motherhood had preserved her from war work. Now, within the social arrangements of an age that discouraged working wives, her world was inviolate.

Just a few short years to go – the sixties and seventies waited to shatter a tired old world with youth-fuelled exuberance – women like Ada and men who enjoyed the status quo, swamped in a rising tide of feminism – a tempest of retribution to drown femininity, then wash it away as anachronistic irrelevance.

Goodbye to the flounce of lace petticoats, stocking tops, stiletto heels and bubble-cut hair, hello to mini skirts, tights, boots and straight curtains of hair worn by young women who seriously believed life could and would hold as much opportunity for them as their brothers. Bless!

None of this affected Mrs Phillips in the slightest. She would always remain true to her beloved fifties. As far as she was concerned that decade – *her* decade – joined the immortals to become timeless.

So, how about it then? Do we stay to while away an idle hour or two in Imogen's company – travel back in time, see what she sees? She's all nice and relaxed now – enchanted by the lovely imagery of recall, but she'll be glad of our company (any company) before very much longer…

ACT TWO

One

Picture the scene... it's a glorious, sunny day in the spring of 1957. The English countryside is bursting with new life – as only the Atlantic-soaked English countryside can burst – given just a bity-bit of encouragement from the sun. One peek round heavy cloud darkness – away it goes like a cork from well shaken champagne – POW!

The French are justifiably proud of their language but let's face facts, their *printemps* sounds like it's limping hesitantly into the year having been badly savaged by winter. As for the Italian *primavera* – too laid-back! Just drifts in, then flows on, all unnoticed, into summer... and beyond.

Ah, but the English *spring*. Now that leaps into the year with onomatopoeic resonance! Winter may well snap and snarl from the periphery, but rage is impotent; deep down, it knows IT IS HISTORY!

Here I go again!

Under this heady influence, gaunt, filigree beauty of winter trees becomes swathed in tiny embryonic leaves to bathe them in delicate green gauze. Sunshine's levity has caused over-eager cherry and plum blossom to tumble from trees now anticipating a less frivolous, fruit-bearing future with matronly superiority – veteran brides discarding unwanted wedding finery, confetti for apple trees now standing in budding pink and white hymeneal innocence.

I hear the trumpets blow again!

And daffodils! (I've got going, so I may as well continue.)

Where did they suddenly leap from? Profusion of eye-catching gold giving the impression of a miser's hoard wrenched from hiding and scattered round to enrich all those dark, impoverished places. Out from sunny, south-facing corners, tulips start to swagger with multi-coloured bombast – safe in the knowledge they will supersede that yellow parvenu.

Nature – that impassioned artist – flings colour at a mud-hued canvas in indiscriminate extravagance of pure, selective genius.

Where were we...? Oh, yes. Now that the scene has been well and truly set, the drama is waiting to unfold. So, CURTAIN UP!

Two

Under the irresistible exuberance of vernal sway, Henry's receptionist has been seduced. Staid, dowdy, efficiency-informed clothes she normally wears have been transformed by a frilly, white satin blouse she teams with her usual serviceable grey skirt – to inadvertently give her the appearance of an over-large pigeon in a presumptuous frame of mind.

To augment such levity, her working environment is decked with daffodils she has plucked by eager, greedy armfuls that morning before setting out for work.

For such a plain woman she has surprisingly large and lustrous, hazel eyes – a pleasing surprise to anyone with wit enough to spare her more than a passing glance. Not for the first time that morning they smile in triumph, surveying golden splendour on coffee tables, windowsills and reception desk. White frills at her bosom swell with purest satisfaction.

Just as vivid as the flowers is Henry's wife Ada, who now surges into the reception on a tsunami of self-assurance. Airily she waves a delicate, well-manicured hand to dismiss the taxi driver who has brought her here, opened all doors, then ushered her onto the premises like royalty. Like royalty too, she never carries cash; knowing this, the driver, touching his forehead with one finger returns to the bower of lingering Dior that is his cab. As always he will get his fare from her husband. Every expense she incurs is dealt with by her consort via his personal account.

Henry, the poor sod, feels deeply privileged fulfilling this function for his wife – taking all onerous consideration from her delicate shoulders is his main aim in life. He thinks that will make her love him.

An astute, even ruthless businessman, with a reputation for striking a fair deal that, nevertheless, gives little away, he's wilfully incapable of restraining her carefree extravagance by even one iota.

She greets Brenda with a wave, bestowing a smile that seems to contain so much sunshine that, half-blinded, the office-bound receptionist instinctively glances at the window expecting to find a morning suddenly overcast.

'Oh, hello, Mrs Phillips,' she flutters. 'How lovely to see you. Such a gorgeous day, isn't it?' Ungainly, she lurches to pick up a magazine to offer, then, perceiving it extra to requirements, replaces it – gratefully retreating once more to safety behind her concealing desk.

Ada makes no reply to the question, but heads in a direct line towards the best easy chair – placed, for her benefit, to face Henry's office door. Seated, she opens the expensive glossy she has brought with her and is immediately engrossed.

No *Farmer and Stockbreeder*, then?

Brenda knows she's forgotten. Doesn't mind. Didn't expect conversation – would have become tongue-tied anyway. But that smile – just everything! She's blushing with embarrassed pleasure – a feeling that rapidly degenerates into despairing regret. Why hadn't she bought a new skirt as well as the blouse? She'd wanted to. That emerald green one for instance. Would have been just perfect. How come she'd allowed prudence to win the day as always? Pensively touching limp, greying, light-brown hair, she makes a mental note to fix an appointment with the hairdresser.

Ada is a good-looking woman. No! She's a *fabulous* looking woman. More, she carries such an aura of glamour that details become almost irrelevant. It's an intrinsic part of fifties ethos, accessible to a very few; Ada's take on it is accessible only to the very rich.

After the initial *wow* factor has worked its awesome magic and scattered wits have regrouped, it's possible to remark that she does have a beautiful face; good bone structure, perfect symmetrical features and eyes, large, wide-set, china blue – seemingly intent on preserving the secrets of the soul in doll-like, expressionless mockery. Adding to the appeal, her figure is well proportioned; legs long, slender – and naturally she headlines that essential element of fifties glam – a glorious halo of platinum blond.

She's waiting with barely concealed impatience that even her magazine fails to mitigate. Her husband is taking her to lunch at the best local restaurant, and his appointments are running late. It's not a particularly exciting prospect… her thoughts run, but then you never know who's going to be there – maybe someone worth impressing!

Impact! Creating an effect. It's an obsession with her. Making the grand entrance; drawing admiring glances from the men, envious ones from the women. That's *her* milieu and all that anticipated attention turns an indifferent meal with an unexciting companion into manna from the gods with Adonis.

She knows exactly what the scene will be. Yes, she can see it all – her eyes will be aglow – she'll be smiling – vivacious. Everyone will get the treatment. She'll miss not one of these, her fervent disciples! They'll all be warm, happy under her spell as she greets them. Even the women will be thinking, *she's so beautiful she could be a film star* – the men will be simply mesmerised. She also knows exactly the effect she'll have on these, her creatures. Some will go so far as to murmur among themselves, 'Just look how her clothes suit her. Isn't she gorgeous?'

Think she'll be unable to hear them? Think again!

It all goes to fuel a cannibal ego that engulfs and consumes any competition. Regardless of wealth, lacking Ada's single-minded dedication, no other self-esteem in small-town 1950's England has the audacity to even contemplate contest anyway. She's just the one sleek, flashing fish in a small pool – and all the other pond life know their place.

Ah well, her musings continue as she glances at the still-closed door, at least she'll brighten the day for them. With a sweet sigh of resigned virtue she returns to the shining pages of wonderland she holds in soft, slender hands.

Madam is wearing her latest little extravagance – having just returned from a Paris shopping spree. Her admiration of the French knows no bounds. How on earth did 'chic' survive the war? *Incroyable*! What a nation!

Visible evidence of her visit is demonstrated by handbag and heels in matching brown crocodile skin together with a blouse of feather-light, beige silk – all of which complement to perfection her newly tailored suit in a delightful shade of darkish pink.

Discrete glint of gold with diamond-highlighted pearls emphasize marble smoothness of neck and perfectly manicured hands.

Madam is, of course, acutely alive to the danger of ostentation! For this reason, yet another trophy carried back from the Capital of Chic proclaims itself in the merest waft of exclusive French *parfum* as she moves. Mmm, sublime!

As always, Ada's complexion is flawless, echoing the delicate beige of her blouse. Lips and nails the same pink as her suit, shaped, feathered eyebrows and lashes are mid-brown, whilst eyelids have the merest smudge of pale blue-grey – all add definition to her eyes.

The tints of complexion, lips, eyebrows, lids and lashes, nails and hair owe nothing to nature, but are the artistic product of a true aesthete.

Henry's office door opens. At last! Impatient as she undoubtedly is, it will never show. Languid, she slowly glances up – to become acutely aware of a man's intense scrutiny. She's used to admiration, but this is far more profound; well beyond mere spontaneous flattery. Caught completely off guard she comes as close to being flustered as she's capable, but still manages to note the perfect combination of dark-brown suit, cream shirt and tie in the most delicious shade of pink.

In that instant, deep conviction borne of total self-absorption takes root. He must have seen her before – fallen for her! She *knows* if she were free of life's restricting influences, this tall, handsome, beautifully dressed man with adorable ardent, dark eyes (an exact match to the suit!) would, without a shadow of doubt, declare his passion and claim her for his very own.

Swept along by a heady mix of fantasy and sexual attraction, she fails to equate her 'restricting influences' with husband, children and home; that realisation will come later. Just now it's like some beautiful, romantic film. Oh, how she just loves the movies!

And this, *this* is the moment when Ada and reality, with which, in any case, she has only ever had a somewhat tenuous relationship, finally go their separate ways – never to meet again except for the occasional stilted moment, like long-estranged life partners.

Three

At the moment Ada first saw Charlie Elrington he was emerging from a bruising session with her husband.

Bust a gut, he had, trying to persuade the son of a bitch to increase the order. 'They'll make sowing a doddle. Sell like hot cakes, they will!'

Enthusiastic fool!

'Well, if they don't, you can have 'em back.' Henry hated extravagant claims, no matter if they might prove eventualy justified – set his teeth on edge! 'Hot cakes become stale cakes all too quickly in this business. Not in my larder, thank you. Sale or return – and that's my final word on the matter. You know as well as I do that farming tools are evolving at a rapid pace. My customers are a conservative old lot, take a deal of persuading. They're not about to get stuck with a prototype that'll lack later improvements, and I don't blame 'em.'

For Henry, every small detail of function was essential and he had a mind like a computer for intricacy of perception. No half stories or hyperbole – just facts. 'You can leave the prognosis to me!'

Charlie had shifted uncomfortably in his chair. 'Increase that normal order – be a winner!' Recalling the usual pep-talk in the safety of the sales office that morning angered him. Oh, sure! Piece of cake! Huh, piece of shit more like!

Later, limping towards a door that seemed to have retreated a mile or so since his enthusiastic entrance, his thoughts were far from charitable. The bastard made me sweat for it! Still, I got me a decent order – the commission'll be good. Reaching the door he straightened to his full six feet, turning his head to look over his shoulder as he did so. 'Cheerio, squire. Delivery next Tuesday – see you next month. Any queries, just ring the office.'

Henry, impatient, knowing his wife was waiting, failed to reply or even look up from paperwork on his desk. The wave of his hand was more a signal of dismissal than farewell.

Charlie smiled as he turned to open the door. *Arsehole!* Still, never mind him. I've met my target for the week – and then some!

Relaxed, expansive, he began to contemplate a nice scotch and soda – with a good cigar. How about that? He passed through the door narrowly resisting a childish impulse to slam it in irritated triumph behind him.

His transient voluptuous mood evaporated with sudden violence as a blast of wondrous envy gripped his guts. Deprived of breath he dithered, staring at the vision in front of him – the overwhelming vision of artistic genius that was Ada. Halted in his tracks he could only stare like a dumbstruck youth – lost in a wonder of admiration. Suddenly aware that she was looking at him he half smiled and somehow walked away towards the exit, oblivious of anyone else there, even forgetting his usual smile and wave for Brenda whom he recognised with pity as one of nonchalant Life's throw– away victims.

As he emerged into blinding sunshine, Charlie shaded his eyes as he began to think. Women were so lucky! *They* could be as colourful and flamboyant as they wished. No one would even raise an eyebrow.

For Ada, enduring love at first sight. For homosexual

Charlie Elrington, a mixture of resentment and reluctant admiration – appreciation of one artist for the work of another.

Reaching his car, he unlocked the door and settled in behind the wheel. His mind already busy with other questions. Would *he* be at the pub? Would *he* speak? Perhaps just a little smile of recognition? Yes, he'd settle for that! After all, their paths had crossed quite often recently (not exactly by accident!) Maybe, just maybe, that smile holds something warmer than recognition. Invitation even! Charlie was sure he hadn't been mistaken…

By now he'd completely forgotten the rainbow woman; lost in a fever of anticipation she had ceased to exist – wiped from his memory by the bleach of desire.

And the lady herself? Because of the secret nature of her passion, she could ask questions of no one, so never did discover her new lover's actual sexual preference. She only had brief, unsatisfying glimpses of him after that fateful day, but thanks to a prodigious imagination, she remained steadfast in conviction of his faithful worship.

Now that's *real* farce! None of your soubrettes and gigolos. Just pure travesty.

* * *

Her husband became delighted – amazed by the amount of interest she started to take in day to day running of his business – calling in on a regular basis, checking his visitors with Brenda, bursting into his office unannounced with, 'Sorry, I thought you were alone.'

To his joy he was also reinstated regularly in the marital bed where her usual bored acceptance of his advances following his ritual humiliation was replaced by a great deal of voluptuously active invention.

Condoms were discarded in the blaze of this growing need. He was amazed as he enjoyed her creativity, but noted that her eyes were usually closed or glazed over as though she wasn't actually seeing him. Also, he quickly found he could do anything with her so long as he was silent. The only bedroom sounds came from her, soft sounds of pleasure followed by a whimpering cry of joy.

In spite of all her manoeuvring she never actually met her lover – a pity, since reality would have blasted the dream to glory and gone. Instead she waited patiently – long after her husband had ceased to exist – long after (unknown to her) Charlie himself had died.

On and on, year after patient year, as increasingly heavy make-up effected grotesque travesty on sagging skin – or *anyone* glanced at her with anything resembling admiration or envy. True, some stared – in fascinated disgust, many sniggered; most averted eyes in pity. Ada neither knew nor cared about the effect she had on others – secure in a dream of Elrington's adoration.

Four

'They must be trying for a baby – it's the only explanation.'

As far as Ella was concerned, what went on in the big house stayed in the big house. She'd never been known to gossip about her other family – not even with her Bert. Now she was incapable of keeping quiet.

'And at the rate they're going on, it won't take long either! I reckon there's going to be the patter of tiny feet pdq.'

'Oh, yes. What makes you think that?'

'Well, his bed's never slept in these days – and you should just see the state of their sheets of a morning! It's like they were randy teenagers.'

'What, like us you mean?'

'Do stop. I'm being serious. He used to use condoms. Thinks I didn't know about it – always put them at the bottom of the dustbin. And judging by the number got through, they were always pretty keen, but this is something else! There'll be another bun in the oven after all these years. You mark my words.'

'Isn't she a bit long in the tooth for that?'

'Oh, no – I'm sure she's not. Still has her bleed – regular as clockwork.'

'How could you possibly know a thing like that?'

'It's obvious. I have to change the sheets every day for three weeks, then nothing for a week – unless they get impatient towards the end that is. Then it's like there's been a massacre. Blood everywhere. I reckon it happens at least three times every night. I'm surprised he's got the energy to get up and go to work of a morning. She's always asleep till about ten. When she does get up, it's like she's in another world, always smiling and sighing.'

'Holy mackerel! By the way, haven't *you* got another bun cooking? All the signs are there.'

'I didn't want to say anything till it was confirmed, but I've a strong suspicion we'll have another in spring next year. Mind you, I wouldn't be surprised if they get there first at this rate!'

'I can hardly believe it of them. He's all quiet refinement and she always strikes me as being regular hoity-toity, a real ice maiden.'

'Oh, she's lovely when you get to know her and he's a real sweetheart.'

'All the same... '

'Promise me you won't say a word to anyone.'

'All right. Here, all this talk about other people's sex lives has got my pecker up!' How about it, eh?'

'All right then. You go on up. I've got one or two things to do then I'll be with you. We'll have to be a bit gentle about it though – don't want any upsets at this stage.'

'Try teaching yer grandmother how to suck eggs!'

Five

Cometh the hour, cometh the adolescent. A zit-obscured interloper seeking lost identity – new identity – any identity. Questing that weaves with terrifying unpredictability through labyrinthine ways – awash with random sexual desire and hate-fuelled, unidentifiable yearning.

Childhood certainties melt like candle wax in a furnace, coming to rest in coagulating pools of embarrassing body fluids. An overwhelming need for freedom alternates disconcertingly with the melancholy of abandonment – to manifest itself in bloody-minded truculence.

'A teenager! It's a teenager!' Not a lovely little boy, not a sugar 'n' spice confection. No, it's a teenager.

Suddenly aged parents, tremble with apprehension, mourn the loss of beloved children who may, or may not achieve renaissance as likeable adults – whilst domestic harmony stands on its head and shows its knickers.

Well, it wasn't always so – not in 1950's Britain it wasn't. The generation that had fought for national liberty wasn't about take any old buck from its kids.

'You just be thankful, my lad – you could have been under the jack boot – never mind goin' out just when you want. This is my house – you'll do as you're told in it.'

And so, in resentful impatience containing nothing resembling gratitude, adolescents lurk in guilt-ridden, sulphurous quiet.

Undisturbed by teenage angst, dear old Dad 'n' Mum

degenerate gracelessly into cardie 'n' slippers to the uninspiring strains of Semprini's *Serenade*, whilst the not-so-young-any-more stalk the periphery of family life, thinking their own impure thoughts, surreptitiously listening to their own music – trying not to be noticed.

Those were the days my friends!

Mind you, finally away from school, feeling power in their own financial worth, *some few* young males rebel. Wear their own uniform – draped jackets, drain-pipe trousers, chunky, crepe-soled suede shoes and hairstyles with rude names – playing their own loud music – on their own radios! Thus armed, they outface the impotent wrath of ageing warriors.

'Whilst you're under my roof… '

'Yeah, yeah, yeah… My money's as good as yours! See yer later, alligator!'

'Well, yer call-up papers'll be arriving any day now – a spell of army discipline'll do you a power o' good – maybe even make a man of you. Huh, some hopes! Still whilst there's life… '

'B**l**ks to you!'

Like the majority, Robin has no argument with anyone – except himself. Lost, disorientated, propelled headlong into a white-water, white-knuckle torrent heading for Adultsville, he's temporarily stripped of the security of certainty that is his relationship with father and sister. In this perplexity he starts to wonder if even the barren wasteland of his mother's attitude isn't preferable to this uncharted territory; at least he knows where he is there!

But it isn't long before Imogen joins him. At eleven she's more than ready to abandon a childhood that seems to have lost much of its fulgent appeal, fearlessly diving headlong into murky depths that have already swallowed her brother, she follows her idol without a backward glance. Together there, they graduate to the jukeboxy delights of coffee bars and greasy-spooned cafes, where, for the price of an espresso, they imbibe fifties culture. The forbidden cup of rock and roll with its blatant, irresistible, raw animal sexuality barely comprehended, or the relative intellectualism of what they call trad jazz – they drink deeply of both.

'Splitting the atom' they call it. Deep, interminable discussions. Books, ideas, ideals, religion, politics, life in general and their own in particular. Opinionated discussions of mind-blowing naivety – arrogant as only the naïve can be. 'Wait till our generation take over – we'll show them!'

Blissfully unaware of future pain, guilt or regret, they alone have all solutions. Beauty of untarnished life emerges from the constraining chrysalis of childhood to paint a rainbow future – shimmering with all the clarity and substance of new-blown soap bubbles.

With so much reliance on these precarious certainties, initial university experience is decidedly disconcerting to eighteen-year-old Robin. His first two months are a steep learning curve from which he emerges some ten years wiser.

Six

'Where are you off to? Your brother's home for the weekend. Surely you'll want to be here when he arrives.'

'Eh? Oh, no. I'm meeting Valerie, we're spending the evening at her place. Er, is he bringing anyone with him?'

'I don't think so, he never mentioned anything.'

'Well, anyway, tell him I'll see him later. Bye.'

As Imogen disappears into the evening her surprised father turns to his wife. 'There's a turn-up for the books! I thought she'd want to be here.'

'You can bet she's got her own fish to fry. She's not your little girl any longer you know.' Ada makes a shrewd guess. 'I'll bet she's discovered the opposite sex.'

Henry starts violently at this first contiguous concept of his daughter and sex. 'Oh, go on! She's much too young...' After a sly smile, his wife merely shrugs in reply. That's given him something to think about!

Now thoroughly upset, Henry deals alone with a growing alarm. He has already been unsettled by his daughter's lack of academic achievement. Now this.

'Well, she's going to be beautiful anyway – no trouble getting a husband... ' His Indulgence, influenced by received wisdom of the day coinciding with the prejudices of both parents, he continues. 'But she should be getting better reports than these – it's almost like she just doesn't care.'

Ada, now thoroughly irritated by the whole subject of her daughter's antics, answers him. 'She probably doesn't, but I for one refuse to concern myself with her nonsense. I'm the last person she wants to discuss anything with.'

'She doesn't talk to any of her family – even Robin's in the dark.'

'Well, I'm quite content to stay in the dark. Please leave me out of these discussions in future. I want to hear no more. You would insist they be educated locally... '

Insufficient intelligence? More like total lack of intellectual ambition! The fact that no one considers university for Imogen is no surprise – except to Robin. Outraged, he storms, 'They don't know you like I do, Imi. 'Course you've got the brains – are they blind? I'm surprised at Dad... he just smiles and changes the subject.'

Imogen is on her own learning curve! From time to time, faint guilt recalls a brother's image. Then she misses him – course she misses him! Trouble is she now spends increasing amounts of time studying her effect on his friends... among others.

Any activity that excludes sexual attraction finds her stricken with overwhelming inertia. Tidying a bedroom – dire enough, but the mental burden of academic study? It hasn't a chance!

In unconscious imitation of her mother, she sits at her dressing table for hours – just gazing into the mirror. In admiring tribute to what she sees, she daydreams. Dreams of love, dreams of happiness – as of right. *Knows* she is pretty and so, will always witness a happy world.

Up close. Eyes light-brown with flecks of green – lovely, expressive eyes. Abundant, rich, dark-brown hair alive with glints of gold waving gently to greet an admiring world – hair that will never fade or lack today's lustre.

No question-marked future ever menaces reflected self-assurance in youthful beauty. At this age, innocent vanity will briefly enhance the world – even if it's just a skirt that makes her bum look smaller.

Meanwhile, secretly busy with her own plans, Imogen decides to enrol in a secretarial course – simply because she anticipates it will result in a lucrative job – quickly.

Oxford – just four miles from home – a different world! A world of bustle, excitement, and what she perceives as sophistication.

The grip of adolescent claustrophobia has become almost unbearable – a burgeoning social life needs to be removed from the confining atmosphere of home and village.

She holds her breath through her parents' initial surprise – past token opposition, to satisfaction – then on to grudging approval.

After a look of triumph at her husband that alters to withering scorn for a fool, Ada drawls, 'There, I told you not to worry! She's more than capable of deciding her own future – and an acceptable one at that.' Turning to Imogen she just says, 'Marvellous, dear... marvellous.'

'But you're a grammar-school girl, you know, could do anything... Are you sure it's what you really want?' Henry's not quite so sure.

Imogen transfers her sole attention to him – a tougher nut to crack. 'I'm never going to do any better at school, Dad – not even if I stay there for a trillion, trillion years. There's nothing for me round here any more.'

Realising a hurtful blunder she gushes on, 'Job-wise, I mean... It's not as though I'd be leaving home, is it? I'd never, never want to do that... '

He understands her motives – probably better than she does. Smiling, he says, 'Well, all right. But just you listen, young lady, you're still our little girl – whether you like it or not! We only have your best interests at heart. Always remember that!'

Arms round his neck, words muffled in his jacket, only he hears her response, 'You're so wonderful, Dad. I love you. I always will.'

Realising most of her emotion results from relief, he is comforted all the same. Feels her move to free herself from the embrace – holds her tighter for a few seconds longer in stubborn parental demonstration.

As we know, Imogen's friends have never visited her at home, an embargo that has sometimes seemed unkind. 'Better not ask, eh, you know what she's like. She won't have it, but she'll get mad anyway and we'll all suffer after!' Robin's warnings always sufficient.

Now, for the first time, this situation becomes not just irrelevant, but downright welcome. The interests of her and her clique have gone to live in the city. They need to follow – or just *die*!

Intrigues of no substance assume overwhelming interest – to be abandoned at a moment's notice in favour of… something equally, fascinatingly banal.

'Let's go to jazz club.' Imogen's usual Wednesday suggestion – always greeted as unique innovation by her coterie. Rhythm-pulsing, semi-darkness-enveloped, she dances – always with the same boy in that intuitive togetherness of jive where two become one in pseudo-sexual abandon.

As if to prove she's her father's child, it pleases some contradiction in her psyche never to know her partner's name, but she will never forget him.

Coffee bars. Great meeting places smelling of a lotta things – bar coffee! Damp, crumbling, garlic-informed walls. Distressed, over-worked Victorian drains. Unwashed youth attempting camouflage in cheap perfume – only to succeed in amplifying the offence. And lurking beneath it all, a suggestion of disinfectant to mingle in edgy distain with the whole malodorous works.

Excitement of a clientele disporting itself around, on, or underneath chipped, Formica-clad tables contrasts in pathetic mutual need with sneering contempt in the staff.

'Coke, please!'

'Uh huh... two straws, I suppose? Get offa my table there! Little bastards... '

Lack of welcome? All part of the fun – as is parental disapproval. 'Hanging round those places... You'll get yourself a bad name. And don't try to deny it – your clothes reek!'

As though influenced by such warnings, Imogen occasionally leads her motley crew to 'take tea' at the Cadena. Sipping tea, nibbling dainty sandwiches, 'indulging' in iced walnut cake in an atmosphere of demure, ladylike quiet – a tableau to charm any parent.

One way or another and for most of the time she fails to miss a mere brother, but if he is home for longer than a fleeting visit, her friends lose her – to drift rudderless from one boring day to the next.

'How long is he staying for this time? Anyone got any idea?'

A question echoed by his mother.

Seven

Robin the bringer of jollity. Robin the raconteur. Robin of the witty rejoinder. Always cheerful, considerate, kindly, ever the optimist – bright early morning sunshine, that's Robin Phillips at this time in his life.

'You should have just seen it! We stepped out of college and there, balancing up on top of a lamp post, was a bicycle! We were all hooting with laughter when Beryl suddenly said, "Damn it all, that's *my* bike!" Well, that was it – we just couldn't stop. God knows how anyone got it up aloft, but it took two blokes with two ladders almost an hour to get it down.'

He reduces his father and Imogen to helpless laughter – even his mother can be caught mid-way to an involuntary smile.

Like his sister, he adores his father. The bond between these two almost palpable – fine, beautiful.

Numberless mutual interests ranging from gardening (well, roses anyway) to chess and poker, with music their grand passion. Hours spellbound by the sounds of radio and gramophone, followed by the serious matter of picking through a performance with forensic precision... 'I bet Schneiderhan wishes they hadn't recorded *that* performance.'

Henry, who loves Robin's enthusiasm, also knows what it's like to put heart, soul and sinew into such work only to be assailed by sick dissatisfaction and self-doubt, demurs ruefully. 'Ah well, son, we all have our off days.'

This affinity with his father has become the most precious element of life – more precious even than sister or friends. Sisters have their own mysterious agenda, friends come and go.

About his mother he's neutral – philosophical. With unconscious accuracy he tells friends, 'I must have been a difficult birth.' Assuming a droll expression he adds, 'Anyway, she doesn't care for anyone very much – but I'm just that bit further down the to-o-o-obs!'

* * *

'Must he bring all his books in here – cluttering up the place. Henry, tell him to take it all back to his bedroom – at once!'

'But he's got exams next week – and it's only three books. It's too chilly to swat up there.'

'I don't care how cold it is – he'll have to put on extra clothing. I'm not having this room messed up. We might well have visitors. The Bellinghams said they would call in sometime this weekend.'

Henry's smile is rueful. 'Sorry, Robin...'

His son wordlessly gathers up the contentious volumes. As the door closes behind him Ada's smile becomes sweet guile hiding triumph as she looks at her husband. 'You do understand, don't you?'

He doesn't answer, but his silence tells her he's resentful. Ah but, resentful and silent! She enjoys playing her particular games with the people around her – especially these two. Her thoughts harden. I'll teach him to be resentful!

As always in such circumstances, Robin willingly forgives his father for not protecting him from his mother's blatant injustice, knowing it results from Henry's love for Ada; has long since understood and accepted it as inevitable. He forgives, but Henry's weakness in this respect constitutes the only flaw in their relationship – creating a certain awkwardness between them from time to time. This he does resent.

Blissfully unaware of any undercurrent, Imogen is always desperate to be included in their activities. Future years will mask her true feelings with a 'poker face', the envy of any gambler, but at this stage, thoughts and feelings flit cheerfully across her face – school kids on an unexpected holiday.

Always convinced she'll one day win at cards, she never gives up hope! The effort is valiant but only succeeds in becoming a family joke. 'Look at that, Dad. I do believe our Imi's got herself a bad hand!'

'So she has, Robin! Never mind, Imi – better luck next time, eh?'

Music though – she can share that as an equal – just so long as she avoids ignorance-revealing autopsies afterwards! Failing to understand what they understand or feel what they feel, she can still hear what they hear. Still and silent under the threat of expulsion – past all human endurance and beyond. On and on into the semi-consciousness of total self-negation just to keep these two happy, share something precious with them – avoid being classified with her mother.

Eight

Robin graduated amid predictable glory – a double first, wouldn't y' just know it? Equally predictable offers of employment. Almost dismayed by speed of transition from student to employee, he was!

'Been looking forward to a few weeks freedom!' he told his father. 'I'd be a fool not to, though. Newson's have an excellent reputation. It's a real piece of luck!'

'Huh! Ollie's the one with the luck – and he knows it!'

Without doubt Oliver Newson (Newson Heating & Refrigeration Co. Ltd, North Oxford) was a good judge of character. Everyone said as much – especially Oliver Newson. Family friend of long standing, he'd watched Robin mature in ability and intelligence – wanted these qualities for his firm. And what Oliver Newson wanted, Oliver Newson got.

Something of a self-opinionated old fart really, but he intended to pay the young man well so we'll let it pass.

Cornering his quarry during the last vacation before exams, he boomed, 'Be sure to come and see me first, my boy!' Then, impatient of events, fearful of predators, made a formal offer of employment even before results were known – and was accepted.

Henry was hurt as Robin moved in to the top floor of a house in suburban Summertown with Duncan Macaulay, another employee at Newson's. His brief comment contained a world of wistful hunger.

'This is your home, Son. I've been looking forward to seeing more of you. Come on back here – see how you feel in a year or so.'

'Oh, Dad, you know it's better this way. In any case, I won't be all that far away – be able to entertain *you*. We'll see so much of each other you'll get sick of the sight of me!'

Henry's fleeting smile failed to hide pain adequately, but all Ada's frigidity had revived at prospect of her son's permanent proximity. Since she made no secret of her attitude, he could hardly be under any illusion as to his son's motive. Leaden resignation doused him with the chill of inevitability. 'That'll never happen!' he replied with joviality he was far from feeling.

As usual Ada attempted to hide aversion under a bushel of altruism.

'He just wants his independence – we really must think of him, dear. Let him go his own way – so much better for him than being stuck at home with us watching his every move. Anyway, he'll be here at Christmas, won't he?'

'I never intended watching his every move – what gave you that idea?' The message was very clear; he'd lost a son but gained domestic tranquillity. Peace with a heavy price tag.

Ada drifted from the room leaving a saddened Henry to console himself with thoughts of Christmas.

* * *

Duncan was a year older than Robin. 'Been working for old man Newson for an age… well, long enough to know the ropes anyway! Take my advice – ignore the old sod if he asks you to stay late. Give him an inch, he'll take the pro- verbial!'

Thickset in a rugged kinda fashion, Duncan favoured suede Chelsea boots with tailored tweeds – and a Cowardesque cravat, which he thought gave a certain lift to his outfit but which merely succeeded in tipping debonair into downright pretentious – a sartorial accident that belied his character. Here was a young man who could always be expected to be pragmatic – and uncomfortably candid in his sincerity.

Facial features pleasantly irregular, his unruly, light-brown hair evoked a mothering affinity in the opposite sex, which he exploited shamelessly.

'Always keen to run their little fingers through it. Keeps 'em happy – till I'm ready to make my move!'

Enjoying his edge of superiority over Robin – naturally taking the lead when it came to girls, booze, fags – oh, and rigging the electricity meter. He airily informed Robin, 'We never pay more than we have to, old boy!'

'Women? *Cherchez la femme*? Don't be daft. Take my advice, don't waste yer time looking for 'em. They'll soon find *you*!'

Robin was a quick learner... 'What, love 'em and leave 'em before they have time to get any ideas?'

'*Now* y' talkin'!'

As month followed month, Robin followed the simple rules – soon acquiring a proficiency to win Duncan's wholehearted approval. With remarkable dexterity he avoided pitfalls that can endanger a young man's progress as rake. Real man-of-the-world stuff this. No complications, no entanglements.

Until Kathryn.

Robin and Kathryn. Kathryn and Robin. Immediately inseparable. Incandescent. In love.

He cast aside his way of living – along with puerile

advice and boorish company, but typically, Duncan didn't really mind. Obviously his young friend was a lost man. So be it! Last thing he wanted – company of a nauseating pair of cooing lovebirds. Cramp his style!

Not that he gave up immediately. 'You're too young to be going steady. Only twenty-one, just out of university – talking about engagement rings! Are you mad?' Mr Cool briefly forgot his chill factor as originality deserted. 'Rings! Huh! How about one for yer nose as well, sir?' A rude gesture, then gone – house door slamming behind him. Next time they met he was his usual affable self, the incident never referred to again – but fun was over.

Duncan the blunt. Duncan the unapologetic – never afraid to speak his mind – discarding the cushion of compromise as superfluous. Admired for these very characteristics. Admired yes, but never loved – not even by Imogen, who considered it a point of honour to fall in love with all her brother's friends.

The cooing lovebirds? Hardly even noticed his disapproval for the short period it was in force!

Happy in a world of blissful compatibility, they were almost identical intellectually and where interests differed there was joy in assimilation. But the way their appearances harmonised! The impact was breathtaking.

Robin's dark good looks complemented the contrast of her fair beauty in a way immediately pleasing to the eye. To see them together was somehow gratifying – lightened the heart, brightened the day.

Kathryn worked at a Church of England school on the outskirts of the city – went there straight from teacher training – been there for just over a year. Here she bestowed on an adoring class of six-year-old 'mixed' infants the unmixed joys of abstract and concrete illumination.

Protected by the enthusiasm of novelty, loving her work (as yet untouched by the world-weary finger of cynicism that eventually seems to beckon most teachers) she smiled at the world, and the world smiled back in mutual affection – and why not?

Golden blond hair rippling to halfway down her back possessed a strange ability to shine even without light to reflect lustre – persisting even without a moon to give instructions. Perhaps the hair was informed by her sunny personality – certainly together they could illuminate the darkest room.

A light that danced just everywhere – everywhere except in Ada's heart. She automatically hauled out the shackles. 'Tarty!' her considered opinion.

Hitherto undisputed queen of all she surveyed, contemplating the natural quality of that hair, vivid unadorned complexion, long slender legs and pert shapely breasts, she realised comparison did her a disfavour. Self-esteem tottered as stealthy desperation crept, momentarily un-rationalised into an erstwhile cloudless existence.

Both Imogen and her father regarded Ada with startled disbelief. Her daughter was the first to speak, 'No, she's not. She's lovely. Tarty! How can you say such things, Mummy? She's not just lovely, she makes Robin happy too and I for one would love her just for that – if nothing else. In any case, she's so ladylike. Nothing tarty about her!'

Thoughts now seemingly elsewhere, Ada made no reply, but father and daughter smiled at each other in the comfort of complete agreement.

Noting treason, Ada's dislike for its cause hardened, but ignoring the inadvisability of judging others by autonomous standards, pausing by the door she decided to go for the caring mother approach and a worried expression. 'She's just looking for a meal ticket! How come I'm the only one to see it?'

Ever noticed how some questions fall on stony ground?

Nine

As Robin's visits became ever more infrequent, it seemed as though home had lost all charm as Imogen began to spend increasingly prolonged periods away.

She slept in a room at the family home, ate the family food, used the family bathroom and the family phone, but to suggest any further intimacy would be to mislead.

Universally acknowledged is the fact that the average child, one who has hitherto delighted loving parents with that quality of sweet ingenuity and depth of love only total reliance can produce, turns overnight and without warning into a shite without conscience. A shite additionally devoid of all consideration for, or understanding of, the hell of grief and worry it visits on parents it still loves.

Demonic process – as deeply mysterious as death itself. Akin to permanent departure of sleep at five of a Sunday morning as the week's only lie-in stretches hours ahead in wakeful derision.

* * *

Imogen's secretarial course ended June '58 and whoop-ee-time started.

Heady with freedom, partying energy seemingly inexhaustible – assisted by an inability to emerge from bed until gone noon – she had a booze 'n' fag-fuelled ball. Out all night, running wild, staggering home stealthy – bedewed by the early morn.

During the bleary-early hours of May Day 1959 – under a bush someplace along the muddy banks of the Cherwell, Imogen lost something precious. Pointless to search. When virginity goes missing it's never seen again.

She figured the sacrifice part of some grand Oxford tradition – in the same category as jumping off Magdalen Bridge – but a tad less uncomfortable. 'Well, the water's chilly – but he's hot stuff!'

Besides, she was oh-so-deeeeply in love. A pagan marriage, no less – sanctified by ethereal beauty as a choir sang from way up on top of a tower.

T'was love profound; to last an eternity! Well, two weeks anyway – that's when differing interests dragged them asunder. By the middle of June – 'Whatever was that guy's name?'

Somehow in all the fallout, she presented for an employment interview (she never understood the hows and whys). For some inexplicable reason a large firm of lawyers were keen to offer employment to the bleary-eyed apprentice bag-lady stinking of tobacco with an undertow of not-so-stale alcohol, who presented an hour late. Not just late, but with *attitude*. Love me or leave me – and see if I care!

Could the firm's boss have been visited by a Damascene vision? Or was it that quiet conversation with his old pal, Henry Phillips, over a beer or three that engineered the miracle? To avoid the charge of nepotism we'll opt for the former proposal.

Okay. Suit yerselves…

Our favourite joined the firm of Chalmers, Woodgate, diving straight into the typing pool – there to amaze with an uncanny ability, to swim in uncharted waters. Went on to create such a genuine splash that within six weeks she was offered opportunity to train as legal secretary.

Bubbling over with delight, she gushed all over an amused brother, 'There's no reduction in salary while I train – and *just think* of all that lovely lucre when I *do* qualify!'

Robin's reply? Eloquent big-brother silence.

No doubt about it, the proposal talked Imogen's language! With the prospect of serious boodle to spend, all that separated her from her mother's philosophy was the desire to earn it herself. Childhood's implicit financial reliance was something to leave behind as incompatible with independence.

Dazzled by her prospects, she became reformed character. Well, almost reformed. Weekday evenings became sober, almost circumspect. Television or a book now made routine; a cinema visit an occasional treat – straight home after! Riotous company eschewed with commendable determination, no alcohol or tobacco to sully the lips. Parties and uproarious excursions banished – until the weekend. All weekend. Every weekend. Monday morning would find her at her desk, upright in protean prodigy, smelling sweetly of mouthwash and Ada's perfume from (not unnoticed!) that lady's overloaded dressing table, outwardly her usual efficient self – secretly trying to focus properly.

Not everyone was fooled. 'Her work's full of mistakes on a Monday. I've got my eye on that young lady.' Her irritated supervisor suspected the boss of collusion, but could prove nothing. Impotent whatever.

Another secretarial trainee nodded sanctimoniously. 'I don't blame you. I've seen her head nodding when she thinks no one's watching!'

Self-orientated as any new-born infant, weekend Imogen was seemingly unaware of inflicting parental pain – so absorbed that even truly outrageous indiscretions avoided camouflage in lies – carelessness not resulting from her intrinsic honesty, but a mix of a teenager's desire to punish – together with simple blithe thoughtlessness.

'What are we going to do?' Henry's appeal to his wife was mere rhetoric, Ada's reaction a predictable mix of irritation and disinterest. 'You worry too much about the wretched girl. She's only doing it to be noticed. Ignore her… I can assure you that's what I intend to do.'

Probably good advice but Henry was hurting. First his son had left home, now his daughter's presence was negligible. He could see no prospect of her voluntarily easing the pain and since he was no tyrant father, would do nothing to enforce compliance.

Most parents have no other option than to flounder in unreason's gloom, searching for a glimmer of illumination. Argue – try to engage the little darlings in equable dialogue – in face of the inevitability of all-out war, as the sinking sensation descends from wary optimism, through pessimism and down to the murky depths of total despair.

But Henry had money – lots of it. He craved melodic harmony. Never mind Schoenberg – just give him Sibelius! With the simplicity of pure genius, he bought his errant child a horse.

He led the spectacularly beautiful piebald-grey mare through a drift of fallen sycamore leaves up the drive to the front door calling out Imogen's name in a deep solemn voice as they progressed – like some grand piece of medieval theatre. Certainly Ada, who emerged from the house with her daughter to see what all the commotion was about, thought all he needed was a fool's cap.

Wordlessly lifting her shoulders in a contemptuous shrug she turned back through the open front door and shut it sharply behind her – to shut out the lunacy as well as the cold. 'Spoiling the little madam!'

Speechless Imogen. Love-at-first-sight Imogen. Not the usual five-minute-wonder-love Imogen. This was the real deal! Pure, selfless, total.

Amongst initial joy and wonder there lurked uncomfortable understanding of her father's motivation; shame in the perception informed her she definitely didn't deserve such generosity – any generosity!

Arms clinging to his neck she murmured through her tears over and over, 'Oh, Dad… Oh, Dad,' as she left teenage disorientation behind.

Henry had thought of everything.

'It's all so easy – why didn't I think of it before?' he asked a furiously silent Ada. 'She's always loved horses, always been after money for riding school… Remember? I've organised stabling and pasture – just down the road at Tom Rhodes' place. Saddle, bridle and a whole lot of other essentials.' He ticked off each item in his head. 'After all, if I don't know what horses need, no one ever will!'

Smiling, he went on to think of other needs he'd anticipated – seeing her resplendent in immaculate beauty – beaver-dark hard hat, jodhpurs, hacking jacket and shining leather boots. He beamed in anticipatory pride – then in a spasm of protective reality added rubber boots. 'Mustn't forget those Wellington boots. And waterproofs! She'll be out in all weathers.'

Busy with his thoughts, he was no longer looking at his wife. Glancing up from her magazine, her eyes contained nothing but malevolent contempt as she looked at him.

Thus he gave a world complete, leaving this daughter-of-fortune to create a new order for herself within it. By doing so, he ended Imogen's chaotic social life. She left it behind without regret, backward glance or one moment of mourning. Henry Phillips was one wise father.

Imogen began to take pride in her job – enjoying it for its own sake, not just as a means to a salary. She became noted for efficiency – her earlier detractors silenced under a welter of universal approval (coincidentally allowing boss Harry Woodgate to relax!). They all smiled indulgence as at five o'clock she would shoot out of the office door. 'Anyone would think the office clock has a starting pistol in its works. Clear the court!'

Tansy. She called her darling Tansy. 'Why? Just seems to suit her... ' Mucking out Tansy's stable – fragrant joy. Grooming, cleaning tack – utter contentment.

Five of a morning, her alarm clock assumed the importance of the office clock – launching her into exclusivity of horse/human co-existence – to experience that delicious, murmuring-silent isolation known only to pleasure-bent early risers – silence faintly broken by the subdued stamp, snort and regular squish-squish of the sleepy milking parlour across the yard where, bathed in low-watt, yellow-mellow, cobweb-festooned electric bulbs, two rows of willing bovine captives served to emphasise freedom's exhilaration.

Bathed in the charm of astringent-damp autumn mornings with the sun struggling to assert itself over a burden of cloud, they would set out on centaur travels – mutual animation vibrating to create a glowing warmth against the chill.

All aglow again?

The season changing to winter brought the first frosts. A fairyland of ice heralded Christmas. Sure-footed, snorting with sheer exhilaration, the mare never hesitated – glad to be alive! From her position of vantage, Imogen marvelled at the silver sparkle of a transformed world, radiating in the wonder of *joie de vivre* it generated; the obfuscation of adolescence forgotten as the self-assurance of womanhood illuminated her rite of passage.

Yes, definitely all aglow again…

Happy, happy Imogen – had she given the matter thought, she would have acknowledged that a consuming passion for sex, drink and rock 'n' roll would have been hard to maintain exposed to the elements of the British winter… You'll just have to take it from one who knows!

Henry didn't get to see much more of his daughter than previous to his brainwave, but his heart was light.

Ten

'I'm so sorry, darling. I'd much prefer to stay with you and your family, you know I would, but I keep imagining Mum and Dad without me… all on their own! It's no good. I just can't do it to them.'

The Christmas arrangements. Arrrgh! Complex enough for the experienced, total perplexity for fledgling adults – as loyalties become disconcertingly divided for the first time. Inclination tends towards novelty; guilt-endorsed sentimentality urges sacrifice to Mum's cooking with nest-empty parents – who probably dream of the Costa Blanca!

'Oh, no, Robin! You must persuade her. You really, really must! Don't give up… Ask her again. Go on – just don't give up!' A sister's gushing grief.

His family all make regretful noises – only Imogen is sincere. She finds the older girl fascinating, been looking forward to impressing her in some singularly spectacular way – to be admired as well as admiring.

Suddenly inspired, she now makes the ultimate concession 'I know! Tell her to bring slacks – then she can ride Tansy – as much as she wants!'

'Wow! Steady on, our Imi – she'll begin to think you're just a bit too keen to get rid of me! In any case, it's no good you trying to tempt her, she just can't come – and that's that.'

Imogen's chameleon face mirrors tragic loss in unconscious, comic gloom. Robin smiles grateful affection.

Considerably heartened, Ada's thoughts are far from

charitable… Pity he doesn't go to her parents too – why does he need to come here? He left home, didn't he? Still, at least we're spared that stupid girl…

Words scattered amongst a trill of laughter. 'Never mind, if she doesn't want to join us, we'll just have to soldier on without her.' She then walks away humming a snatch of *We'll Meet Again.*

Henry has previously struggled with an uncharacteristic, almost panic-stricken jealousy. Not ready – not yet! Need to welcome change, though – after all, the lad's made his choice – no matter he's far and away too young. Yes, accept it, welcome it – welcome her. But welcome her to share our Christmas? With my family – my Ada – my Imogen – *my* Robin? No, please not yet… Fortress Phillips! Just once more – in the good, good old way.

Relief intensifies guilt as Kathryn refuses reluctant hospitality. He wrestles his conscience. So, just this one year more – then turn a new leaf – New Year's resolution – really keep this one! With that promise in mind, guilt lifts to a more comfortable level.

Turning to his children, he says, 'Come on, you two. Less of this gloom. It's a real shame, but it can't be altered. Now then, lots to do. I need you to help with everything.'

As usual his enthusiasm carries the day – lifts the mood.

Henry is a kid for Christmas – more traditional the merrier. Carol singers, holly smothered in red berries, midnight Mass followed by Father Christmas; next day – mince pies, sausage rolls, roaring fires, presents, turkey, a massive, flaming plum pud, iced fruit cake – all, if possible, amid an outside sprinkling of snow – just sufficient to emphasise indoor glow.

He relishes the lot! Sees no reason why this year should be any different. Might be last of its kind!

Following annual custom he's found the district's largest cut fir tree, confidently hauled a half-barrel of sand to the sitting room's furthest corner. 'It'll be perfect next to the piano!' Next, stagger in under the weight of a massive arboreal invasion. *Not enough ceiling height!* Outside for shortening treatment – back. *Damn – bit more!* Front door now accustomed to standing open – Henry overheated, everyone else shivering.

Fifth attempt – floor awash with pine needles and sand. The customary, still, small voice of reason. 'I bet it'll look much better in the hall – kind of welcoming, don't you think?'

Ella, keen to promote domestic harmony – also aware the clean-up will be her prerogative, reminds herself she has a home of her own to go to!

Finally in correct location, the tree is lovingly adorned. 'Pass me the fairy, Imi – it'll have to go on just below the top… not enough room… '

Front door gratefully closes on the elements. Too late! The fireside has already lost most all pretence of cosy appeal; Ella completes devastation with a campaign of vigorous clean-up. Same old tradition! Year on year.

Ada, whose only motive for staying is to be justified in righteous indignation, now makes haughty, strategic retreat. Pausing at the stairwell she turns to Imogen. 'Will you tell your father to be careful on those steps – there's been enough mess and excitement already!' Knows her words are part of this idiotic tradition even as she utters them – realisation increases exasperation as she heads for her cosy boudoir.

Nervously watching children ignore Ada's instruction as just so much wasted breath, knowing words – any words – will be unheeded by a gravity-defying Henry.

Work complete, he stands back to survey transformed branches coruscating with lights and baubles, an abundance of presents scattered beneath.

'Now isn't that a picture?'

Artistry, reflected in the eyes of his speechless children – it's all he wants. As he stands with an arm round each, the three of them are aware of reaffirmed magic; that gives him more pleasure than any present he might otherwise receive.

Henry's tasks also include all the cooking – all except the cake. Tradition decrees that is Ada's job. Surprisingly she not only does it with good grace, she does it well! Her moisty-fruity creations, cooked to perfection, marzipaned and iced to a standard high enough to achieve professional approval, are one of the main features of a perfect Christmas. She is secretly proud of the fact.

This year she has excelled herself. The finished masterpiece stands in splendour in the centre of a sideboard cleared of all but two humiliated decanters on one end and a large cut-glass fruit bowl the other, all filled to capacity – but totally outclassed.

Years of producing the Phillips' Christmas lunch have resulted in a kitchen equipped with the largest oven outside the catering trade – of such titanic proportion that startled visitors secretly suspect it capable of Wurlitzer capabilities – descending into the ground after use whilst triumphantly producing the 'lost chord'.

Previous to its arrival, there have been occasional near disasters – massive turkeys arguing bitterly with roast vegetables about over-crowding, sulking in the oven till tea-time, by which time all have become too hardened to care. Even now there is hardly enough room for all – but aided by *legerdemain* of no small skill, Henry triumphs!

Boxing Day is open house. Welcome one and all! Jingle

bells – deck the halls – dreaming of a white Christmas – bedecked with bay and rosemary – jingle *all* the way!

Brookfields reverberates to the sound of greetings, clatter of crockery, tinkle of glass, laughing, happy voices growing louder in alcoholic zest. 'Cheers, Henry – grand do, fantastic spread!'

There's never any reserve to Boxing Day invitations; no ulterior socialising – just the glow of genuine friendship. Open house it is! Lots to eat (no leftover turkey!) and although he rarely touches it, alcohol flows freely for everyone else.

Constantly on the move, checking refills, urging food. 'Have you tried the blue cheese vol-au-vents? They're good!' Joke here, laughing response there. Light flirting with the wives to make them blush with pleasure – concurrently delighting husbands with unspoken compliment. Hmmm, yes, my old girl does look good today – I chose well all those years ago. Trust Henry to notice – the sly old dog!

In the onerous capacity of celebration-fest hostess, Ada is fully occupied maintaining her usual static glamour. As always she has told Henry he seems to have invited the entire district. 'I do wish you could be a little more selective. Some of these characters…!'

Secretly she enjoys holding court, especially with the men. 'Lovely to see you… do sit and talk to me a while – I seem to have been deserted by my husband.' Mock-plaintive complaint followed by clarion laughter. 'You men are *such* scamps and he's worse than any. You should watch out for your wife! No, no, don't go – I was only teasing… '

As always she manages to convince herself she's bored. No matter how content she may be, however stimulating the company, she invariably persuades herself the whole experience is wearying. Seems she has to obey rules designed for her governance only; rules convincing her she possesses intellectual superiority – that merely rob her of any real enjoyment in life.

Catering for his friends in this gloriously open-handed way is food and drink enough for Henry Phillips. 'Just look at him!' Robin's pride and love obvious in spite of happy exhaustion. 'He's just a compulsive feeder,' he laughs. 'Nothing for himself… all for everyone else… Look!'

He and Imogen stand in the sitting room doorway, both trying to recoup enough strength to advance with reinforcements on the hungry multitude. 'It's no good – I'm whacked! D'you think anyone will notice if we slip away for a minute – get some fresh air?' Imogen's hopeful question only just heard above the tumult.

'No, course they won't.'

His reply dispels vague guilt. *After all – just a few minutes respite… we won't be long… not desertion… not really…*

'Go on,' he urges 'you slip away first. Here, give me your tray – I'll put it with mine on the table – they can just help themselves for a while. I'll follow in a minute – don't want it to look too obvious… '

Out of the corner of one eye Henry notes the desertion and grins. Lack the old man's stamina! They're good kids, though – couldn't have managed without 'em. Hope they'll be back to help with the washing up! He shudders at the thought, then arming himself with a flashing smile and a further two bottles of cheer, charges fearlessly at the phalanx of dangerously emptying glasses.

Eventually – farewell's crescendo. Happy New Year! Had a lovely time. Thanks for having us. Wonderful party, wonderful! Thank you again! Goodbye… Goodbye… Goodbye…!

The profundity of silence! Don't break it. Speak in whispers. Quietly gather debris. Tiptoe to the kitchen. Shushhhh!

Alone in the drawing room, Ada moves to the window to watch the last of the departing guests. This is the part she really enjoys!

It never fails – Art Brown is always the last to leave. This time he has two companions just ahead of him. The three wise wives have long since vanished into the night.

As usual, Art is tipsy. Noooo, Art is drunk! Skunk-drunk. Plastered. Motherless! He wavers down the drive, trying to maintain dignity, remain vertical. Until – wait for it… YES! 'Bingle jells, bingle jells, bingle orla wa-hey!' And gone!

The lost Art! In Ada's quirky imagination the unseen hand of lust has dragged him into the bushes, there to have its wanton way – every year, at the same point in the drive. 'Art's in the bushes as per usual!' she calls towards the kitchen, amusement's clarion shattering the spell of silence. 'Where the devil's Art?' The other revellers reach the gate and turn. 'Art! Art? Where the devil are you?'

Retracing their steps they find a bewildered Art and haul him out of the shrubbery. 'Come on, old lad, the girls will be home by now!'

'Watch out juss there! Chrisht – ish slippy!'

'S'all right, we got ya.'

As they pass from view, the pleasure of Ada's Schadenfreude cools to contempt. As Henry reappears to check for empties, she turns from the window. 'Silly old fool – break his neck one of these times – serve him right! And him a church warden too… A fine example!'

'Hmmm?' A shell-shocked Henry fails to hear her opinion properly, or understand its cause.

'This house smells like a four-ale barroom!' Ada follows him to the kitchen door, idly watching her family busy at the sink for a minute or so. Catching Henry's attention, she smiles slowly and half turning, gives him the full effect of her magnificent silhouette in the doorway. He notes again how her simple black dress accents every delicious curve – breasts enlarged by a low-cut neckline; legs long, slender and shapely in those sexy high heels! Still smiling in his direction she huskily drawls, 'I'm just off for a bath before bed – see you later. Don't be long… '

Hands still in warm soapy water, feeling the old familiar stirring, he's glad of a camouflaging apron. She won't need any encouragement, not tonight – not with all the men ogling her, flirting like it's going out of fashion. She knows she looks extra seductive in that dress too. Old Graham Harper almost had his hand all the way up her skirt once or twice when he thought I wasn't looking. The dirty old sod. Not that I'm blaming him.

He gives his children a wry comical smile, 'She doesn't even know what a four-ale bar is – never been near one in her life.' Makes them giggle.

'Went like a bomb this year, didn't it?' he continues. 'Tell you what, why don't we finish this first thing tomorrow. Think I'll have a shower and turn in myself. It's been a long day. Off you go – before I change my mind!'

* * *

Their love making is ardent, soft rejoicing.

As usual these days her eyes are closed, a fact he barely registers. Gazing up at her body moving sinuously as she straddles him he notices the bulge of her belly and enlarged breasts for the first time.

Questioning is immediately subsumed in mutual sexual dissolution.

Afterwards with a sigh of total satisfaction she turns on her side away from him, drifting off to sleep.

He lays behind her for over half an hour whilst she slumbers – his question returning with urgent force. Could it be? After all these years?

His hand creeps across her shoulder finding, caressing the drooping breast nearest to him. She murmurs, 'Darling,' softly as her nipple hardens, making no resistance as he turns her on her back.

He looks questioningly down her body. Yes – a definite thickening! Pregnant! That's why her breasts seemed so large this evening. Apart from that she looked slim as ever. Must have been wearing a corset of some kind!

Her body begins to respond. Proudly he arches himself above her – in the glory of the moment shattering his self-imposed protocol of silence with the imperative of speech he cries, 'My darling! Oh, my wonderful, wonderful darling!'

Abruptly her eyes open. As she focuses up at his face, languor vanishes in alarm. Knocking him aside, she abruptly sits up. Looking down at him lying at her side again, she says wonderingly, 'Henry? What are you doing here?'

She's confused – just woken up. Confident, he continues caressing the breast now just above his face – the breast that will soon give suckle to his baby! It's a dream come true!

Her reaction is cold rage as she hits his hand away. 'Leave me alone, you disgusting animal.' Looking down his body she continues 'and how dare you come near me without a condom?'

'But—'

He is about to remind her it's well over two years since

they've used one, when she continues with a low, guttural snarl, 'Go to your room. Now! I don't want you anywhere near me.'

Eleven

'Ella's got the extra day off; think I'll have one as well. They'll just have to manage without me! Well, after all, am I the boss, or aren't I?'

In a singular spirit of self-indulgence, Henry has awarded himself an extra day off. As his family, too fragile after the previous day's efforts to dignify rhetoric with reply merely stare in his general direction, he wonders if he's made a mistake. Here's anti-climax as its most anti. He's still in catering mode – and no one to cater to! Leaves him twitching.

Watching them pick a subdued path through demoralised salad and cold turkey (no wonder he's twitching) a mammoth syringe of inspiration zaps through his veins. 'I know! Let's go see Auntie Clara – take her a bottle of port – keep the old girl warm of an evening. Oh, and a few bits and bobs – pork pie, sausage rolls, mince pies, ham, pickles and – and such-like.' As his enthusiasm takes off on another supersonic flight, Ada's attention becomes absorbed in the dining room curtains – his children experience what they know to be doomed reluctance. Like most young people, they shrink from the prospect of visiting an old maid. So bloomin' ancient – not even our aunt, but Dad's!

Ever since they moved near to the village where she lives, his attempts to persuade the old lady to join the family Christmas have been consistently unsuccessful. Thoughts of her lonely observance occasionally seep into his consciousness with a nebulous but stubborn melancholy.

'Oh, come on!' Henry senses a certain reluctance here. 'She's the last of the old 'uns – poor old dear might not be here next year!'

Ada's wrapt contemplation of the curtains evaporates in a surge of righteous indignation. Turning majestically to face her family she almost spits out the words – vicious words that have accumulated over the years.

'That would be no loss. That wretched old woman – she's invited here every year – but does she favour us with her company? Oh, no! And why not? Because this way she's sure of being noticed. It's all she wants!'

One glance at her husband's face tells her she's overstepped the mark, and it's routine policy to keep him reasonably placated. Neatly turning from vehement principle to affectionate pathos she continues, 'Well, I've watched you, Henry, I know how it hurts you. Anyway, take no notice of me – I'm exhausted… all that bustle yesterday. Think I'll have a quiet afternoon on my own, if you don't mind – recharge the batteries.'

Instantly mollified by concern, he smiles acquiescence. 'Good idea, darling – you have a nice rest.'

The children patiently wait for the charade to end, never expecting her to join the expedition, but knowing better than to interrupt the flow.

Any disinclination Robin might have felt dissolves with Ada"s words. Not only is he unwilling to stay in the house alone with her, but his customary desire to protect his father from Ada's callousness surges in suppressed irritation. As usual he wonders why his father tolerates her – always making excuses… Out loud, he says, 'Fine by me, Dad. It'll be nice to see her.'

'Me too!' Comic predictability from Imogen. If they're going, so is she!

The afternoon at the stable she has planned can wait till tomorrow. Her regular visits bearing edible gifts for Tansy have kept the mare informed of all household excitement, but neither have had any recent exercise and both feel it well overdue. Tomorrow. All day tomorrow, she promises.

And so Clara Phillips' three unexpected visitors go to prepare the gifts they will bear – whilst Ada goes to the cosy sitting room to prepare for an afternoon of recuperation in front of a substantial hearth.

Henry collects his bottle of port (make it two!) from a cabinet behind the settee where the seated form of his wife waits with barely concealed impatience.

Bending to kiss the velvet softness of her cheek he says, 'Thought you might like some Chrissie-cake later – with a cup of tea or something. There's lots left – I'll put it on the table beside you with a plate. The knife's there – you can help yourself.'

Sighing, Ada swivels her body to lay, feet up, among the cushions. With his customary sweet indulgence he says, 'That's right, darling. You have a nice rest. Do you the world of good. We won't be back till six-ish. We'll have a serious talk then – about – you know… '

She manages a wan little smile that hides contemptuous impatience. All that food and drink – you'd think the old fool was in danger of starvation! Serious talk? About what? What on earth have *we* got to talk about? The man's an imbecile! She says nothing.

At the doorway Henry turns. 'Goodbye, darling. We'll talk later – there's a lot to discuss you know. '

He's now fighting a growing reluctance to leave her. In the soft woollen dress she's wearing today it is obvious she's carrying. He wants her again – her condition makes her even more irresistible. Still unnerved by the conclusion of last night's bliss, he wavers, trying to rationalise her reaction… She was just protecting her baby. Women are like that when they're pregnant. Too much might be dangerous.

Still, maybe the children can go on their own. Why not a lie down with her instead? A little gentle love making – be nice for us both…

'Shall I stay, darling? We could go upstairs. There's a fire on in the bedroom.'

His question goes unanswered. Silence indicates she has dozed off whilst he has been deliberating. Ah well, appealing thought! But maybe it's best this way. Don't want to upset her again. It's obviously all been a bit too much for her – pregnant and all.

He tiptoes across the hall to his waiting children raising a finger to his lips, 'Shhh… ' Together they softly leave the house.

'At last!' Ada's words a sigh of relief.

Some little time later, only the dull thunk of heavily expensive magazine falling to a carpeted floor mildly disturbs the silent house as she drifts away into her dreams.

Twelve

Old Clara Phillips is an unemotional woman whose expectation of pleasure is limited to her immediate environment.

Her promise of a happy life of mutual, human love terminated in the freezing embrace of a blood and water filled hole in Flanders. In defence of king and country, they told her. Realisation that neither entity cared a tinker's cuss for the sacrifice added bitterness to heartbreak. At first resentment mingled with grief almost to madness, then she gradually became pragmatic, self-contained and eventually content with her own company and that of a succession of lovably ugly, stray mongrel bitches. Behind this wall of female unity she is completely fulfilled. 'Don't bring me dogs – we have no room for them.'

If outsiders feel pity, they are mistaken!

The only tie of affection she has with humanity is reserved for Henry and his children (and only because they are his children). Yes, very fond of young Henry she is, but for the life of her she fails to understand his devotion to Ada.

Conversing with her acquiescent mutts she often vigorously debates. 'Vulgar beyond recall that one! Don't you agree? And to think, he's given up music for her... the wretched woman lacks even one ounce of spiritualism. It's certain she doesn't love her husband... never has! A thoroughly unsuitable match if ever there was one... ' Tails thump the floor. The verdict is unanimous.

'And you know how I feel about Henry pestering me

to join their Christmas. But don't you worry, I'll never go. What! Leave my girls all alone?' Four pairs of eyes fix on her in complete, loving reliance.

'He means well, bless him, but imagine all that noise! And then that awful woman will ignore me till lunch is over – then turn on the gracious condescension. It's more than flesh and blood could stand!'

It's an annual embarrassment that fills her with dread. She's not used to human socialising – besides, she knows her girls will be miserable without her. She's read somewhere that canines become increasingly distressed when their humans are absent, convinced they are abandoned; a pack without a leader. True or no, she'll never put the hypothesis to the test.

Her sitting room is immediately inside the front door, and hidden within her smile of welcome as she opens it is something very near panic. Since they lack her good manners, the dogs slink away with churlish haste – abandoning a warm berth in favour of chilly privacy in the kitchen.

Seeking divine inspiration the old solitary's first thought is, *Dear God, how on earth can I keep them entertained?* And the answer to an old maiden's prayer? *Of course! I'll get the photo albums out – they always like looking through them.*

Like so many of her ilk Clara has become the willing repository of old family photographs. Well, no one else wants the bother, do they? Not to mention the dust and clutter!

When inevitably the family produces an individual desirous of discovering ancestral roots, there comes an interesting point of family history in itself. Disaster is discovered! 'What a shame Auntie's gone; she had lots of old photos – what on earth happened to them?'

Ah, but these irreplaceable images have fallen victim to the zeal of some harassed, middle-aged, now forever infamous woman delegated the unwanted task of clearing out the dear departed's old lumber – and we're talking *real* old lumber here, that which is left after systematic extraction by peripheral family members, who materialise to lay claim to whatever Auntie always promised them.

Valiantly, Imogen fights to conceal yawns as the visit stretches ahead in mind-numbing boredom. Oh, no! Please! Not the photo albums!

However, her examination is steadfast and thorough. Well, *someone's* got to check no interlopers have infiltrated the pages since last time!

'All present and correct, Auntie Clara,' she says, using one of her father's favourite expressions. Now suddenly shy, she gives her first genuine smile of the afternoon as she murmurs, 'I love looking at them.' That's genuine too.

Once accepting, there's no escaping the sepia brigade she always finds their fierce charm beguiling. Loves the structured seriousness of the turn-of-the-century ones best, before people realised they could smile at the camera without harm – coincidentally shattering the illusion of grandeur with inane reality.

'See this lady here – behind these grand old ones? She looks so sweet.'

'That's my Aunt Hannah. I loved her dearly – she was so kind. She looked after her parents until they died and was dead herself a few months after Grandma went – as though she had nothing more to do in life.'

'Oh, how sad… You could say she had no life of her own!'

Clara's heart has now completely melted. Henry's lass

might seem a little madam but she's a love really – not her mother's daughter after all.

'She was a happy woman nonetheless… In those days, people found fulfilment in duty.'

Realising there's nothing for it but to offer the iced biscuits she and her girls have promised themselves for a treat, Clara brightens resolutely, chiding herself as she remembers the basket of goodies… enough food for weeks!

'Now then, I expect you could all do with a nice cup of tea!'

'Oh, lovely, Auntie – shall I make it?'

Starting eagerly to his feet, Robin makes his customary hopeful offer. But it's no good! – she won't hear of it. This is her home and she knows the duties of hostess! Resigned, he sinks back into his chair as she shuffles into the kitchen to be greeted by the vaguely hopeful eyes of her dogs – tails a-flutter in subdued greeting.

Reading signs from the selection and filling of the large kettle, they emulate the unwanted visitor and sink back down with world weary sighs.

She's so slow, it's half a yawning, shuffling, scratching, stretching hour (aren't dogs and humans alike in so many ways?) before she returns with tepid tea and biscuits that have to be thoroughly examined for dog hairs.

'Thank you, Auntie – perfect!'

Time to go! Embarrassment. Eager reluctance. Coats on. Edge towards the door. 'It's been lovely to see you,' they chorus in unison. 'We'll come and see you again soon!'

The last thing Clara expects is to see them again for at least another year. They all know what she thinks and acknowledge inherent truth. Remorse makes them uncomfortable – especially Henry. Suddenly he turns to embrace the old lady with an enthusiasm that astonishes her. He murmurs, 'Don't stay to wave goodbye. You'll let all the warm out.'

'Goodbye then, Henry dear.'

The closing door is signal to her guests. Embarrassed reluctance rapidly alters to cheerful relief as they set out at a brisk pace for home. Clara feels relieved too, but it's a relief tinged with an inexplicable poignancy. The dogs, hearing the all clear of departure feel no such reservation, silently reappearing at the fireside, they settle contentedly into normality of unruffled, cosy somnolence.

The Phillips family make an appealing sight as they pass under village street lamps on their journey home. Laughing in that sense of happy freedom that conclusion of a charitable act brings, they are light-hearted. A tall, still-handsome, middle-aged man with his two attractive, grown children. Glowing, powerful in health and beauty, they form a joyful trio of invincibility.

As they near the farm halfway between village and Brookfields, Imogen's plea, 'Come with me to make sure Tansy's okay,' creates resistance, but no surprise.

'No, thank you, *very* much! It's going to start snowing any time now.' Henry's pace never falters. 'You go if you like. Auntie's fire isn't big enough for my liking. I'm for home!'

Indecisive, Robin slows his pace then starts to turn with his sister into the farmyard. 'See you later then.'

Henry simply waves without turning or even slowing his pace; very soon his rapidly moving figure is swallowed in midwinter darkness.

'Hmm, we can't possibly neglect Tansy now, can we? Much more important than a mere old aunt don't you think?'

It hasn't occurred to Imogen that moments during the afternoon when her face has revealed bored irritation mixed with an underlying sanctimonious charity have been noticed. Robin has seen! 'Sometimes you're a bit too much like our mother for comfort! His comments cause an unwelcome spasm of guilt.

Suddenly stricken, she hesitates, dithering in the gateway. But now, brotherly love and awareness of her elemental sincerity silences further reproach. Smiling he urges her. 'Come on then! It's all right. I didn't mean it. Dad's right, it is going to snow soon.'

They stroke the velvet opulence of the mare's nostrils, inhale the musty fragrance of her breath and experience a mutual, loving tranquillity.

Thirteen

First flakes of snow leak reluctant through cosy cloud blanket; fat, virgin white, they seesaw gracefully down to a grim, impatiently waiting earth. Henry smiles welcome. Uh huh – too late for Father Christmas though!

With unfaltering feet, his thoughts concentrating on his waiting wife and home, his need to be with Ada has now become urgent. He's glad they'd found time for old Clara, though. Been the right thing that visit! He briefly feels a warm glow of love and pride in his children, then perverse guilt for a neglected wife returns with increased force.

In his chastened imagination she'd been looking more than a bit peaky. Hope she's not sickening for something. Got to think of the baby now! Wish one of us had stayed with her.

His lone and unmistakably brisk footsteps sound crisp on the still-frozen gravel driveway as he hastens towards the focus of his solicitation.

One of the nicest things about Henry Phillips is his habitual sensitivity to the sensitivity of others. After quietly shutting the house door behind him he removes shoes and thick overcoat in the hall then silently tiptoes towards the sitting room – resisting his natural impulse to switch on lighting. Shh! No sudden shocks…

There she is! Enveloped in shadows of the darkened

room, gazing into the fire – lost in thought. Just the ticking clock for company...

As though seeking to exclude any lesser sensation, egoism of his love fetters his stomach with inflexible knots, constricting his chest to make breathing reluctant and shallow.

Under no illusion, he knows she has never felt the same way about him. In the humble arrogance of his ignorance he doubts her capable of his intensity. Far from saddening, the thought is reassuring, convincing him that at least she'll never love enough elsewhere to seriously stray. That's consolation enough. He'll always gratefully take and devour whatever she cares to toss his way.

Unrequited love – it produces an exquisite quality of pain that courses through the veins like heroin, to become as essential to the lover as superficial to the beloved – and he knows he's hopelessly addicted. Just as fish must have water, he must have Ada – or die. Simple as that. The need hasn't lessened with passing years. On the contrary, like any helpless addict he only ever craves an increased dosage. Torment is critical to his relationship with this beautiful woman – he accepts his fate without regret.

Watching her from the doorway he momentarily feels like some profane interloper and almost turns to go – give her some warning of his approach – but lacking any real volition, fascinated, he stays the impulse.

Seemingly unaware of his proximity she sits like some glorious pagan goddess – remote in dreams – hair gleaming in the light of the hearth's flames – eyes glowing in softer reflection.

His movement towards her is now irresistible. Soundlessly he pads across the carpet thinking she will turn and smile at him – that special smile of hers; the one that says she does love him – in her own way!

Gently, hesitantly he reaches out a hand towards the satin sheen of her hair.

Fourteen

He makes no attempt to defend himself. Willing sacrificial totem. Three slashes to the upper body fail to kill Henry Phillips; a fourth, higher, nicks the carotid – filling the air between them with fine, red mist; the next severs it completely. His life-blood drenches them both, spraying walls, soaking the thickness of hearth rug to carpet beneath, hissing in the fire – suddenly released steam from a stationary locomotive; in red-racing desperation it leaves his confining body.

As though in one last, futile attempt to endow barbarous proceedings with some semblance of dignity, his legs wilt beneath him. With balletic grace he settles into a pool of his own gore – unscathed arms flung out in a gesture eloquent with elegance. Genteel crucifixion.

His face in death still registers humble adoration.

During the execution Ada's face has remained impassive – save for occasional spasms of pure hatred. As he sinks to the floor she regains her seat, gazing at his lifeless body with serene detachment just as she'd regarded the fire earlier – still clutching the knife as though on the alert for any sign of returning life.

Slowly her face registers total triumph. Her hand relaxes. The knife – in a previous world used to slice Christmas cake (a confection newly resplendent in pink marbled icing), now falls, discarded – redundant.

Ada's children enter welcoming warmth of their home

– glad to be out of the cold, quietly laughing in relief at the contrast.

Duplicating Henry's earlier actions, shoes and coats are discarded at the front door, then, smiling in anticipated greeting, Imogen moves softly after her brother towards the magnet of sitting room fire.

Unlike his father Robin pauses to switch on the light and is immediately transfixed. In an instinctive gesture of protection his arm shoots out across the doorway to halt his sister's progress.

So absorbed Ada's contemplation of her handiwork, there's a fraction of interval before she fully realises the light is on and she's observed. Immediately her face assumes the mask of bewildered distress it will wear during following months, but for that split second there is just pure, malevolent satisfaction. This her son has seen – and she knows it.

For the rest of his life he'll be haunted by that transient manifestation of evil within his mother.

'What's the matter, silly?' Still-smiling Imogen playfully ducks under his arm – to be confronted by a strangely distorted scene to the one she anticipates. Initially, she fails to register her parents' presence at all. Discounting surrealism, instinct demands, *What's the time?*

In absorbed fascination she stares at the white face of the mantle clock – trying to understand why its hands have vanished to be replaced by a straight, dark red line that includes the frame. And that grey fuzz round the edge? Numbers? Trying to escape...?

How's she to understand? A fast congealing gobbet of blood has landed top centre, then run straight down its face in a fine line – to obscure hands standing exactly on six o'clock.

At that very moment chimes strike the hour, releasing

her gaze to wander in stupefied wonder, seeking some feature of normality where none exists. Tracing great, red, condor wing splashes on the wall, it settles on the figures of her mother and father for the first time – figures that appear to be the centre of some meaningless tableau...

At a loss, she returns to the clock-puzzle where a timid minute hand now peeps from behind lurid camouflage.

Recovering from shocked paralysis, Robin races to the prone form of his father. Kneeling, he tries to find a pulse at the wrists. Aversion and fear of increasing injuries make him flinch from any examination at the neck – where gentle oozing from the final gash tells its story of hope and life departed.

In dogged optimism, he yells into the silence, 'Get some help!' Looking round at his sister still dithering in the doorway his command rings out across the room. 'An ambulance – 999 – get someone! QUICK!'

An Olympic sprinter, she races for the phone in the hall. Beneath confusion she has absorbed all relevant details. Now calmly focussed, she explains the whole situation in detail to an operator – chatting to her best friend, reluctant to say 'goodbye' till clamour around her indicates help's arrival.

Within whirling confusion of noise and flashing lights, coloured illumination of a bedecked Christmas tree has paled into insignificance – in sudden irritation, she switches it off.

Simultaneously – as though touching a switch within herself, shock reduces her to a gibbering, quaking mess. Alone in a void of darkness incapable of coherent thought as vague flickering lights advance and retreat she totters to the wall; sinking to the floor she presses her back against its solid, cold comfort.

With instinct borne of dread she stares at the floor,

unwilling to look up in case her eyes wander willy-nilly towards the sitting room. Not even for Robin's sake will she go back in there again! Where is Robin anyway? We should be together...

He's gently but firmly led out to join her. With the immobility of an artist's model he stands for almost a minute gazing at the darkened tree, attempting to determine what aspect has changed. Then with a start, his eyes search wildly around in increasing alarm – small child suddenly realising that familiar, necessary face is nowhere in sight. Lost!

Terrified, uncomprehending vision disregards the hunched figure of his sister, but he hears her urgent whisper, 'Robin – I'm here!' Lurching towards the sound, he sinks to her side. Mute, they convulsively cling to each other.

At some stage of the now detached pandemonium around them, they're vaguely aware of Ada being led away. A sleepwalker, she passes through the hall without a glance at them. Later they watch too as their father's covered body is stretchered away.

Exhausted, both tumble into the welcome oblivion of unconsciousness as their vigil ends.

Police, ambulance crew, doctor – all have been tenderly kind. Hardened to tragedy, they can yet feel pity for these youngsters.

In the sanity of his own home Detective Chief Inspector Howard, a man of little imagination beyond that required for his work, labours to describe scenes in that other 'home' in terms his wife can comprehend. Describe those two huddled children? Suddenly inspired, he reaches for her hand. 'They looked just like *Babes in the Wood*... in that dark hall... all shadows... with that huge, dark tree – massive it was! Poor little devils... what a start in life, eh?'

'Where are they now?'

'The Cottage Hospital – sedated up to the eyeballs.'

'Best place for them.'

'I guess so… '

'Come on, it's late. Let's go to bed. Want to make love?'

'Yes, please.'

Fifteen

Sister Bellamy is a dragon – a real dragon. Not the modern, woolly, touchy-feely version. A real-life, breeze-flappin', spark-spittin', momma of the 'old school'. She's in vaguely recognisable human form; the effect is distinctly disconcerting! An enormous bank of boOOsom a-bristle with pens, scissors, watch and other assorted sharpness, blends into monolithic neck muscles that hold a large head in slight abeyance – permanently flexing to strrr-rrike.

And eyes – large, fearsome, hooded, all-seeing eyes – constantly flickering round the periphery, but seemingly concentrating on her immediate vicinity. Add to this a *nose*. Awesome! Ponderous, deep red, with wide-splayed nostrils. Regular fire-breathing gear!

Few dare further examination. Come to think of it, few dare get thus far; some can't even tell you the colour of that hooter! – so for them and the rest of us we'll note that her body is large and, er… stocky (it's the kindest word!), whilst her legs are so thin, it's a miracle they've kept her bulky 5 ft 11 inches vertical to date. Pins of steel!

She has a self-assumed assignment – will never flinch from the task – not her! Invincible, she will guard the lives of any mere air-breathers who enter her domain in need of protection. With redemptive dedication she stands guard; straddling colossus at the gates of the after-world – and *no one* is allowed to slip through on a one-way ticket. Only the most determined have ever succeeded – and that only after one helluva struggle.

Should iron cladding hide a softer centre, it remains, like her first name, a profound, solemn mystery. Amen to that!

* * *

On this snow-silent morning we discover our dragon guarding firmly closed entrances to two adjoining mini-lairs containing the sedated forms of Robin and Imogen Phillips. She has no fear of them slipping into the next world. No, their danger has a more prosaic temporal aspect. Reason for her present vigilance is awareness of a circling vulture.

'Yes, Officer – and what do you seek here?' Snorting derision she allows herself a smile that would send a charging rhino into a dither. He decides to ignore obvious sarcasm – got bigger fish to fry. With assumed courage, he blusters his priority. 'I need to interview those two. Now!'

Stupid waste of breath! Only a daredevil doctor has been allowed near her charges – and that only on distinct understanding that dragons know best. As far as she's concerned, Detective Chief Inspector Howard is no menacing predator – just another lightweight! Maintains he has the law on his side, does he? Hah! (again that smile!) She's the law round here – there'll be no mitigation!

'Certainly not. They're both still sedated. It'll just have to wait till they're well enough to see you. I will let you know as and when that might be.'

Although events of the previous night have assumed a slightly less nightmarish quality under the calming influence of an understanding wife, normally phlegmatic, George Howard is still distinctly unsettled – to the extent he just wants his enquiries complete – draw a line under 'em.

'It's essential to my enquiries. I insist on seeing them,' he asserts. In sudden panic he looks behind him, lamely appealing to colleagues who have so far remained silent and firmly intend to stay that way. 'Well, either of 'em will do – after all, they arrived on the scene together, didn't they?' His unanswered question betrays seniority's lonely incubus.

For a brief, yearning moment he considers circumvention's possibility. He knows there *is* a higher authority somewhere in the hospital complex – a shadowy, God-like figure with a passion for administration. Ah, but this 'being' understands delegation's value, appreciates dragon-esque qualities, consequently, a strict policy of total non-intervention prevails. With a sigh in which frustration vies with resignation, he accepts an appeal in this direction would be pointless.

'I've told you, I-will-let-you-know-when-they-are-ready. Now, if there's nothing further… Some of us have work to do!'

Since he's still experiencing unaccustomed fragility, our 'tyrant of the local nick' knows he presently lacks the balls for an attempt on dragon fastness. Not today, he decides. He's been scorched before – badly scorched! He shudders like he's ice cold.

There she is! Standing her ground. All unconcerned. Pretends she's forgotten me – like I just don't matter. The bitch! Ah, well, I'll just have to wait my moment. Patience, my lad – patience. Might outwit her yet!

Only the flicker of her ever-watchful eyes betrays vigilance. His heart sinks to new depths. *Knows* she will remain so rooted until he leaves the hospital grounds – and what's more, her uncanny intuition will warn of any sneaky attempt at return. Damn her!

He's well aware that time distorts vital facts. Unadorned facts – they're what he needs. Facts. Not the 'whys' and 'whatnots'. None of that new liberal mumbo-jumbo – just facts. With a shrug of realistic resignation he heads for his car – a defeated man.

Had he but known! Oh, had he but known – how close victory – a dragon defeated! Within twenty-four hours of her introduction to Sister Bellamy's brand of TLC, Imogen already wants out – big time!

Sixteen

Throughout childhood, strangers had mistaken them for twins. Little distinction even now. Robin stopped growing at 5 ft 10 inches, Imogen, already over 5 ft 6 inches, wouldn't be far behind. Average for a male, slightly tall for a girl – although not enough to give her a complex. Both moving with the fluency of natural dancers – lean, fit, jungle cats, burning bright with good health and youth's over-generous optimism.

Testament to early teendom's auto-homophobia – before sexual orientation is decided factor, Robin had opted to have his luxuriant dark-brown hair crew-cut when he discovered his looks left him vulnerable to slander. Free of such consideration, Imogen could wear her bounty to below shoulder length – did so with evident satisfaction.

Large, wide-set chameleon eyes, full of hazel flecks, sparkling with intelligence, changing hue with mood or colour of clothing – framed by long, dark-brown lashes, and high, prominent cheekbones to give them a disconcertingly Slavic appearance, speaking volumes for Henry's east European distant ancestry.

'They're *nothing* like my side of the family and just look at her hair – it simply refuses to curl! I've tried everything! Still, never mind, at least she can do something with the colour later on. You'd think I would have blond children, wouldn't you…?' A mother's unanswerable grief.

Yet in spite of same-pod appearance, there existed

previously un-remarked but fundamental differences in both character and temperament – differences becoming starkly emphasised after Henry's death.

Imogen's personality had tensile muscularity – a calibre that had occasionally found her judged shallow by the casual observer. Now that quality flexed, giving with the blow like a good boxer – paradoxically strengthening character, bestowing spirituality to become her ultimate defence and grace.

And Robin's temperament? Totally different metal – one that glowed with promise – precious, fragile, with the kind of ultra-sensitivity occasionally accompanying high intelligence; one that would flourish in a sympathetic milieu, maybe even achieve greatness, instead it shattered under the impact. Reason and flexibility departed – with them any hope of redemption, leaving him that most pitiable of humans – the autonomous victim. His reactions became those of a wounded animal, seeking cover from an outside world of pain – strategy to forever deny him sanctuary.

Although inundation brought a corresponding depth of grief and pain to both, Robin was completely swamped without his chemical life-jacket – Imogen could swim on her own.

With narcotic barrier between him and reality, Robin floated in safety. Should that barrier show signs of disintegration, he became fearful and distressed. As a result, portentous medical decision, 'Keep him sedated – for his own safety.'

Conversely, after a good night's sleep, Imogen began to fight cloying drug-induced euphoria. People were trying to help. The wrong help!

Pain out there wasn't going away – merely waited.

Besides, pain equated with understanding – understanding that might carry mitigation.

'I don't need anything any more – thank you so much. I can go now.' Shy, but determined, in a world suddenly insane, she reacted by attacking the dragon from an unexpected direction – from *inside* the lair. Doing so, she won both her freedom – and everlasting condemnation.

'Base ingratitude – that's what it is!' roared the dragon. For the rest of her life she would refer to Imogen as 'that callous madam'.

Poor little moo! Apart from a basic desire for autonomy, Imogen nursed an obstinate affection for the fabulous creature who had first given her sweet life then brought horror into it. Convincing herself there was an explanation she merely wanted that knowledge – and there's nothing, particularly callous in any of that!

As narcotic fug lifted, nauseous revulsion threatened to fill the hiatus, creating a brief interlude during which she loathed her mother. Fought that too – just as she'd fought the dope.

Pity. How about pity? Pity for the mother promised solace for the daughter – offering a suggestion that should it be deserved, comfort might be apposite. A daughter's comfort? Imogen needed to be needed. Waiting for ever-faithful Ella to collect her, she silently prayed. *Please – give me hope… something to cling to.* Over and over, a mantra of desperation – to shut all else out. It brought strange comfort that bordered on faint, flailing optimism.

Pitiable craving – focus of brutalised perceptions, it helped her mind crawl away from stunned horror, but was also to have tragic, unforeseen results, introducing a corrosive element into the beauty of her relationship with her brother.

During Robin's first lucid moments, chatty Imogen concluded her theories, 'I'm sure there must be some logical explanation, Rob. I'm going to see her tomorrow – then we'll know.'

Having listened to her with growing disbelief, he covered his ears wailing, 'I don't want to hear this. It was murder… surely you realise that. You're talking rubbish. Don't believe a word she says – do you hear me? Not a single word!' Exhausted, groaning, he turned his head to face the wall and wept his grief and frustration.

Making things worse! Change the subject… 'I'm staying at Ella's for the time being – wasn't it kind of her to take me in?'

But he was asleep again.

After visiting Ada, she tried her project again – with the same result.

'I've told you, I don't want to hear this nonsense. Didn't I tell you not to believe her? I knew she'd pull a stunt like this. She murdered our father – how many more times do I have to tell you? The woman's a monster – a murderer!'

Now his screaming violence really scared. Refusing to relinquish what had become necessity, she ceased to raise the subject with him. She was learning fast.

There were other imperatives. A father gone – a home destroyed – and what about the business? *Anything – but don't upset him again – else he'll never get better!*

Too late! Knew just what she was thinking behind diversionary tactics. Since she refused to do so, he would raise the subject – then they would argue – bitter, hostile.

Disaffiliation – grit in the Wellington boot of life. Unable to find escape, it chafed and festered, becoming a gross, suppurating cause for dissention. Although they could discuss all other problems amicably enough, this one lay, a coiled cobra. Waiting. Watching.

Initially, desire to spare Imogen further pain sealed his lips. Her refusal to accept his word soon became betrayal. No longer caring how much pain he inflicted, knowing her opinion uninformed, he took perverse pleasure denying information her logic demanded, still hugging the truth to himself – hair-shirt of a zealot nearing ultimate salvation.

'It's treachery, that's what it is – and from my own sister too! It seems you can't trust me after all we've been through from that woman. Now you take her side against me. Truth is, when the chips are down, you just don't trust my judgment. Where's your loyalty in that?'

As always, these altercations ended with Imogen wordlessly staring at the floor – dumb misery in every gesture.

Interpreting silence as wilful intransigence he unknowingly subscribed to the dragon's verdict, 'Base ingratitude – that's what it is!'

Thus, doomed love having achieved denouement, Henry's journey to the morgue forced his children to share the mantle of ultimate victim with him; shroud for the dead – and the living.

Grief's comfort is withheld when death arrives in violence. Illness-inspired passing, whether long anticipated or even sudden has sad logic – a thing of soft beauty by comparison. Conventional mourning remained tauntingly unattainable for brother and sister.

As Imogen took her first faltering steps into this new world of malevolent chaos, she experienced raw fear for the first time. And lonely... so, so lonely.

Having refused sedation she discovered that a fatigued human mind creates its own numbing defence, allowing brief respite – a facility initially offering no lasting relief since returning awareness results in promethean punishment bringing tearing guilt for a grief neglected. But eventually rational thought loosens its shackles – creeps haltingly back.

Ella was there of course, dear constant Ella, but hampered by a natural lack of complete comprehension, she felt shock's devastation, but from outside looking in; so, knowing any comfort given would be inadequate, ever pragmatic, Ella merely concentrated on the practical.

Inside Imogen's world, no father now to still trembling in strong arms, no understanding brother to console – not even Ada's limited caring comforts her – just the silence of loneliness reinforcing fear's dominion.

Seventeen

Ada has become blithe spirit. Fame – infamy, what's the difference so long as the spotlight is correctly focussed?

The glamorous 'she', centre of attention, cynosure of the universe. *The* star! Relishing drama as only a consummate actor can, she plays her part to perfection. Word, gesture, glance, tears, inarticulate sorrow – and all the time, *that* face – pained, grief-stricken bewilderment blending with naivety.

Acutely aware melodrama will be fatal, nothing is overdone. Never a foot wrong, just occasional stumbles – within the proximity of strong male arms. Piteous sobs, trembling, weeping and stuttering always accompany the unvarying story.

'I was gazing into the fire, lost in thought – in a kind of reverie… You understand what I mean, don't you? Yes, in another world. Absolutely no idea what time it was…' Deep, trembling breath. 'My darling husband – he was out with the children – walked over to see dear Auntie Clara… She lives on the other side of the village, you know – about two miles away. I didn't go – just had to have a rest. Well, I was tired out with all the work over Christmas. You men can never understand just how much work there is… '

Indignation mingles pathos. 'Well, I was expecting them to come home together. How was I to know he would come home alone and creep around like that?'

Full flood. Deluge. Unstoppable. Mesmerising. A takeover. Her statement gushes on – over them all.

'I heard a slight movement somewhere at my right-hand side… I was blinded from looking into the fire – couldn't see a thing in the darkness! Really thought it was an intruder. Well, I'd heard nothing before – no sound of anyone coming honestly in by the front door!'

Now, slowing to soft reminiscence, 'Such a peaceful afternoon it was – all by myself… '

Pause to meditate the scene, then – a wild rush to finale. 'I was terrified, I tell you! Groped for the cake knife – knew it was with the cake on the table at my side… where dear Henry left it… Oh, dear! Just chance I found it, you know – in the dark. I struck out wildly in the direction of that movement.' Pause. 'You must understand, I was absolutely terrified!' It's all been too much – strength is failing. Ah, but pathos returns to rally defence. 'Truly, I didn't mean to kill *anyone* – just protect myself.'

Then muted, almost inaudible, one last, forlorn rhetorical question, 'Oh, my poor darling, what have I done?'

Pointless canvassing of the 'dear departed' is invariably accompanied by an ever-ready supply of tears. Never sufficiently violent as to spoil looks – more noisy than moisty; useful facility too in case interrogation becomes over-enthusiastic with uncomfortably near-the-knuckle questioning.

'Why such a long, sharp knife – just to cut a cake? For Christ's sake, who did the baking?' A derisive snigger.

'Henry left the knife with the cake when he went out – I didn't choose it… '

'And why continue to strike with such force when this "intruder" made no move against you? Panic? Huh, you don't seem like the kind of lady who panics – a real cucumber!'

Ada feels a spasm of near panic as questions continue. Mockery unnerves her, she hasn't anticipated this. 'Surely, Ada love, you would know your own husband – even in the dark?'

Such insolence! Ada love? Iron self-control rallies – never to desert again. Turning piteously reproachful eyes on her 'bad cop' she repeats well rehearsed, rapidly becoming apocryphal lines. 'I tell you, I didn't mean to kill anyone, least of all my darling husband.'

Hostility of questioning falters, then withers like unwatered plants in prolonged, full summer sunlight.

Never going to be too tough for someone like Ada anyway – she has 'authority' in spades as birthright. The unlaboured, almost lazily cultured accent of the era's middle classes give her words a ring of irrefutable truth. There's little but respectful sympathy for her throughout an all-male station.

Initial investigation complete, a psychiatric assessment follows to ascertain fitness to plead. Ada enjoys centre stage here too. A charge of murder is brought, the plea 'not guilty'.

Bail? She has no desire to go anywhere anyway. She's at home with her new friends in the remand centre where a fatherly barrister (the best money can procure) assures her, 'The police have failed to present a creditable case – I anticipate no problems.' His words reinforce her confidence in a comfortable outcome to the trial.

* * *

After Imogen confirms her mother's story about the knife the Crown finds it impossible to prove intention to kill or endanger life. Where's motive? A pregnant, happily married woman with nothing to gain, who has obviously loved her husband? The charge is altered. Manslaughter.

The bewildered daughter attends the inquest – gives evidence as first witness on the scene. They're discussing strangers! She fails to register any relevance to her family in proceedings. Fails to register anything much.

* * *

Under sedation, a hospitalised Robin fails to register anything at all. When he is awake, listlessness is fast claiming him. Soon nothing interests at all. Sits for hours staring vacantly into a corner of the room. No movement save an occasional involuntary blink. Everything too much effort – eating, drinking, talking – even lifting his hands – until some kind soul returns oblivion to its rightful place.

* * *

Henry's lawyer, family friend, arranges the funeral. When consulted, Ada merely stipulates cremation. 'Less fuss...' At this stage even she eschews conventional posturing, preferring to get down to business.

'I would be so grateful if you could organise closing the house down too. The sitting room will need cleaning... Oh, dear, yes... redecorating... '

'Leave all that to me. Don't you worry about a thing.'

'We'll have to do something about selling the business as well... '

'Yes, of course. We've already had a lot of interest in it.'

'I expect we have! Even so, it's not going for less than value just because of circumstances.'

'Leave it all to me. You've got enough on your plate!'

Henry's mother has been dead some five years – his violent death has precipitated a major stroke for Aunt Clara who will shortly follow him. Ada is offered release under escort, but declines the opportunity. 'I just don't feel I deserve to go – besides I can't take any more upset – in my condition… He wouldn't want me to lose my baby.' With Robin still sedated, an ashen-faced Imogen is sole family mourner at her father's funeral.

* * *

The will is a surprise. A few weeks before his death, in another of his tax-avoidance schemes, Henry has transferred the business to his wife then set up large trust funds for the children to be held for the benefit of both parents for the duration of their lives. Plenty of time to do something more substantial for the youngsters later…

House and contents are Ada's already. Small change of his estate amounting to a little over £2,000 will eventually be divided between the children.

When Robin finally understands, his face contorts in a smile of pure cynicism.

'Well, she's taken everything else from us – she may as well go the whole hog. Huh, the bitch will probably outlive us anyway… '

Interest fades.

However, there are some things Ada can't control. After twenty-seven weeks of pregnancy a badly deformed male foetus crosses the threshold of existence for a few struggling minutes before inevitable retreat.

It's as though she's unaware of her loss – until visited by a chaplain.

'Please can you baptise my little boy. His name is Charles.'

'Now, now, my child – it's much too late for that.'

'But what are we going to do about him – funeral-wise I mean?'

'Don't you go worrying yourself about things like that. Everything has been dealt with.'

Eighteen

A grieving widow and newly bereaved mother stands in the dock appropriately dressed in black – coincidently creating a foil for carefully applied make-up that itself achieves a lovely pallor. And someone has done her hair – blond curls, worn a trifle *dishabille*.

Tout ensemble, Ada is fully aware she creates the desired impression of forlorn innocence as she pleads 'guilty' to the lesser charge.

During the trial she hears herself lauded by character witnesses, local 'notables' who praise her as wonderful wife and mother.

'Pleasure and a privilege to know her!' enthuses old Major Smythe.

What a sweet old half-wit, she thinks, beaming gratitude at him. That smile warms the fraction of intelligence that remains to him – will continue to do so for another few months – until his wits regroup on senility's furthest front.

Robin alone knows what farce the whole proceeding is, but his voice, which might have proved disastrous, has been silenced by severe mental breakdown – leaving a defence built on Ada's charm to carry the day before it – fox with a lifeless chicken in its jaws.

Judge Abercrombie has presided throughout the case with a face of grey severity that matches his wig and gives the festivity of his vivid-red robes an appearance of incongruous menace. His impeccable reputation, his authority, his utter respectability are expressed in that face – but nothing more. No compassion, no anger, not even interest. It disconcerts Ada.

Heavy, bushy brows overhang eyes seemingly fixed on the ground in front of the dock. Questions, issued *soto voce*, are heard and answered with the immediacy of orders thundered on a parade ground.

He's enjoying this case.

Maintaining the strictest order throughout, he has idly dallied. In his imagination he has been escorting a beautiful woman like this defendant on a triumphant arm to Lady's Night at the Lodge! All blond, willowy, pliant, feminine. Mmm…

'SILENCE IN COURT!'

Figure of dread, symbol of legitimate vengeance. On occasion it has donned a floppy black cap to pronounce ultimate penalty on some shivering wreck of humanity. Now it sits in all pomp and glory. Dreaming of beautiful, forbidden things…

A fat, bejewelled hand pulls the lever. As he teeters on the edge of the trapdoor he glimpses an awful vision of grey-permed, squat, rotund, tweed-bristling, quiet spite. Daydreams end in jolting nightmare. For one fleeting second, his eyes open wide before gratefully closing in rediscovered legitimate sanctuary.

With a sigh of submission that alarms the ever-watchful court, inspiring even deeper vigilance, the great man wonders, as he so often has… *whatever happened to Love's young dream?*

Asking if she has anything to say before he passes sentence, for the first time he appears to pay attention. Heartened, she gives it all she's got. 'I'm heartbroken to think I've inadvertently killed the only man I've ever loved… '

But even then he isn't really listening, just musing. That murder charge – she might well have been threatened with the gallows. *Unthinkable. Preposterous – but it's happened before – not so long ago either. Damn it all, this is a lady – one of us!*

With another sigh, this time of regret, he sentences her to five years imprisonment.

'COURT RISE!'

Nineteen

Robin's illness lasts months. Then, spring growth after rain, our lad becomes stronger – looks forward to visits – takes an interest in life – even manages the occasional smile. His doctors begin to hope. Hope loses its tenuous quality, grows increasingly robust until the Wise Ones can tell an impressed Imogen, 'We anticipate full recovery...'

This then, the moment! Awaited with impatience and concurrent trepidation, the moment he will have to know everything. With tears in her eyes she first tells him, 'She's had a baby, you know – our little brother. He died just after he was born.'

'A brother? A brother, did you say? Well, I'm blowed...'

'Yes, I was as surprised as you are.'

If she hopes poignancy in her news will disarm him, she underestimates the virulence of his antipathy.

'Surely they were too old for that sort of thing? I'll bet it wasn't his! That explains everything! You mark my words, there's a man in all this. I bet she wanted to run off with him. Don't you understand – she wanted to make sure of the money before she did! It all makes sense now...'

'No, you're wrong. I'm sure the baby was Dad's, and the house and business are in her name anyway. She's gone to prison now. Thank goodness, that awful murder charge was dropped – no evidence. Manslaughter.

The effect is electrifying. All his hatred resurges – boils over in one long wailing scream amid a cataract of mucus

– saliva and tears of impotent rage. 'It's a lie!' Again and again. Mouth hanging open, producing unearthly noises; not exactly the howling of an animal – not human either.

Oh, my God! What have I done? She clutches the side of her seat fighting an urge to run. Following familiar sedation he focuses with difficulty on his sister's horror-shrinking figure, wailing, 'How could you let it happen?' She gazes at him in mute misery, making no effort to answer unanswerable rhetoric. His voice fading but still emphatic, he adds, 'It was cold-blooded murder, I tell you. Why can't you see…?'

It would be so easy. Just agree – fingers crossed like a child. But, even in her abject loneliness something stubborn, resisting the ties of fidelity, refuses even this compromise. In dumb misery she returns his stare. His eyes gradually falter – then close. After that he just weeps quietly.

She isn't sure which is worse – tears or rage. Wretched with guilt, unable to offer the comfort of accord, she creeps silently away.

The paradox is, far from causing relapse, Imogen's news and contrary attitude actually aides Robin's initial recovery. At least he's feeling something! Anger.

Soon he burns with growing fury, vowing to be heard, believed by his obstinate sister at least. With no ambition to see Ada punished (even he stops short of invoking gallows justice) yet he wants her condemned – by those fools lavishing blind sympathy. It is all his desire; his heart's yearning. *His* justice!

After a lifetime's slavish endorsement of his every suggestion, Imogen clings to her convictions with limpet obduracy. When, in a rage of frustrated irritation he eventually tells his story, it merely reinforces her defensive stance.

'Oh, Robin. How can you condemn her on such a pretext? A fleeting facial expression! You must be mistaken.'

Voice rising with his words he answers, 'You didn't see it. You should have, then you'd condemn all right! *Then* you wouldn't be so damn stupid!'

His yelling arouses alien anger. She yells right on back. 'No, you're right there. I saw no such thing. She looked devastated when I saw her. Anyway, how come you've taken this long to tell me about it?'

'Never mind all that. I'm telling you now, aren't I? Had you been seconds earlier you'd need no convincing.'

Now speaking slowly – loud, distinctive staccato – as though to a half deaf, half-wit, he reiterates, 'You – would – need – no – convincing!'

'Well, I didn't see any such thing! And there's no need to be insulting – I'm not deaf – or daft. Maybe I just lack your vivid imagination… '

Knows he's going about it all wrong – but can't alter. 'That woman's a murderer. Why does no one believe me?'

It's a question he asks any who'll listen. Unanswerable, it becomes cause of considerable embarrassment. With the passing of time it degenerates into humdrum rhetoric – unheeded, or worse, laughed at. He feels the searing isolation of the votary ignored, exacerbating endemic isolation within his illness.

His mental state deteriorates again, but in a different way, alternating destructively between inertia and blind rage. He begins to experience perverse justification in denying his sister, his best friend, any further discussion – or affinity.

The passing of time will carry awareness of her mother's actions and motive to Imogen. Then she calls herself FOOL! Too late… Her folly is her need. A daughter's need. Belated comprehension, potent with realisation of Ada's mental aberrations will conceive a forlorn pity to grow within her. Foetus of illumination, child of forgiveness, it will cause much anguish, but glow on undimmed – year after year after year.

No such soothing emotion to soften Robin's virulent hatred. Understanding the full depths of his mother's depravity, knowing she's dragged him down into a special hell where she's comfortable with her fall from grace, he alone suffers the tortures of the damned. Only her denunciation can release him. Her liberty tightens his bonds, leaving him helpless in scalding mire – trapped, suffocating, floundering – cursing his life – and the woman who had so reluctantly given it to him.

As the chasm between Henry's children grows ever wider, Imogen's ultimate comprehension is ruined for him by her forgiving.

What on earth do you mean – understand poor Mother? What's to understand for God's sake? She's a cold-blooded killer – she murdered our father! That's all you need to consider!'

His constant ranting breaks something inside, reducing her to quivering victim in his presence. Distress becomes resentment, mutates to aggravation and eventually becomes justification for not seeing him too often. 'We need to heal,' she tells him – when she can edge a word or two into the flow. 'Learn to forgive, like me. It's the only remedy.'

Innate charitable bias creating a growing pity for this same mother is helping to heal her pain. She considers it time for balm – he just wants the wound left open.

* * *

INTERMEZZO

In magisterial splendour Dr Capman's substantial, black, early 1950's Rover saloon slowly pulls up outside Ada's apartment block. It might be elderly, but it and the driver understand each other, care for each other, rely on each other.

'Manufactured back in the days when cars were built – not slotted and bolted together Meccano fashion. Never a moment's trouble!' he often tells unimpressed junior colleagues – as if reinforcing gracious, sagacious ascendancy – like he's giving a lecture to mildly intelligent students.

The great man emerges with ponderous ease. Clunk. Even the door closing has a supercilious ring suggesting awareness of a pivotal function – that of retaining a comforting, warm ambience in anticipation of the returning hero.

Exuding despotic authority, he strides towards Ada's building – frigate, full steam ahead, on a wave of pomposity – trailing a foaming wake of self-satisfaction. A sight to inspire the dying with the will to live.

Literally worshiped by older patients (of a generation unused to free medical assistance, who cling in awed, fervent gratitude to the quaint principle that 'doctor knows best') in total contrast, he's shunned by the young as an arrogant bastard.

He's undoubtedly an excellent physician – that's undeniable, but one who remains sadly incapable of modifying an all-pervading aura of superiority that conflicts with his mental picture of himself as a friendly sort. Well, we all know just how much we appreciate a condescending friend!

Stranded in a hiatus of natural evanescence within an ageing patient bracket, he has to acknowledge he's avoided by younger patients in favour of younger practitioners – huh! As though they hold the key to perfect heath with their chummy first-name terms! Necromancy aside, he can think of nothing to kickstart a renaissance.

So, in spite of an unblemished record, he's becoming an anachronism – a phenomenon he is aware of, resents, but just can't fathom. *Early retirement – that's the answer. But why should I? I'm still in the prime of life!*

Of slightly over middle height and somewhat stocky in build, he knows he makes an imposing figure – but is also uncomfortably aware of medical penalties for those even ever so slightly overweight – and at a certain age too! In consequence, his long-suffering wife's existence is one of constant care, catering for his ever-changing dietary requirements – something to be achieved in tandem with caring for the health of herself and their children. He adheres diligently to convoluted, self-imposed culinary regimes within the confines of home, but happily for domestic harmony – and the sanity of his stoical spouse, he's often obliged (his word) to eat away from home.

With colleagues, medical and or golfing cronies, or at the lodge, he becomes a different creature. Acknowledged by all as a true *bon vivant*, in effect he simply becomes a latitudinous glutton. So, in spite of Mrs Chapman's thraldom, he remains stubbornly overweight.

Oh, my God, just look at the buffoon! Imogen's daydream shatters as she catches sight of her mother's doctor approaching. *Imagine having to see him when you're ill! Oh, well, come on girl, got to get it over with...*

Firmly subduing a nervous giggle, she walks towards the door telling herself sternly that he'll be expecting conventional, doleful anxiety.

As he nears the apartment our dignified doctor is also experiencing difficulty controlling a comic conflict between monolithic irritation and a rebellious imp of hope. Ada is his curse.

In spite of efforts to meet the occasion with dignity, nerves make a dog's breakfast of composure as she gushes. 'I'm so sorry to bother you, Doctor,' (now why do we all say that?), 'I think she's dead.'

Without a word of greeting or acknowledgment he pushes past her making for the bedroom.

'She's in the sitting room. We moved her bed in there the day before yesterday – it was easier... ' With a grimace of irritation he swerves into the appropriate direction.

Examination is cursory. One touch of Death's chill is enough! As he leans over the corpse, images of messianic intervention bring that giggle dangerously near the surface once more as she imagines his victory over dark forces – and a mother revived. Heaven forbid!

Dr Chapman turns towards Imogen, who is standing in the shadows of the sun-filled room. Unable to see her properly he merely speaks in her general direction 'Yes, you're right I'm afraid. Dead. Sorry.'

Sorry? Sorry? Liar, liar – pants on fire! You're delighted. Quietly, she says, 'I thought so.'

His florid countenance aglow in sunlight clearly tells of an incubus removed. Now plagued with an urge to laugh long and loud, she moves from shadow towards him – managing a sweet smile of gratitude to equal anything Ada could have achieved. Iron self-restraint resulting from years spent concealing her true feelings helps – a lot!

As Ada's doctor completes the necessary paperwork with almost indecent haste, he glances at Imogen's placid countenance. He's thinking, poor cow's free of the old horror at last – and so am I! All nice and straightforward too. Death confirmed 1.30pm, Monday 16th September, 1992. Cause of death? Well – old age, heart failure… take your pick! With a flourish he signs the statement.

'Cremation or burial?' His bald question both startles and affronts her. What a thing to ask – and in front of *her* too! Nervously she glances at her mother's placid face. Reassured, she mumbles, 'I can't think at the moment.'

He carries on talking as though she has remained silent. 'You'll need another doctor to sign for cremation. I'll bring Dr Curtis up to speed. He'll pop down – it's not far. Merely a formality. Just phone the surgery.'

'Thank you, Doctor.'

He doesn't hear the words, but is aware they've been said. His ego counts every 'Thank you, Doctor' in like chickens into the coop of a night. You didn't acknowledge each and every bird, but you damn well knew if one was missing!

Snap! Bag shut. After one last satisfied glance at the bed and its burden, he makes for the door and almost bounces through it. Remembering himself in time he calls, 'Goodbye,' over his shoulder without awaiting reply.

Through the window, Imogen notes a new spring in his step and smiles with wry understanding. She doesn't blame him. No one could! Probably the only one of the doctor's dwindling flock he's not sorry to lose.

Adulation he's used to, but this old bird falling from its perch removes what over the long, weary years has become a doctor/patient relationship of nightmare proportions – in direct contravention of his preferred self-image of good-natured toleration.

Walking towards his waiting car all this falls away. He hears the clunk of the closing door as his car welcomes him back. Ego fully restored, he turns the eager ignition.

Alone in a silent apartment with just a uniquely quiescent mother for company, Imogen rings her office to explain absence – half listens to conventional condolences, responds with conventional thanks, then in genuine gratitude kicks off her shoes and sinks into that seat in the sun.

Necessity of a doctor's formal attendance over, she can regain comforting languor. Right now, no outside influence will interrupt except the tyranny of passing time – and even the clock seems to be dragging its hands! The thought brings a slow but irresistible smile to illuminate her normally impassive face with real beauty.

Mind you, there's nothing ephemeral about her beauty – that has ignored marching time as something immaterial.

Never uses or needs make-up. Never messes with her hair – allowing its dark abundance to fade at nature's dictate in a loose knot at her neck. Unaffected by middle-aged spread, her movements supple, she has the mien of a gracefully aging ballet dancer or model.

Clothes, necessarily inexpensive – on her they acquire éclat that is the envy of women rich or poor, young and old.

Like her mother, this fifty-year-old is gifted with serenity. A constant friend, occasionally forced to become part of a defence system creating an artificiality she always resents, otherwise it has remained a soothing companion – even during dark vicious times when logically it should have been destroyed; over time developing into a valuable asset, allowing her to successfully juggle home, family, job – and a mother who gives no quarter.

In true reflection of tenacious inner emotions she presents the world with a calm, caring, cheerfully optimistic face. Outwardly she seems almost, well... boring! Utterly dependable. On the surface, never upset, never flustered, never obviously taken unawares.

Constant grinding financial worry has only ever been relieved by occasional bargain-basement holidays of the kind that neither relieve nor satisfy. With the prospect of limited spends expiring within hours of arrival, she has always met her family's clamour for restaurant meals by adopting a bright, forced smile. 'How about lots of picnics on the beach? Won't that be lovely!' Where's the relaxation in that?

Yes, boring. Plodding on through never-ending drudgery – without thought of complaint. None of that 'Why me!' stuff we're all so good at. But-but-but that monolithic calm obscures just one teeny-weeny enigma, 'cos like the rest of us she's an occasional visitor to fantasy-land – that pleasure-dome of escape for when the going ain't going no place inviting.

In the aftermath of her father's death she embraced the quotidian as a friend in need – shelter from fallout – antidote to the Chinese curse. Enough excitement to last a lifetime!

That death, coming at a critical time in her emotional development has profoundly affected life choices – but they are choices she has never regretted.

Amid ensuing cares and drudgery, there exists a tiny, private world to give mundane life that itty-bitty extra buzz. Fact is, no matter how pervasive her everyday rationale, it fails to blind her to admiration she inspires in men.

Realisation that she arouses such homage without giving a morsel of encouragement is balm to a battered ego – proving her normal after all!

That's as far as anything ever goes, though! Prefers her feet on solid ground… but it does soften the impact a tad.

Right now, Imogen makes no attempt to halt a mournful pilgrimage of youth's memories, but the lovely smile falters as her placid mood assumes a fitful shade of melancholy. Almost bitter realisation that this present balm of perfect tranquillity has been absent from life since, well, *taken more than half my lifetime to return!*

Sitting forward she stretches, cat-like, in the sun, slowly rising, she pads towards the kitchen. Now. How about a treat of some kind? Tea? Coffee? Hmm… hot chocolate… how 'bout that? Steaming mug in hand she sinks back into total opulence.

Weightlessness of total relaxation lifts her mood – which then became a plastic carrier bag of memories caught in the breeze. Hither, thither. Effortless sailing.

Not to last! Total relaxation takes years of practice don't-cha know!

The buoyant bag falters, losing direction in a darkening sky, before becoming ensnared in thorns of menace, creating a further chill of sleet-sharp recollection.

She's experienced this comforting cushion effect before! Yes… that time when power of drugs had filled her with a terror worse than any reality!

Within the chair's warm comfort, her body tenses. My God, how she'd fought! Panther with threatened young. Guarding reason, lucidity – life itself.

Over years, distrust of an authority that insisted on cloying sedation for doubtful benefit to brother and sister has developed into aversion – which now, quite unfairly, includes all manifestations of the medical profession. Absolute necessity apart, she invariably avoids it like contamination.

A spasm of anger disturbs her mood still further. Forgive what was done with such casual arrogance? Never!

Instead of using intelligent consideration to help them cope with inevitable psychological fallout, it chose to blunt effects with facile overuse of a pharmacological cudgel – cheap, easy option, creating unnecessary fug of confusion for her and reducing the brilliance of her brother to a state of befuddled dependence from which he never recovered.

Not one doctor able to observe what had been obvious to her! Her qualms swept aside with high-handed arrogance as just so much immature hysteria – merely earning her an undeserved reputation for neurosis.

Forced to watch him deteriorate, she had known terrible, helpless anxiety. Later she'd raged. And now? Mostly just a profound graveside sadness at the impotent inevitability of it all.

Relaxing again, eyes moist with loving gratitude, she remembers how lucky she'd been in the benign influences that helped to heal a fractured life – softening impulses with the sweet fragrance of selfless love.

ACT THREE

One

Within hours of tragedy Ella Adkins abandoned her own hearth and family. 'You lot can manage without me for a while.'

Putting a spell on our dragon, she proceeded to divide her attention between chicks – waiting for the first crack to appear in shells of chemical opacity.

Robin disconcerted – his reaction to consciousness so violent, much against her will she was temporarily inclined to agree with received wisdom – continued sedation till things improved. Imogen was another matter altogether. Her efforts to escape the lair had Ella's wholehearted approval and it was into her care the hospital released its reluctant ward.

Ella's older children were fast leaving home and her latest little boy would probably be her last child. There were certain signs!

'Bert and me are thinking of fostering – but that can wait. This is your home for as long as you want it.'

Repeating life's earlier actions, kindly Ella poured the excess of her mother-love over the poor waif – so abruptly and cruelly in need of loving *loco parentis*.

'You can have the girls' old room. Couldn't be better! It don't half seem empty without anyone in there any more... I don't mind telling you I had a little cry when Angie left too. You'll be doing me a real favour.'

Her mind busy with adequate bedding – don't want her

getting cold of a night… and food – she won't want anything much yet, poor little mite… tasty and often, that'll be best… she concluded 'Yes my love, I'm sure you'll be comfy.'

With tears of gratitude blending with those of shock and loss, Imogen drifted into safe harbour – just like the mother ship so many years before. Grey, dust despair of isolation found no resting place with Ella around. Muck in the doormat. One thwack… gone! No matter how many such efforts might become necessary, she had strength to persevere – for however long.

'And don't you worry, my darling, we'll soon have Robin out of there as well. We'll find room for him too if necessary. Oh, and I nearly forgot – Tom Rhodes says he'll take Tansy off your hands – so there's nothing for you to worry about there. Oh, my love, please don't cry again… '

Two

'It was a dreadful mistake, darling. I was frightened out of my wits. Honestly, I thought it was an intruder going to harm me – maybe kill me! How was I to know it was your poor father? He never said a word! Not one word!'

Settled in Ella's care, inquest and funeral over, Imogen found enough emotional strength for a visit to the remand centre. With a child's need to esteem a parent, she listened with eager greed as Ada's well-worn tale of woe gushed out – drowning Robin's accusation in the tumult.

'Oh, Mummy, what a terrible mistake. Oh, you poor love – you must be devastated!'

Ada's 'truths' brought comfort – proof that a strong enough need can facilitate acceptance of half-truths or even downright lies.

But, in the quiet of her room at Ella's – caught on query's wondering hook – came pain in a fleeting but familiar doubt... Saccharine blandishments she was used to – oh, yes, more than used to *them*! *What if it's more of the same? What if this isn't real? What if... what if...? No, surely not? She's got to be genuine this time! Yes, she's utterly devastated – you can tell! Can't you?*

Reservations persisted for two more visits, but each time Ada was loving and welcoming. As a result, Imogen's reaction began to lose all suspicion as she became her mother's regular, willing visitor.

Understanding based on deceit illuminated the chaos

of incomprehension. Under this fallible but consoling influence, fragile courage began to convalesce, allowing previous concerns to resurface.

'Mummy, I'm so worried about Robin. I'm sure he's having too much medication.'

'Medication? What on earth does he need medication for? Is he ill?'

'No, but he's so upset by Dad's death. He's being sedated all the time.'

All of Ada's antipathy was in her reply. 'Great heavens! As though I haven't enough problems of my own to cope with. I'm surprised you want to add to my troubles! He must sort himself out – he's all grown up, isn't he?' Imogen's lonely, carping, sorrowing worry impelled her to persist.

'But surely there must be something we can do. Talk to his doctors or something. I'm sure he doesn't need all those drugs.'

'What on earth do you think I can do from here? In any case, no one's forcing him to take them surely? No, of course not. It's all just self-indulgence! Just feeling sorry for himself when we need his help. Typical!'

Seeing Imogen's despair she added more softly, 'Don't worry, darling. He'll be all right – you'll see.'

Henry had always marvelled at her skill avoiding unwelcome subjects of conversation. Not only was his son a taboo subject, but now, except in application to her trial, he also was banished – and that really hurt the daughter.

Surely it's natural to discuss a mutual loved one? Instead, a rapid change of subject! Again, why?

However, such spasms of uncomfortable apprehension were gradually subsumed in the seduction of a mother's unprecedented need.

'I really look forward to your visits. You won't desert me will you?'

'Never! You're my mother. I love you.'

Imperative topic of conversation between them not unnaturally concerned the mother's immediate prospects, but right from the start Ada evinced her usual blithe insouciance – containing no hint of apprehension.

'I'm certain to get a prison sentence – after all, I did kill him… God forgive me. But I'm sure it won't be for long. In and out you know!' Words not intended to comfort Imogen (such consideration would never have occurred) just mere reiteration.

In early 1960's Britain the gallows tree was becoming anachronistic, but it wasn't yet legal history! It loomed massive with threatening horror in public perception, but Ada was unfailingly unconcerned – and as we already know, her assessment was correct.

* * *

So visits, remaining more or less mutually soothing, became routine. Until…

'I wonder if Elrington will visit today – I'd love you to meet him.'

Oh, so casual.

'Elrington? Who's that? Is he a lawyer? Can't say I've ever heard the name before.'

'Now just look at that woman over there – the one with the mousy straggle of hair. Charged with the murder of her husband. Stabbed him in the stomach with a massive kitchen knife then stood back and watched him bleed to death. Maintains he was hurting her. Well, there must be a hundred ways to burn your arm and fracture your ribs.

She never talks properly to anyone – not that I'm exactly looking for sparkling repartee – not in here! But all she does is constantly snivel about her children. It transpires that if she's convicted she'll lose them. All I can say is, she should have thought of that *before* going into the kitchen!'

'Oh, how dreadful – that poor woman!'

'Well, that's as may be, but imagine being stuck in here with all that misery.'

But scattered In amongst trivial chatter that name kept coming back. Imogen would ask, 'Who is this Elrington? I've never seen him, have I?'

Always ignoring the questions, Ada would dreamily simper, 'He'll be here any day now you know!'

That Imogen was unable to participate in discussion of a total stranger was immaterial. Amid blushes, just saying that name was sufficient. The daughter simply became aware another visitor was expected – confirmed by Ada's constant eager glances towards the door. No one.

Time eventually arrived when the mother was contentedly telling her daughter with brisk, cheerful decision that she would have to wait for the pleasure of meeting the mysterious He.

'Why didn't I think of it. He certainly won't want to meet you here. He's quite right of course – I'd hate it too.' In dreamy, smiling submission she concluded. 'How like him to want to spare my feelings. He knows how embarrassed I'd be. He's so sensitive, you know – so considerate…'

Now considerably alarmed, but realising questions were pointless, Imogen could only take refuge in disquieted silence.

Fantasy can't tolerate meaningful debate, although there are occasions when it flirts with delicious danger, dropping hints, defying exposure, skirting its subject, dropping loosely veiled hints like brightly plumed birds in dense fog – to be relished as both succulent hors d'oeuvres and the apogee of discourse. In reality, it relaxes behind sound defences, always confident with them established it will remain ultimately inviolate.

As years progressed, Ada concocted defences aplenty for her creation.

There could never be any doubting the tactician's skill; a full armoury ranging from selective deafness through rage to sulking silence and lacerating sarcasm invariably greeting the slightest opposition. Harsh experience soon taught the long-suffering daughter to avoid introducing reason into this or any other issue on which her mother's imagination was engaged, but at this stage she was just a rookie.

* * *

The sun shining on her chair is still as warm, but now Imogen shudders as memories reluctantly settle into inevitable new captivity – dragging with them a hoard of miserable memories. Reluctantly, she recalls raging scenes that any perceived opposition would provoke – even when opposition hadn't actually existed. Initially shocking, over years they had degenerated into bitter routine.

In self-mockery she smiles, recalling terror of those early years. Terror that during one of her rages Ada might banish her. Huh, fat chance! The voice of jaded retrospection. Isn't retrospection a smart arse?

From that first mention onward, the Elrington subject remained active but unexplored between them, one trying hard to ignore it, the other obsessed.

That Imogen never confronted her mother is easily explained. She was Ada's daughter. Simple as that. This was a time when to be older was to be automatically superior. Rarely would a child contemplate confrontation with a parent – no matter the provocation.

Within her isolation she rapidly learned there were occasions when self-survival required abject capitulation. In any case, it only happened occasionally, didn't it? In those days, most of the time Ada's company was delightful – delightfully worry free.

But it was a blow. No denying that. An assault on the belief structure supporting her recovery. In the surreal game of snakes and ladders that would become their relationship, she now found herself perilously teetering on the business end of her first reptilian let-down.

Attempting to ignore dread's obdurate lump now increasingly oppressing her, she would adopt an expression of mild interest as delighted, always fragmentary confidences persisted; but for the first time she began to understand there was something very wrong with her mother. Something dangerous… something frightening!

Her own need for comfort forgotten in the urge to protect Ada, the 'unknown' confronted her yet again with subtle terror as she searched for some kind of explanation. It wasn't long coming. Lady Luck was with her! All smiling – and bitchy with it.

Three

Wandering slowly down dreary, rainswept Cornmarket, Jane Paget glances upward. After briefly acknowledging affinity with an inconsolable sky, she returns to contemplation of her plodding feet. Lowered umbrella isolating her in gloomy meditation, she fails to notice angry reactions as other pedestrians, forced to take avoiding action, curse selfish introspection.

Nothing to do. Nowhere to go and coming from the same place. Nothing to think about – nothing except a large-looming probability of employment as sales assistant.

A shop girl! What a come down! And at my age too. Still, the rent's got to come from somewhere…

Ever since Henry Phillips' violent death dumped her in the slot marked 'middle-aged – unemployed', all office jobs within her capability have vanished. Aggrieved at fate's cruelty, even, paradoxically with the victim himself, a spasm of anger makes her wonder why people can't just get on with a respectable life – same as her?

Contemplate the unthinkable? Relinquish the Council tenant's tenuous hold on lower middle-class respectability – swap 'the office' for an irrevocable slide into working-class servitude behind the bacon counter? *What would Mum have said? Never thought I'd end up glad she's gone.* She lifts her head at thought of her mother, who always told her, 'Look the world in the eye, my girl! You've got nothing to be ashamed of.'

Imogen obeys her first instinct as the rotund figure of her father's erstwhile employee bowls towards her on collision course; turning towards a shop window she gazes in fascination at nothing in particular. Her action is involuntary – always disliked this woman! Just can't stand the thought of talking to her – even acknowledging her.

Then a thought… If Ada's mystery man has some connection with business, here's the best person to consult!

She'd gone to visit Henry's receptionist with her delicate enquiry in mind, but it proved too painful talking to doubly bereft Brenda Cosgrove – incoherent in illegitimate grief. They had simply wept together.

Now turning with a show of surprised pleasure, she greets the woman she'd wanted to avoid seconds earlier.

Plain Jane. Unemployed Jane. Jane with a clerk's penchant for small details – and, being Jane, also a passion for gossip. She craves the self-confidence bestowed by conviction that should a subject be even ever so slightly incomprehensible, it is, by definition, inferior, making it 'up for grabs' for redefinition and general dissemination.

Plain Jane. Now in enforced leisure she's even more interested in lives and activities of others – lives containing the elementary accommodation of being more interesting than her own. Given opportunity, she will joyfully pick over every morsel found along the way – a chicken occasionally released from a barren coop, scratching, pecking in frenzied ecstasy.

Finding a tasty morsel occasions life's only other imperative – another hen to dig the dirt with – or better still, an impressionable audience, one willing to listen without butting in with awkward reality.

The office *milieu* has been ideal. It isn't just the wage she misses! Perceiving Imogen long before she herself has been seen, also noting recognition and consequent clumsy avoiding tactic with the socially inferior's amused cynicism, she now finds herself unexpectedly noticed. Pride occasions slight resistance – a mood immediately swamped by flattery inherent in Imogen's welcome.

Accepting an offer of coffee, to her joy, she unexpectedly discovers in this shy young woman the audience she craves.

She fails to notice how or when Elrington's name enters conversation. All questioning is subsumed in the delight of imparting superior knowledge. Jane's face becomes even less attractive as it assumes an expression halfway between smirk and sneer. Imogen knows she's stuck gold! Out it pours. Unstoppable!

'Oh, yes! I know him all right. Ever so la-di-da – him in his fancy togs. Got no call to be so very superior, though. He doesn't dress up like that to impress the ladies – got no interest in them… Prefers boys, he does – if you catch my drift… '

Oh, lovely Jane! Outraged but triumphant. Bigot sovereign!

Maintaining a mildly interested expression, Imogen valiantly tries to hide disgust. *What an awful woman… she's positively slobbering at the mouth! Still, got to find out more, can't give up now. But keep it casual…* 'Oh, yes. I understand you all right. Shocking!'

Feigning a fleeting, amused interest, she probes with unconcerned lightness. 'Do you think my mother would know him? I remember Dad mentioning his name once or twice – blowed if I can remember in what context, but I never heard her talk about him.'

'Huh! She wouldn't want to know him! 'Course, your dad had no option – but she's too much of a lady for the likes of that one!'

Like everyone, Jane adores Ada – the only character 'off limits' to the assassin within.

Constrained by a sudden awareness of pathos, Jane is silent for a moment, then continues in more subdued tones. 'Ah well, queer or not, he'll miss the trade he did with the firm… We'll all miss the old place… I know I'll never get such a nice job again.' The prospect of job hunting looms large again as she continues with unassumed grief, 'Mr Phillips was a lovely man to work for.'

Glancing at Imogen's disintegrating face, a spasm of contrition makes her blunder on in hasty embarrassment, 'It's such a terrible tragedy for your family – your mum's trial starts soon, doesn't it? You know, we all loved your dad. I'm so sorry… '

Private! Trespassers trampling her loss! Lurching to her feet, Imogen gasps through her tears, 'Oh, I'm sorry. I didn't realise the time. Supposed to be in Beaumont Street – dental appointment. It's been lovely chatting – must fly – see you again some time.'

Leaving a cup two thirds full of tepid bitterness, she stumbles out to crowded privacy in a sullen Cornmarket, where a shock of cold water from the end of an awning gushes down her neck. She doesn't notice.

Back in the café, contrition merges with regret as Jane, solitary once more, curses her lack of tact aloud, 'Me and my big mouth!' Looking round embarrassed she winces, as to hide confusion she hurriedly drains cold dregs in her cup.

The bitter taste reminds her of earlier thoughts. Of her empty house and a mother, dead these two years – still achingly missed. No one there now to share news with – just an empty chair and the fast-fading echo of a loved voice. *Still, it's been good chatting. Nice kid that! Hope we meet up again sometime.*

Imogen's thoughts are much less charitable. With a violent movement she rubs treacherous eyes on her sleeve. At the same moment distress merges with terror! Desperately she tries to review the interview. *Shown too much Interest? Created suspicion? No, I don't think so... What a risk I took! Well, I'll make quite sure I never have to endure that particular company ever again. Disgusting old muckraker!*

Four

'Get that would you, Imogen my lovey – I'm never going to get dinner on at this rate.' Preparation of one of Ella's famous meat pies has reached a critical point; she isn't about leave it to providence!

The loud noise of doorknocker has startled Imogen – not merely because her nerves are still badly shaken but because she's unused to a house door so near the sitting room.

Steadying herself, she opens the door and stares blankly at a total stranger. Tall, dark, handsome, mid forties – smiling kindly like he's known and loved her all her life. 'Hello, Imogen. My name's Charles Elrington. We've never met, but I was a business associate of your father's.'

Her face pales. Tightening in the chest temporarily deprives her of breath, making her grasp the doorframe for support. For one terrible moment she's certain Jane has brought him and is sitting outside in his car. One wild glance beyond him reassures her. No one there!

'Oh, I'm so sorry. Have I startled you? That's the last thing I wanted to do. I'd have come to see you earlier but, well, I figured there'd be a lot of folks round – family and so on… Didn't want to get in the way. Anyway, I had to come and say how very sorry I am for your loss – see if there's anything I can do to help. Found out your address from Miss Cosgrove.'

'Oh, please… it's me should be sorry – keeping you on the doorstep. Won't you come in?'

As shock subsides, she becomes aware of immediate rapport between them, quickly making her relaxed, comfortable in his company. He follows her into a sun-filled sitting room. Pie now safe in the oven, Ella walks from the kitchen, drying hands on her apron, a look of enquiry on her face.

'Ella, this is Mr Elrington – used to know Dad. He's come round specially to offer help. Isn't that kind?'

Ella beams a huge welcome. Her chick is going to need all the friends she can get! 'How do, Mr Elton, nice of you to call. Won't shake hands – they're all wet.'

'Happy to meet you. Please, both of you – call me Charlie.'

Ella, who has baulked at what she considers a 'mouthful' now grins cheerful relief. 'Charlie it is then. You'll excuse me a mo, I've got the beds to sort out. Leave you two to have a good chat.'

As she moves towards the stairs she calls over her shoulder, 'I've got some little coconut and cherry cakes just out of the oven. You'll stop for a cuppa.' It isn't a question.

Smiling, Imogen gestures towards an armchair and seats herself in the other one. Charlie relaxes. What a charming young lady – but so pale and thin! He's needed all his nerve for this visit. Tricky situation to say the least. And the circumstances – ye gods! But now, completely at his ease, he repeats his offer of help. 'After all, I've got a company car. I expect you often need transport – and the buses are hopeless. There's so much business to see to – I know what it's like from when my mother died. Endless! And, of course, you have to visit your mother. Only got to say the word.' She starts violently. *He doesn't mean to actually visit her himself?* Then relaxes once again. *No silly – just take me. That's all.*

Imogen's gratitude is in her smile – her eyes sparkle.

Initially she's been reluctant to accept help from this man – of all people! But the realisation that he can know nothing of her mother's feelings sweeps that away and leaves her with a full appreciation of what she knows instinctively to be genuine concern for her.

'I do remember you now! You were at the funeral… It was so good of you to attend. 'Fraid most of that day was just a blur to me, though.'

'Of course it was. I'm surprised you noticed anyone. Anyway, that's all behind you now… and your mother will be back with you soon. Her sentence is bound to be short – and with good behaviour, well, home in no time!'

So they chat on. By the time Ella reappears with tea and cakes, they are family. Later as she waves to his disappearing car, both bask in the glow of good fellowship. Both know they've made a new and much needed friend.

five

After sentencing, Ada's next home is HMP Holloway; glorious Victorian assertion of outraged public morality – soon to be demolished to make way for soulless modernity with the same message.

Arriving in a closed van spares her the outside image of ornamented impregnability or massive jaw-doors opening to swallow a tasty new morsel of misery. Her resulting initial impression is of an interior bleakness crowding in with clinging caresses of perverted welcome.

'Gawd almighty! What *have* we got here?'

Two warders behind the induction desk grin knowingly at each other.

Foolishly Ada decides to go for charm. 'Hello. I'm so pleased to meet you. My name is Mrs Phillips.'

'Oooo, there's hoity-toity! Don't worry Phillips, we know who you are all right. Now, come over here to the desk and stand still. You speak when you're spoken too – understand? We've got a lot to get through here.'

Defiant courage sustaining this day of sentencing drains away as a blasting chill of fear rushes to fill the hiatus; fear that once conceived, quickly subdivides to grow – propagating in an orgy of auto-reproduction.

'We'll start with yer posh handbag. Up here and sharp about it.' She carelessly tips sacred contents on the desk like so much garbage and starts to enumerate for her colleague's benefit. 'One lipstick, one powder compact, one purse

– with three one-pound notes.' Each item is laboriously written down.

'Now then, let's have a look at you. Well, for a start we'll have yer posh little hat. French, I suppose.' Turning to her friend she adds, 'They don't make 'em like that here in Blighty.' To Ada, who now knows better than to speak she barks, 'Take off yer shoes – and the rest of yer fancy duds.'

Though guiltless, her hat is imprisoned in a cardboard container, together with the elegant suit, specially worn to give her last day in court that 'Wow' factor; into obscurity they go, along with other morale boosters – handbag, hosiery, heels – all stripped away to be replaced by a number – and prison garb that has the immediate effect of making her feel and look twenty years older. Shivering with cold and nerves, but picture perfect, photos are taken to record a happy occasion. 'Not so bloody la-di-da now, are we?'

Hot-foot after personal belongings go personal identity, personal thought, personal reaction, personal feelings. Process of institutionalised flaying that leaves mere instinct – to blindly flounder in humanity's guilt.

In pathetic contrast to the brisk march of the warder in front, shuffling, reluctant footsteps, hampered by unfamiliar footwear scurry along the slamming, rattling progress into grey fastness. 'Keep up there, Phillips. You're not here for a rest cure.'

To the bewildered Ada, who has never received an order in her life, each turning lock on the journey separates her from normality. She hears shouted commands – half hears, half understands. She puts hands over her ears and stops walking. A shove from behind! Someone following? 'I've told you to keep moving. Think we've got all day to mess around with you?'

In her terror Ada responds by running a few steps looking wildly round to get her bearings. Obediently mobile now, she becomes aware of a smell... Getting stronger, stronger – makes her stomach heave... What smell? Just that well-documented miasma of cheap disinfectant endeavouring to conceal the odours of confined humans. It fails, but the two vie constantly for pre-eminence, combining to become defining fragrance of prison. The smell of putrefying hope.

An endless corridor? It terminates in sudden scorn within the vastness of a grey-painted, brick-built rotunda encircled by grey-painted metal walkways – one above the other – stretching imploringly through layers of grey-painted wire netting to glimmering obscurity in grey-painted sky far above.

The unnerving impressions of a giant spider controlling a vast web of interconnecting corridors stretching from the rotunda (to where?) is no illusion. All is permanently exposed to scrutiny. Panic-induced thoughts of escape wither at this realisation, finally dying in an agony of suffocation as the cell door crunches into place and the prisoner becomes aware of an intermittent watching eye.

Abruptly severed from shouting, rattling and clanging, the loss is cataclysmic. Alone in silence she sinks to the floor weeping, desolate in desertion.

But as hours pass, she gradually becomes accustomed to isolation; oppression alters to growing relief. There's privacy of a kind here – in spite of an occasional eye in the door that locates her then closes with a snap. Comfort. Breathing space. Time to reclaim scattered thoughts. Not so bad after all!

Crash! As the door opens, all tentative optimisms scurry for cover. Witless, she stares. In total silence her cellmate climbs deftly to the top bunk, throws Ada a glance of territorial menace, settles her head on the pillow and shuts her eyes.

So even solitude is denied! For the first time she has become aware of significance in bunk beds! Claustrophobia a silent cell has failed to inspire now claims its prize.

Ah, but our Ada is made of sterner stuff. Before many hours she escapes into a comforting nether-world of imagination in which outwardly she passes though the discipline of prison life without complaint.

An automaton eats prison food without tasting and as a result, defecates without disgust into prison facilities. Without seeing, it looks into a prison mirror, uses a prison comb, washes in prison water using prison soap, meticulously obeying all prison rules as only an automaton can. As a result, Ada quickly becomes a model prisoner.

Penitent exterior hides an individual that admits no guilt, who laughs at an automaton's actions, sneering at hoodwinked fools who believe them her own. With its help she can wait – insulated from reality. Safe. Inviolate. Serene.

Six

The remand centre holding Ada pre-trial was that species of sterile no-man's-land designed to consider sensibilities of the as yet uncondemned, but without hypocritical pretence of reassurance. Accustomed to warm welcome wherever she went, Imogen found its bleak ambience repellent.

By comparison, change to Holloway Prison categorised these visits light-hearted social calls.

Unlike her mother, she had liberty to approach that exterior on foot – experience its salutary effect to the full. Not a freedom to relish.

Fighting an urge to turn and run, she concentrated on thoughts of her mother waiting inside; thoughts that held her advance steady.

With nervous, faltering smile she approached a guardhouse. 'Hello, I'm here to visit my mother. How do I get in?'

Polite, timid enquiry resulted in curt direction to a previously unnoticed, straggling queue of patient humanity standing in the rain – she obediently faded into its obscurity.

Looking for more information, she tried conversation, but failed to make eye contact with anyone. All simply stared at the ground as though mesmerised. No chit-chat here. No socialising. Little more than furtive glances by way of introduction, each absorbed in a hell of worry and shame that excluded the concept of camaraderie in adversity. The 'unclean'. Sons, daughters, husbands, lovers, lining up in the rain – waiting.

1960's Britain. Mary Quant mini-skirts, 'pill'-informed sexual freedom, love and flower power growing in Carnaby Street and that queue growing in the rain – all within sound of Big Ben.

In one of life's more sick paradoxes, visitors were relieved to get inside out of the rain, away from that glowering façade of respectable outrage. Dubious comfort of limited duration since the interior, although dry, was designed to repel – with a vengeance.

For some inexplicable reason, Imogen expected to find her glamorous, vivacious mother little altered. Preoccupied with seeking this image among drab uniformity pouring into the room, she was irritated with – tried to look beyond the stranger who, with averted face, slunk into the seat opposite her own.

Refocusing – as though entering a darkened room direct from bright sunlight, with slow reluctance she gazed in vague recognition at this apparition – taking in details of travesty. Used by now to profound shocks, this one almost paralysed her. 'Hello – Mummy?' She couldn't keep the question from her voice.

In a particularly unaccountable innovation, Ada's hair had a left-hand parting. It had the unfortunate effect of revealing a small, shoddily plebeian margin of nondescript roots from which lack-lustre but still patrician locks of blond were in determined retreat. Ultimate humiliation for a woman who had preserved an inflexible peroxide identity for so many years.

If only that were the full extent of mutation! No vestige of make-up hid a putty-hued complexion – obviously estranged from soothing face cream. In baleful mockery,

Ada's favourite red nail varnish glowed in flaking remnants on broken nails of already-roughened hands.

Ordeal in that first visit continued unabated – compounded by Ada resisting all attempts at conversation. Mute throughout, she stared fixedly at her daughter as though struggling to identify a stranger.

Watching as Ada was led away, Imogen noticed flat shoes for the first time. Of all the day's searing images, that one was her undoing. All resolve, all courage evaporated – to leave her weeping in poignant pity for the down-at-heel degeneration of a once fashion-obsessed woman.

Seven

Within weeks of sentencing, deemed to pose no threat to anyone, Ada was transferred to a small, new-built prison in the Buckinghamshire countryside with modern, liberal attitudes – not exactly come and go as you please, but positively relaxed by comparison with its London cousin.

Too late! By this time Holloway's indelible mark was on both women.

Permanent blight created two manifestations in Imogen – a king-sized inferiority complex plus a massive boost to her ever-growing mother-pity.

As for Ada, well, outwardly her spirits revived with a changed regime. In her new home she was allowed, even encouraged to take an interest in her appearance. Hair regained blond glory and although she never again achieved the artistry that had so impressed Charlie Elrington, reclaimed use of pallet and manicure materials revived her femininity with the touch of pure kindness. Consequently, Holloway's influence was initially unnoticed.

However, her retreat into the sanctuary of mental chaos and consequent unwillingness to venture out (a snail surrounded by salt) was soon noticed in a more relaxed atmosphere.

Not everyone wanted to acknowledge it. Imogen didn't. Put mental blinkers on – clung to limited peace of mind. Obstinate, cowardly, wilfully obtuse… In any case, Mother was relatively normal in her company!

But at other times Ada would laugh uproariously for no obvious reason, hold long, murmured, one-sided conversations with an unseen companion – or simply stare in rapture at nothing in particular.

Spent a whole heap of time doing just that.

Consequently, other house guests rapidly decided to avoid too much contact. Well, isn't it accepted as fact in many sections of society that mental illness is downright contagious? A wide berth recommended? Among Her Majesty's guests being a 'nut' is a definite deterrent to socialising. In their world – as with so many others – it's only too easy to be condemned by association. Yeah… a *very* wide berth!

Aversion fully reciprocated! Ada wanted no socialising with 'these people' as she termed them. Imogen's anxious enquiry, 'Have you made any friends yet?' was greeted with a look of such withering scorn it was never repeated.

Ada's conventional snobbery, creating a bizarre analogy with disinclination in fellow inmates, ensured the privacy she craved. Human companionship had never been priority. Not for her the unburdening chat with that special confidant. Always unnecessary – now potent with danger! Besides, none of them could possibly be useful when she was released.

She'd undergone many vicissitudes since her husband's death. Holloway alone had fundamentally distorted much of her ideology, but, in spite of all, ability to categorise humanity remained immutable as her fingerprints. Under a cloak of very real psychological problems she remained as shrewd as any captain of industry.

Meanwhile, her new prison authorities, considering themselves guiding guardians to those who have erred and strayed like lost sheep, noticed the new lamb's idiosyncrasies and singled her out from the flock.

With 'enlightenment' as guiding principle, they and the resident psychiatrist held prolonged meetings, used jargon-coated language – and made no advance whatsoever.

In Ada's funny farm it was the shepherds who got hopelessly lost, until, after profound deliberation, it was decided that unless this particular errant one created actual mayhem in the pen, it would be advisable to ignore any behavioural eccentricities – for the time being.

'She's no danger to anyone… not suicidal either. We'll keep a watchful eye, review the matter in six months or so.'

Thus did good old-fashioned pragmatism eventually come to the rescue – ensuring nothing got done.

Sadly, the only real result of all hot air was that Ada's very real psychological problems continued to be ignored – being left to flourish and multiply undisturbed.

But now, for the very first time, Imogen basked in the glow of a mother's love. Entering the visiting room to find her daughter waiting, Ada's face would lose its habitual shut-in aspect and light up in delighted greeting.

For the first time also, there was a mother's genuine interest.

'How is life at Ella's?'

'It's fine – I'm being looked after like royalty.'

'I'm so glad you went there. Any special boyfriend yet?'

'No, no one in particular.'

'Any new friends? Anyone I haven't met?'

'No.'

'Well, how are all the old ones? Do you see anything of Cynthia Fullerton or the Buchanan girls?'

'No, they've all left home – moved away.'

Questioning, blithely assuming Imogen's life unaffected by recent events, continued, oblivious to the blight her actions had created.

Even friends she'd known all her life were now failing her. Overwhelmed by embarrassment, they had all distanced themselves from her world – by a galaxy or three.

Insensitivity aside, in her naivety Imogen was pathetically pleased with novel fellowship. Real friendship was blossoming, tentatively revitalising brutalised perceptions. Too early yet to know that 'glad to be alive' feeling, but there was definite improvement.

The 'enthusiasm of youth' woke, yawned and scratched its loins – as yet unwilling to get outta bed, but at least starting to think about what it would wear when it did.

By blinking at Ada's mental deterioration she could confront her own life – just about. What matter that Mother sometimes lost track of the conversation? Just momentary drifting. So what her sudden replies to forgotten questions? Understandable, wasn't it? After all she's been through! Hardly worth the notice. And the Elrington thing? Just some kind of silly misunderstanding.

Eight

Charlie Elrington? Yep. Good as his word. Imogen needed help? There he was.

Sweet, tender attachment soon established – the kind that can flourish between homosexual man and non-threatening woman. He became comforting father figure – for a beloved daughter, impossible of proclivity necessary for conception.

Hitherto, father or brother had been confidant of choice, now Charlie took their place with butterfly modesty – giving her life an echo of its former beauty, answering an aching need with genuine, delicate, unobtrusive sympathy borne of his own pain; understanding her need to talk as graceful maturity informed his responses.

After her father's death, people had crowded in with intrusive sympathy – only just disguising excitement with endless dissemination. (For many, Henry's death would eclipse any future sensation – including their own demise.)

Embarrassing, distressing, unanswerable, unstoppable verbal incontinence. 'Ah, yes, terrible, isn't it? I was at the funeral, y'know.' Blah, blah, blah…

It's a universal brand of sympathy which, if not borne of excusable embarrassment, often ends in irritation because it fails to comfort – as though the bereaved were guilty of underhand ingratitude.

'You must try to buck up, my lass – put it all behind you. He wouldn't want you to grieve like this, y'know. Anything I can do? Only have to ask.' Offers relaxing in the comforting certainty of being unaccepted.

So, of all her parents' friends and acquaintances, only Charlie Elrington proved genuine. Only he was willing to listen patiently to broken outpourings of confused grief – and without embarrassment or crass sentimentality.

As the quiet benevolence of this new friendship grew, confidences eventually became reciprocal. Charlie dared to tell some of his own secret life – including his brief encounter with Ada.

'I remember the first time I saw her. At your father's office it was. She looked absolutely fabulous! I've never seen such perfect make-up – and her clothes! What harmony... That lady is a real artist! Made me so envious... 'Fraid I stared – hope I didn't embarrass her... '

Imogen flushed.

Noticing her discomfiture he quietly whispered, 'I'm sorry. I didn't mean to upset you. Take no notice of me.'

Quickly recovering, she smiled bright encouragement at him. 'No, no, please carry on. It's just memory... You know... '

Unstoppable now, floodgates open for the first time, despair poured out.

'I'm hog-tied. Have to be totally discrete. Makes meeting anyone much too difficult – too dangerous. Huh, "the love that dare not speak its name." Love is love – should never be ashamed. But I'm such a coward... '

Momentarily forgetting his role as comforter he revealed glimpses of timid desolation.

'I don't want to upset anyone – just want some happiness like anyone else. But I've no rights in this stupid world – no rights at all. If I was a woman, or black African, or... or, well, anything but what I am, I could proudly fight my cause without people thinking I was disgusting.' Sightless, he stared into his hell. 'Yeah, it's the aversion I can't take. So I live alone – in silence.'

After Wolfenden there were to be eleven more years of frustration as men like him continued to be incarcerated in a cast-iron closet. Pitiless iron maiden, made all the more unbearable by beckoning freedom. Malicious, mocking siren to tempt the impatient to destruction.

Awed by the man's grief, Imogen realised it was her turn to comfort – made her feel oddly comforted – and sweetly privileged too. But she was now forced to confront the ludicrous character of Ada's passion (flimsy structure of her father's scaffold) as harsh comprehension finally removed blinkers.

Also came concomitant realisation! She must forever keep her own council on the subject. Seemed like birth of a kind of deceit!

In addition, she had to gradually face up to odious comparisons between profundity of dialogue with Charlie and poverty of that with her mother. With sharp regret, she perceived the hindrance Ada's secret fantasy inflicted on their relationship – and now she must bring her own discretion to the feast!

* * *

Charlie Elrington lived in the rambling Victorian house on Iffley Road that his mother had bequeathed him.

'I know I should let a room or two...' he would murmur with affected irresolution allaying a perverse guilt. 'So much room for one!' Meanwhile knowing nothing would induce him to share his privacy... Unless!

Sunday tea-times were now special. He would bring out

best bone china and silver tea service for the occasion – for his beloved Imogen.

With the passing years this became regular ritual. He called her his 'duchess', plying her with delicate crustless sandwiches and griddle cakes, which, with elaborate finesse he cooked on a beautiful silver apparatus that somehow managed to combine antique curiosity with efficiency. 'A bit like me!' he would joke.

Occasions, light-hearted, frivolous, giving supportive structure to the somewhat lonely existence of them both. Sedate, she would 'take' her Earl Grey and eat quantities of jam-coated cakes with youth-fuelled hunger.

Well, perhaps not so sedate!

She never told Ada she knew him; instead became the link between them – a kinda lopsided go-between.

Charlie never failed to enquire after Ada – got to know a great deal about her – a great deal that excluded one relevant fact.

And Ada? Ada had her dreams – leave her out of it!

Some years later, when Charlie suffered a fatal heart attack on his fiftieth birthday, Ada remained blissfully unaware of the event, leaving Imogen to grieve alone. Attending his funeral as the only genuine mourner, she had the weird feeling she was also representing her mother.

Having been shunned by his family as an embarrassment during life, his death produced the usual plethora of grieving relatives working hard at a tear or three, whilst busy with fiscal calculation which would reap minimal reward for all – after a long, weary wait!

Like so many of us, Charlie had refused to consider his own mortality, so there was no will.

Perhaps it was his greatest legacy that family gatherings

ceased from this date – torn apart by the rancour of sharing out his material possessions.

Back at his bargain-basement funeral (and how much is this costing anyway?) 'the bereft' regarded Imogen's inclusion in their number with startled suspicion. Two dark-clad females accompanied a droning priest with whispered undercurrent.

'Our brother, here departed… '

'Here, Maggie!… Isn't she the daughter of that lot out Hannington way? You know, the mother took a carving knife to her old man? Reckoned it was an accident… '

'We come into this world… '

'Yes, you're right,' Maggie, mumbling behind the piety of a large white handkerchief, added further interest. 'I think she's out now. Not much for a life was it? The son's a bad lot too – nothing but a drunk by all accounts.'

'take nothing from it… '

'What a cheek, eh? Turning up here… What's she after, I'd like to know? Didn't know he even knew her – did you?'

'Oh, he knew all sorts… never did have any discretion – as you very well know!'

'Amen.'

'ARRRMEN!'

* * *

Smiling at the memories her mother's death have evoked, Imogen's heart warmed with love and gratitude for the man now so many years dead.

Well, she was wrong in so much, but she was right about that – he was a beautiful man.

Nine

So, with a little help from her friends, Imogen is starting to recover from her father's death. You would never have gotten her to admit as much. Amelioration of grief? Treachery! Hug it close – don't part with recognisable company in an alien landscape.

Ah, but it's seeping away – unable to withstand the onslaught of love. Ella and Charlie's loving care, Ada's seeming love and care.

If only repairing the deteriorating relationship between brother and sister were as easy! Robin's grief is going noplace. He tells her straight, 'You're colluding with the enemy!'

In her innocence she has no enemy. It's an impasse spiralling to hell and gone. She and his fiancé Kathryn become mere helpless witnesses as the horror of Robin unfolds. Disintegration of promise, dissipation of glowing prospects, brilliance, replaced by obsessive preoccupation with loss – and utter hatred of what he perceives as its cause. Cussedness apart, his spirit is broken.

The girls search for rehabilitation's strategy – clinging to each other for support, blind fools, equally baffled, dancing in darkness as the band plays *Believe It If You Like*.

Illusory buttress of mutual encouragement founders beneath them leaving the ever-expanding silence of impotent misery to cling to.

But, this poor affinity is Kathryn's only comfort!

Trapped inside a decompression chamber of isolation – bolts wheeled home from the outside – she watches as, unconcerned, the world goes its careless way, whilst the rarefied oxygen of helplessness smothers her.

Her parents' delight in what they had once regarded as a socially desirable match has undergone radical alteration.

'Cut your losses now, darling. We don't want you involved. We can see nothing but pain for you in the match.'

'How can you imagine I'd be so fickle? I love Robin so much. I can't desert him – he needs me now more than ever.'

Through tears of outrage she can clearly see their faces. The shutters of respectability have slammed shut. She's on her own-io.

'Ah, well, you must do as you think best, but Mummy and I don't want to hear another word on the subject. If you feel you must marry him, best do it quietly.'

Duncan loves her. Ah, how Duncan loves her. Wholehearted worship. Honourable, steadfast. Inarticulate – doomed whether or no.

Oblivious of his passion, Kathryn only knows she's uneasy in his company – wary, shy – in a way that precludes confidences. Too innocent to understand, only aware that something is somehow… inappropriate.

Sad, lonely Kathryn. Some of us wouldn't know the real thing even if accompanied by a trumpeter, name of Gabriel. Oh, blow that thing![2]

Whenever Robin emerges from the seeming tranquillity of moon walking, pain hits him with a rubber mallet. Not physical pain. Worse, much worse. Needs a hit of another kind. As months pass, in privacy of his home with his dosage now unsupervised, he is becoming a helpless addict.

Medical professionalism is piqued. Time he was back

to normal. Let weaning commence! Scientific progress. Dosage gradually reduced – compensated by alcohol to bring spiritual solace. No flies settle on our young man! His pain, never going to respond to some fancy strategy, keeps grief constant – hones his hatred, his *raison d'etre*. He just needs it relieved from time to time. Not much to ask, is it?

By the time narcotic weaning is complete, the patient has choice of vodka, or whisky, or gin – or whatever (he isn't particular) to lull him gently into a utopia of forgetting – whenever he feels the need.

* * *

In the immediate aftermath of Henry's death, only Kathryn is available to cope with Robin's grief. Duncan is willing, but embarrassment plus *gaucherie* discount him. A disconcerted Ella, deciding to concentrate on Imogen, leaves no one else willing to tolerate involvement's anguish.

His shame excludes his fiancée. He never will tell of that fleeting image of his mother's evil. Unenlightened – unaware of his rejection, she battles alone to sustain him, hold him close as he sobs his endless torment – torment only relieved by chemical sedation that labels her 'failure'.

When, after Ada's conviction, grief first becomes tinged with anger, she and Duncan share relief with Imogen.

'That's natural progression! It's healthier.' Eager agreement tinged with desperation. Coterie of wistful hope.

Before long, as home life becomes increasingly tense, characteristically blunt, Duncan attempts amelioration, typically opting for the direct approach.

'Listen, mate. Yer dad's dead. All this anti – not goin' to bring him back, is it? Why don't you cool it – for yer own sake if not for the rest of us, eh?' Robin stares steadfastly at the floor, seemingly considering given advice.

Encouraged, soft-sweet Kate joins him on the sofa. 'Please, darling. Your mother's paying a terrible price. Surely you can pity her a little?'

Smiling pleasantly he leans towards her, lips pursed. Expecting a kiss, tension relaxes as her eyes close.

'You stupid bitch!' explodes into the small space between their faces. Eyes wide open in shock she leaps to her feet and standing, looks down at him in bemused anticipation of repudiation – or moderation.

Nothing.

Relaxing now, he swings his legs into the warmth of the vacated seat, deceit in his smile modulating to a sneer.

'You think you're so smart! Know the lot, don't you – you and that clown over there?' Nodding in Duncan's direction. With rising vehemence he continues, 'Well, let me inform you. You know nothing from nothing. Just nothing. And I'll tell you something else. I hope she rots in hell. No! Not just in hell – I don't trust the afterlife! No, in *this* stupid world. Slowly… alive… in agony.'

With quiet menace, he adds, almost to himself, 'You can have no idea how good the thought of her suffering is to me.' Picking up the customary glass he raises it. 'Long life, Mother dear!'

'Let's get outta here!' Duncan hisses, drawing the girl's unresisting form towards the door. 'Leave him to calm down… '

Later he is to ponder why in God's name they hadn't just kept going.

Ten

In the pre-pill hiatus of the early sixties, a relationship that has progressed unconsummated to engagement probably remains so until the wedding night – when total sexual ignorance may well prolong the business indefinitely. Ignorance, a nice girl's best friend, is essential precursor to wedded bliss; hypothesis that assumes the guy knows what he's about!

Youngsters of Kathryn and Robin's background get a lot of hogwash about evils of the unchaste state – code for social death of pregnancy.

In the heady days, before Henry's death killed romance, Robin had reverenced his fiancée's purity – totally committed to veneration of the hymeneal altar. Violation would be desecration of splendour. Her dress should be significantly white – unbesmirched by experience. In his imagination he might well spend many a sticky hour removing it from her yielding nakedness – but never dream of usurping its authority!

No such idealised qualms now. Sex. He needs sex. Sex will be his saviour. Not the sex of a few bargained minutes. He needs a woman to bring the warmth of love to the act. Kathryn. Kathryn's love. Kathryn's body is his need's salvation – rapacious need that remains unsatisfied after the first brutal assault leaves her trembling, nauseated, bleeding.

Again! Again? Dear God, please not again!

Repelled by constant animal demands – and nerve-wracking wait for the safe termination of her physical monthly cycle, she begins to dread Duncan's absence. Sweet, shy desire to comfort sustaining her is eventually replaced by a growing reluctance.

'No? You're just another selfish bitch! Beginning to think you're all alike.'

Violence of rage merely increases reluctance – till it becomes refusal. He stops just short of rape.

Her ideals might never have matched those he's abandoned but they still include love's joyful, mutual reciprocation. Here is no love, and certainly no delight – just perversion. She knows his demands for her total mental and physical submission are ultimately harmful to them both.

Returning to work, distracted by stimulus in an enlarged world, an unusually subdued Robin capitulates to her stronger will. 'You're right. Forgive me? Won't happen again. Promise!'

He chooses a sunny Saturday lunchtime. Midsummer mellow – with the promise of a warm, lazy afternoon ahead.

Trudging from the bus-stop laden with groceries for the two men, happy with a quiescent Robin and influenced by the weather, Kathryn is unusually carefree. She knows that with a morning's work completed, her fiancé and Duncan will be relaxing, deciding what to do with the rest of the weekend. Thinking of it, she smiles.

'Got me a hot date with a jolly little number. Too warm for the cinema… anyway, why waste money, eh? Think I'll just take her up Wytham Woods – let nature take its course.'

Realist enough to know his absence is required, a gloomy Duncan faces an afternoon of arid exile. He's merely wondering how to pass the time till return is safe. Not for the first time, his mind turns to the desirability of finding a new home. Robin, smiling with careless cynicism pours himself a whisky and waves the bottle enquiringly at his friend.

'No thanks, mate – I'll need my wits about me later.'

'Can't think why. Like fallin' off a log!'

Kathryn approaches the big old house where Robin and Duncan rent the top floor. Contented in spite of aching arms, she is planning ahead with something that's almost optimism. *This afternoon for instance – how about a walk by the river? Do him the world of good! And why not a picnic too? Got some beautiful ham... he likes a nice slice of ham with mustard.*

Mind engrossed with gastronomic treats she hauls shopping bags up the last stairs; gratefully putting them down, she opens the door. Resuming her burden she adopts the bright smile that has become habit, then walks forward into the room.

He hates that smile!

Sheer malevolence in Robin's face roots her to the spot. She can only stare at him mesmerised. Sprawling, one leg over the armrest of his chair, drink in hand he calls, 'Hey-up, Dunc. Here she comes! Little Miss Venus Dick-trap herself. Imagine trying to shaft that prissy bitch. Let me tell you, it's possible to get hypothermia of the crotch up there.' In full flood – unstoppable – sniggering. Ignoring Duncan's horrified expression, he drawls, 'Well, I certainly don't want it any more. If you're willing to take the chance – help yerself... She's all yours!'

Groceries fall from inert hands. Turning she rushes headlong downstairs – out into a strange street – away from the hatred in his voice. Unmindful of traffic she fails to hear shouted warnings or screech of rubber on tarmac as drivers swerve to avoid a careering form.

Back in the apartment, his fists clenched, Duncan breaks the stunned silence with quiet menace. 'Go after her you filthy bastard.'

Shocked himself now, kicking and cursing groceries, Robin takes the stairs four at a time out into sunshine. Even half blinded he easily overtakes her directionless footsteps. Grasping her arm he pulls her to safety on the pavement.

'Let me go! Let me go!' Adrenaline fuelled terror rains blows on his head.

'I'm sorry, darling. I love you. I'm so sorry. Forgive me, please!'

Words don't register – just the sound of penitent love. Feet faltering, shivering with cold shock, she allows him to lead her back along the street, up the winding stairway to a world unchanged – obliterated. Once inside, he makes her sit on the sofa before finally shutting the door, then tries to sit beside her. With a renewal of vigour she pushes him away. In a change of tactic he moves to a seat nearby, trying to sooth with softly spoken endearment.

Having retrieved the shopping, put it away and witnessed her safe return, a white-faced Duncan has slipped unnoticed from the apartment. She's in no danger now – not this time anyway.

Robin is astounded by her reaction. He never anticipated this amount of upset! Moving towards a bottle-laden sideboard he pours a large brandy, gently urging her. 'Go on, it'll steady you.' Tentative sips make her choke. Seeing her struggle he takes the glass, drains it himself then pours a refill – downing it in one. 'My God! My nerves need steadying too… It was supposed to be a joke… '

Love becomes the ultimate despot when reinforced by pity. In this disguise it finally claims Kathryn for plaything that sunny afternoon. Cunning, eh? Pretending to lie a-bleeding and all the time narrowly watching its prey.

'Sometimes I don't even know what I'm thinking – let alone what I'm saying,' he tells her. 'Please forgive me – I can't even remember what I said.' To confirm the lie he adds, 'Oh, God, saying things like that to you! Unforgivable!'

She forgives anyway!

As the sun's course moves towards friendly shadow and their world becomes sweet once more, his self-pity resurges. 'I just can't seem to help myself… My life's become terrible… terrible.' Encouraged by her murmured sympathy his lament turns with dreary inevitability towards blame – making Kathryn fidget under the familiar mix of dread and embarrassment.

'It's all the fault of that damned bitch. Just look what she's done to you and me!'

Rising hurriedly, she puts friendly shadows to flight by switching on the light. 'Think I'll make us a couple of sandwiches each. You hungry? I know I am… I got some lovely ham this morning… pity to waste it. It'll be off tomorrow in this heat.' She refuses to see the utter contempt on his face.

Duncan suspects his one-time friend capable of physical violence. In that he's wrong – but then, abuse wears so many different garments.

Prowling Oxford's streets that afternoon, any sympathy for Robin vanishes – to be replaced by a growing contempt. What that sod's been through is no excuse. Used to be a decent type. Real swine now!

'Time he got a grip on it,' he later tells Kathryn. 'Making everyone's life a misery – especially yours!'

'We'll just have to be patient with him – this isn't the

real Robin. He'll come back, you wait and see. Please don't desert him now, Duncan.'

He turns away, hiding a baffled grimace – mix of pity with frustration's gall.

The poor sod's worship had begun the moment he first saw her. It hadn't been long before Robin discerned his friend's affliction. Smug but kindly banter had followed. 'Forget it, old pal. She's not up for grabs… you'll have to find your own. This one's special. Mine all mine!'

When dislike first started to grow he'd fretted. Was antipathy partly due to jealousy? After a while he'd ceased to care one way or the other, leaving hatred to grow unfettered.

Now he realises he must move out or go mad – but leave her defenceless with that bastard?

On the bus home, enlightenment sears awareness of a new dilemma on Kathryn's lacerated understanding. She loves him, yes – but respect? Already eroded by his constant mother-hate, this day's work has finished the job. How can she possibly marry a man she doesn't respect?

Wearied beyond her strength, tears trickling down her ashen face, she stumbles from the bus two stops on from her own and sets out to retrace its route.

From that day Robin begins to derive increasing sadistic pleasure, saving his more viperous outbursts for when Duncan forms an audience. Solitary, dumb and mortified Kathryn fails to satisfy the devil in him, but watching that big ox squirm with silent rage. Pure joy!

Unholy imp, assuming the sweetest of smiles, innocent as a babe, asking, 'Didn't you realise she was only a prick-tease, Dunc?' Adding with assumed weariness of bitter experience, 'No, mate. Take it from me, waste of time getting yer hopes up there… ' Puerile wit creating amendment calculated to send Duncan crashing out of the house. 'Let's face it. Hope is *all* you're gonna find up there! Just look at her – a regular frigid bitch!'

Endurance snaps. Gotta leave this hell-hole – before there really is a murder! 'Come with me, Kathryn, this'll only get worse. He's a lost cause. *Escape* girl!'

Knows he's wasting his breath! Forlorn, empty gesture – designed to make him feel less spineless. Failing.

Leaves his job, leaves the apartment, leaves the city – leaves the only woman he will ever love.

Eleven

Conditioning brings a species of languid nausea to replace terror. Typical victim of brutality, Kathryn endures with stoic patience – waiting for the day it will end. *It will end! He doesn't really mean it, not deep down.*

Her loving pity merely compounds his raging misery. Doesn't know what he wants from her. Not necessarily sex. But sure as hell, not this nauseating, sweet forgiving!

Duncan's departure brings uneasy peace. Lacking an audience, vicious verbal attacks cease. Rather than reassuring, the resultant silence creates a disconcerting hiatus – until fickle hope twitches tawdry skirts. Away goes the wily, flirty, old bird – dancing, chancing, glancing, backing and advancing; wanton tarantella with venom hidden in gaudy display as competent substitute abuse is discovered.[3]

Fondle – fully clothed. No resistance! One, two... all buttons. Hooks undone. Still nothing! With shuddering sigh of ecstatic relief he buries his face in her naked breasts – motherland of consolation.

Kathryn is relieved. She can bring peace to the conflict of her sad, tortured love and keep him off the bottle too! Earth mother – proud, powerful, comforter.

Hours of blissful tranquillity. No more aggressive pestering for sex – just her loving murmurs to mingle his baby noises.

Not to last! For him this coddled status-quo can continue

indefinitely, but Kathryn is a natural young woman. All this activity does is awaken maternal instincts only to pervert them – making lust vie with inhibition to plague with the warm damp of unappeased arousal.

Loving, gentle humour to start… 'But, darling, I want you to father my babies, not be one yourself. And anyway, isn't it time we began to think about getting married – started planning for the future?'

'Later… we'll talk about all that later. Lots of time for that… No hurry.'

'I know, then! How about we go out for a meal this evening? We haven't been out since you came home. Change of scenery. Do us good.'

'Wanna stay in – wanna be here 'iv oo.' The need to keep him happy buckles under aversion's incubus.

'I'm sorry, darling. We've been doing this so long. Really is time… make plans. It's no good… just can't do it any more. It's not that I don't love you. I just… can't… '

Ousted! Rejected! Deprived! Worse, humiliated! Antipathy revives.

'What's wrong then? There was me thinking we both enjoyed it. There's no harm is there? Hell, we don't even have to worry about getting you preggers do we?'

'Well, I just can't go on with it – and that's that.'

Leaping away from her he screams 'No? You bitches, you're all the same! Baby, eh? Well, how's this for grown-up?' Moving towards the sideboard he picks up a vodka bottle and waves her to the door with it.

'Oh, no! Please don't, Robin. Let's just talk about it… '

'Nothing more to be said. Now will you bugger off? Go on! Piss off!'

Turning, he pours himself a drink. When he looks back, she's gone. Rage evaporates. His eyes register infant loss.

Utterly dejected he flops down on the now empty sofa, glass in one hand, bottle in the other. Draining his drink in one gulp he puts the glass down but holds fast to the bottle.

* * *

After this, her steadily weakening trust in their future will revive every once in a while making a perfect cocktail, consisting one part love, one part pity and that essential twist of hope. Brings its own pain to the party – guest that doesn't give a damn it's not invited.

For him? Well, a man can rely on straight booze, can't he? Sister, best friend? They can sod off! As to his once-treasured love – for her, the ultimate abuse. Indifference.

As she cleans, tidies, cooks untasted meals, he will occasionally squint through an alcoholic haze as though trying to identify her. Recognition will create a lazy irritation, 'What the hell are you still doin' here?'

By this time it's nearly three years since Henry's death. For another four months or so, limping, pitying love will keep her constant; but there's a limit to the amount of virulent rejection it can take. Alcohol lards his speech with a venomous carcinogenic that carries slow silent death to her once powerful love.

Independent of each other they decide on surgery. Amputation to terminate putrescent spread.

God-forsaken sot – his course is firmly set towards irrevocable self-destruction. He knows it – doesn't care for himself, but what about her? In spite of contra-indications, he does still care. Tries not to, but hey, there it is. He's inflicted his pain on her long enough. Poor cow doesn't deserve that! Truth to tell, his misery increases every time he hurts her.

He wants her gone because he can't resist inflicting pain on them both and she's suffered long enough.

Overwhelming rage has died, leaving a weary melancholy – and a growing certainty. He doesn't want her on the journey he's going to take. She makes one last appeal. 'Can't we start again…?'

Stupid! Puerile waste of breath. Dear God, as though there's some way back!

He makes no reply, but the muscles round his mouth tighten. This is it! Stony silence – that'll do the trick.

In this, their last ever meeting, she pours out all her regrets – but never a word of reproach. The unspoken words lacerate – he barely hears those whirring round his head. When she's finished, all he says is, 'Goodbye'.

As she stumbles out of his life, Robin sits, eyes fixed on the ring he holds; the ring she has just given back – symbol of the life they should have shared. Tears welling painfully he lurches to the sideboard. Tearing open a draw he thrusts the redundant beacon into furthest darkness, never to see it again. His sigh mingles relief with fathomless regret as he reaches for the bottle.

Twelve

'So, any special boyfriend yet? Anyone nice?'

With her son's life careering towards its threshold of lonely disintegration, Ada's sentence had run well over two years. Quite the old lag!

Thanks largely to Charlie's taxi service and an understanding boss, Imogen managed regular visits, but always winced at the inevitable question.

Of course there'd been boys; several of them in fact – unfailingly forming two distinct groups. First, those initially knowing nothing of her history, merely attracted by good looks – until enlightenment created an overwhelming need for distance. Worse by far, the sons of bitches who sought her company to gratify ghoulish perversion – usually for a bet among their mates. It all left a boundless need... *someone* to love.

'As a matter of fact, I have met someone rather nice... '

'I knew it! I knew it! You've got that extra sparkle about you – thought I saw it last time. You can't keep secrets from me, you know – I always ferret them out!'

A nervous giggle. Out it comes – in a rush to get the task over with. 'Well, if you'll just give me a chance I'll tell you all about him! He's really nice... you'll like him. His name is Geoff. Geoff Parsons. His family moved in to the village a few months ago. We met on the bus home – works in town – like me. We often see each other on the bus and – and well, we've been to the cinema a few times. Last night we went out... for a meal... Italian.'

The torrent of monumental embarrassment slowed, struggling for expression – deepening as thoughts of her date return, leaving her temporarily stuttering, almost inarticulate.

Menu choice! Dreadful mistake for a start. Spaghetti bolognaise. How to look sophisticated or even vaguely civilised wading through *that* face-splatter-er? And knowing all the while 'question time' approached!

She really liked this one, knew he felt the same, but how to explain everything? Things like a drunken brother, a violently dead father, a mother's culpability and imprisonment – oh, and one further consideration. Mother was, well, a bit odd. A lot odd. All right then. NUTS!

In the years since Henry's death, self-delusion had been painfully ripped from Imogen's understanding to reveal Ada's total guilt; a process to concurrently increase pity for her poor deluded mother. And now enlightenment brought new awareness! There would be times when Ada's mental state was going to create endless embarrassment. This was just such an occasion.

Rallying a little, she smiled weakly as her mother's interrogation continued.

'Oh, lovely! Well, darling, he must be nice – or you wouldn't like him. So, what does he do for a living?'

Cut to the chase, why don't ya?

Ah now, come on! In fairness, most all mothers faced with the distinct possibility of in-law-dom will ask that one up front. Like Imogen, she was intuitively certain this was serious. Aware of her daughter's disquiet, she probably guessed most of its cause as well. She wasn't that nuts!

'He's a plumber – qualified, of course…'

'Oh… that's… marvellous! Plumbers are never short of work – name their own price!'

With fixed, bright smile, Ada silently considered. Plumber? *Don't tell me the silly girl's going to throw herself away on a plumber! What's the matter with her – selling herself short? She has looks – of a kind... and intelligence... Yes, she's bright enough! Good family too! Why? What a waste! I bet the oik can hardly believe his luck! And what will Elrington make of it? A plumber in the family...*

Trying to gain some comfort she asked, 'I expect he would like to start his own business?'

'Yes, he has talked about the possibility – some time in the future.'

Instead of reassuring, the reply hardened Ada's prejudice. He'll know I've got money. My bet is he thinks I'll set him up. Well, he can think again. They needn't come looking to me for handouts when hardship hits – as it inevitably will!

Her assessment was correct in only one aspect. He did consider himself lucky – couldn't understand why Imogen would even look at him, was a little in awe of her at this stage.

Of course, he knew all about the (official version) family history – couldn't avoid it. Fascinated debate of village folk starved of drama – becoming evermore apocryphal, caught in an amplification spiral to hell and gone, energised by greedy human imagination.

Didn't care – not him! Face all the horror of her circumstances, which, in any case, made her vulnerable – more approachable – irresistible!

Back in the restaurant he'd smiled his slow, sweet smile as she began to whisper murky depths. Reaching out to cover fluttering hands busy rearranging cutlery and breadsticks, he'd murmured, 'None of that's important....' Willing her to look full into his eyes, he'd continued, 'Only you are. You're so very beautiful… beautiful in every way. You know I love you, don't you?'

Shy, she had turned her eyes away. Gently he'd stroked her cheek to make her look at him again. Slowly, quietly but emphatically he'd told her, 'It's *you* I'm interested in – not your family.'

On the bus home, Imogen merely smiled faintly as he continued rationalising events of recent years like they were nothing. 'You silly girl,' he concluded, 'you mustn't fret so much. It'll all be all right… I'm here to look after you now… '

A spasm of grim fatalism. He would have to keep his illusions where her mother was concerned! She could never share *that* with him. The shame, awareness of danger – she couldn't inflict that cruelty on someone she loved. Maimed, she must forever hide disfigurement of a mother's guilt from a world – that included him!

Chill loneliness of her situation caused a deep shudder. Her smile faltered. Trapped! Trapped in an ever-growing web of enforced deceit. Yes, deceit! She should be able to share every aspect of her life with him like a normal couple, but… integrity's scourge must be endured. Oh, my God – *for ever*!

He misinterpreted her pensive, haunted face. 'Don't worry, love. I'm here now. Together we're strong enough for anything!'

Terrifying courage of youth, eh? Without a second thought he'd accepted the official version of her family tragedy; so armed, considered Ada's sentence too severe. *No wonder the old girl has a screw loose! As for the brother? He'll improve in time… Only started drinking after the accident. If I lost my dad that way I'd probably do the same.*

Back in the privacy of her bedroom after the prison visit, brief, atypical anger flared. Aware of Ada's unspoken reservations, she burned with inherent injustice! *How dare*

she even dream of criticising my choice? And her the cause of
so much trouble – with all her romantic nonsense!

The mood soon guttered. Following visit, chastened by irrational guilt, she shyly introduced them to each other.

If Geoff was daunted by the backdrop to that first meeting with his prospective mother-in-law, it didn't show. A frank, open face displayed nothing but cheerful anticipation as he stepped towards her, hand outstretched. 'How do you do, Mrs Phillips. I've been so looking forward to meeting you.' A faint Oxfordshire burr lent his voice a pleasant ease, making him seem more comfortable than he was. The interview continued harmoniously – with him making a determined, genuinely respectful effort.

Ada was gratified. Long time since respect for her had been routine – or even occasional. Receiving homage again was delightful revival.

She smiled approval. He was more cultured than she'd imagined. *Not bad looking either! Charming... courteous. Yes, not bad – better than anticipated – no doubt about it! What's more, he's obviously in love with Imogen. Hmm, let's face it, he would hardly be here dancing attendance if he wasn't!* Her smile relaxed and broadened as they began chatting like old friends. Yes, could be worse – much worse. Quite intelligent too.

Charlie was delighted for Imogen – delighted because, well, he didn't want her lonely like him. Delighted in spite of fear his loneliness might intensify as a result of her happiness. He needn't have worried, she would never desert him, even brought a comically apprehensive fiancé to meet him on one of her Sunday visits – visits which, with religious devotion, continued uninterrupted for the rest of his life.

Thirteen

Initially, Ada was disconcerted by the loss of her daughter's exclusive company but rapidly began to prefer the new arrangement. Genuine, mutual liking between her and Geoff was destined to become a constant.

In ensuing years, Imogen would often be disregarded – making her smile in delighted gratitude. As her mother became evermore difficult, his unreserved support was invaluable.

If he was fond of the old girl, in spite of her oddness, he wasn't taken with Robin! Sympathy survived just a couple of meetings with a surly, drink-sodden brute. For Imogen's sake he persevered with friendly niceties to a man who made no effort to conceal utter contempt, but ignoring him, growled at his sister, 'Wadja bring *him* for?'

Second time round Geoff had edged towards the door – ready to make good an escape soon as she was ready. *What a joke! That shit thinks I'm not good enough for his sister – as though he is!*

Imogen realised the two men in her life were destined for mutual antipathy; it was bitter disappointment – knew just where blame lay too.

'Don't be so dog-in-a-manger,' she whispered to her brother. In response, loud enough for his other visitor to hear, he asked, 'How can you lower yourself? He's just a country bumpkin…'

Conversely, Geoff never made judgmental remarks

about either mother or brother. She was grateful for that. And he never would – even when confidence in her love might have prompted him to take a risk. Throughout their lives together she never heard him backbite, no matter how provoked. She loved him. Loved him for his calm. Loved him for his gentle kindliness. Loved him for loving her and for never over-analysing or intellectualising anything. Faced with the immediacy of her seemingly insoluble problems, he would tell her, 'There's always a solution – it's hidden now, but never fret, all will be revealed given time.'

'You remind me of my dad.'

His family were added bonus – mother, father, sister Irene. Unquestioning, they emulated the son of the family, loving her immediately – without reservation – first meeting.

'Sit down, my lovey.' His mother managed to clear a chair, reaching for the kettle in seamless action. Never one to waste energy. Just like Ella! Imogen smiled, immediately at home.

'Cup of tea? How about a fried egg or two… and some chips? I've got a lovely, new crusty loaf too – be just right with some nice butter. Hadn't taken her long to discover Imogen's weaknesses – thoroughly approved 'em too! *Poor little mite needs fattening up… far too skinny…*

The welcome filled Imogen with reciprocal love and gratitude she would never lose.

'Let's get married.'

'Okay.'

One afternoon they kept a secret registry office appointment – and did just that.

'We're sorry. We just had to do it this way.' They stood in the family living room, blushing, embarrassed. Sorry? Evident joy in their news made sorrow a fibber – redundant in any event.

'Oh, well… I look dreadful in a hat anyway… ' Ma Parsons' response hid a world of disappointment – till she considered… *The poor love's had no choice. Why didn't we think of that before?*

When you've just turned fifteen, events sanctioning 'dressing up' are valuable. Not so discrete, arms clinging round Imogen's neck, sister Irene wailed, 'I was really looking forward to being a bridesmaid… '

'I know, darling, but we just couldn't have done it that way. D'you see?'

'Yes, I s'pose so… Oh, never mind, you're my very own sister now!' Irene's pretty face brightened at the thought.

'Glad to have you in the family, lass.' Pop Parsons rubbed a certain dampness from his reddened cheek, embarrassed by his evident weakness. Like his father before him – and the son about to leave his home, he was a plumber. Like them also, he was a man of few words, high intelligence, deep feelings, spontaneous generosity and elemental spirituality.

Temporarily sober, Robin refused to interest himself in proceedings. Ignoring Geoff, just focussing on his sister, his words were brief and brutal. 'If you must denigrate yourself, don't expect my sanction.'

They turned and fled, happiness temporarily quenched. Later, hurt subsided as sick irony in his words occurred to her. She forgave, but with reluctance – result of new loyalties. Filial alienation got another fabulous boost from that day's work.

Fourteen

They started life together on the top floor of a rambling Victorian house similar to Charlie's. Unlike Charlie's, it was in a district where better days were long past. In spite of rundown aspect, it retained remnants of elegance... and they could ignore the street – the brawling neighbours, the drunks, the growing drug culture. That was outside! Their two rooms, tiny kitchen and shared bathroom with one elderly spinster – to them it was pristine wonder. Their first home. Sacred memory throughout life.

In privacy, from their eyrie under the eaves, they watched distant river views beyond the meadow. Just below them, longboats on the canal passed the garden end with a soothing putt-putt-putt. Later, exuberance of swans beating the length of quiet, reclaimed water with their wings, would settle calm, floating gracefully in disdainful denial of furious effort.

Drained of energy after love-making's passion, floating in legitimate rapture on the nebulous chaos of their marriage bed, listening to patter of rain just above their heads. Learning to cook; glorying in culinary triumph, laughing at disaster. 'Never mind – let's have fish and chips!' Taking pride in newly learned household skills. Competing with friends – who's better at marriage? Always winning!

Only one thing marred happiness – the constant haunting of a brother's need; always there, omnipresent spectre at the feast. There grew an increasing reluctance for a task she refused to shirk...

Spending time with him – knowing a lifetime could never salve his conflict; persisting anyway – trying to silence her own desire for peace. They had shared childhood's happy memories, shared loss, shared trauma – if she failed to understand his problems, who would? But in those halcyon days of early marriage, his perspective created unwanted contrast that made her feel uncaring... guilty.

'Guilty! Why on earth should you feel guilty? Just because you want to move on after three years. Doesn't make you guilty of anything!' Redundant reasoning from Geoff. Ah, but guilt had loadsa oomph still – only just got started fer Chrisake!

Reason's voice insisted on nagging internal debate. Selfish! Why is wishing for heartsease selfish? Shallow escapism? Surely not!

Robin thought it was.

She could really dislike him for his prohibition, wanting her to share misery in hideous mutuality. She craved the freedom he begrudged.

As months passed, intransigence denied him a brighter future. Instead, life stretched ahead in sour undulations of misery, parched of human kindness. No friends left; from his sister's struggling source, the only love. Worse, he lost desire to alter existence – having grown to need it unchanged. His self-worth gone, in involuntary filial fervour he developed an overpowering need to do penance for the sins of his mother.

That he failed to perceive injustice in vicarious castigation illustrates just how sick his persona had become – as the mind that had once delighted in abstract constructs now entirely failed to cope with personal dilemma.

It wasn't the only paradox of his life at this time! In spite of heavy drinking, concurrent loss of faculty, haggard looks lost under untamed beard, slackened interest in matters of personal hygiene or social interaction, wonder of wonders, he kept his job!

Oliver Newson wasn't ready yet to concede error of judgement – besides, that young man still did an excellent job. True, you couldn't risk his contact with customers, but at the drawing board he was second to none.

Drunk or sober, or anywheres in between, he could still concentrate on intricate details in his work. This then, the only healthy aspect of life – his redemption. Work and drink – necessary as air, sustaining as any food.

Imogen's defection was personal affront. Imi. His sister – boon companion of childhood and youth, as lost as those happy times. If he allowed himself retrospection in her absence, he quite missed her. There might not be much empathy any more, but there was understanding. Better than nothing!

In rare moments of sobriety he would seek her society. His conversation now lost its belligerence, gaining a plaintive quality. 'Ah, Imi. If only your eyes had seen what mine have seen. All right, I know they didn't – I accept that, but you now know she's guilty, so how can you go on with life as though nothing has happened?'

And she would respond with the loving care that guilt, however irrational, inspires. 'I know, Robin, but you know as well as I do what a softie I am. She's deluded, you know, terribly deluded. If it wasn't for that I would hate her as much as you. Just because I can't abandon her, doesn't mean I don't love you or miss Dad – I miss him so terribly… '

Tears would soften him. 'Ah, well. It can't be helped. Don't cry, or you'll have me at it… '

Fifteen

It's something over three years down the line since Ada's sentencing. Good behaviour? Not a blemish! Early release beckons. Having done a perfect job, her automaton approaches redundancy displaying the same care as ever, leaving the boss-lady a perfect record. Only Imogen has reservations.

'It's been ages since she's mentioned Dad – I'm sure she's forgotten all about him – and she just won't entertain the subject of Robin. When I mention either of them it's as though she doesn't understand me, doesn't know who they are.' Imogen is in tears.

'Oh, darling, it just hurts her too much.' Geoff certainly hates his wife hurt!

When questioned about what she wants – where to live on release, Ada is adamant. Aversion informs every syllable. 'I never want to see that place again! Never! Do you hear me? I mean it!'

'Yes, Mummy, I understand.'

Imogen is relieved. Shares her mother's aversion – and then some. Never been back – even avoids the road approaching Brookfields. When, in the aftermath of Henry's death, among so much other business, solicitor George Benningfield had asked Ada, 'What do you want me to do about the house?' her instructions had been quite succinct.

'When it's cleaned up and decorated you'd better organise storage for the larger, more valuable items. Any other furniture will need cleaning and covering with dust sheets. Then I suppose the place should be firmly locked up. It can be sold later.'

'Fine. You can leave all that to me, you don't have to worry about a thing. I just needed to know if you wanted it sold now, but I agree about delay... let the value appreciate with time.' He was also thinking... Let the dust settle too!

All that activity happened in the dim past. Since then, guarded by local, macabre reputation the house has mouldered in uninterrupted silence.

Garden, tended so lovingly to Henry's instructions, now derelict wilderness. His favourite roses hidden under mounds of rank grass that had once been immaculate lawn. Gravelled drive smothered in dead leaves and untrodden weeds convolvulus winding greedily round and over gates to secure them better than padlocked chains.

Poor old place! Given up listening for sounds of children's laughter, music playing, whir of lawnmower, or clatter of cutlery on plates mingling with quiet, murmuring, mealtime voices.

In spite of aversion, Ada is not blind to the cheering fact that Brookfields belongs to her; it and all its contents! In her mind she moves from room to room, with businesslike efficiency recalling every detail in total clarity – furniture, furnishings, ornaments...

Inventory in hand, she moves stealthily – a thief in the night. In an entrance hall designed to impress, every item is ticked off. Then an inordinate amount of time is spent in the sitting room, business ethics discounting ruined carpet and soft furnishings. No fire this time! With sight unaffected, every antique artefact and ornament is in clearest detail. Other downstairs rooms carefully inspected – silver cutlery, cruets, candlesticks… lots more antique furniture. Kitchen? No interest here. Move on.

Climb the stairs – glance at a mahogany refectory table on the landing… Mmm, Chippendale. The glass figurine on it? Oh, yes! Lalique. Children's rooms? Don't be stupid! Pause briefly in the bedroom once shared with her husband. Avoid looking at the bed, but quickly assess remaining contents before hastily moving in to guest rooms. More interest here, more restful – and full of accessories to impress a guest. More Lalique. Some nice bronzes – and, of course, the Sevres!

Saving the best till last, she searches inside two cavernous ottomans – stroking satin sheets and soft blankets with tender, lingering fingers in sensuous anticipation.

Most of us have taken similar journeys of sentimental retrospection (even if sometimes unwillingly) recalling strange cracks in plaster, odd marks on ceilings and early morning bedroom curtains in which a rising sun reveals patterns we didn't know existed. Ada's peregrinations have nothing to do with cheering sentiment – no intrinsic happiness for her in this house! As the door slams behind her, she sighs heartfelt relief.

Nothing will persuade her in there again, but she has what she came for – a fully comprehensive list of what to keep and what to sell with the building. Some things can't be left to a mere automaton! Ada's comprehensive inventory translates effortlessly into a task for an as yet unwitting, soon to be unwilling Imogen.

'This is a list of what I shall want to keep. Take them out first and store them – carefully mind! Then contact the auctioneer. I shall want valuation with reserved prices for everything else as marked on the list, then it can all be sold with the house. Oh, and I shall need a ground-floor apartment – select area – Summertown preferably. You know me well enough to know what I'll like. When it's all done contact Benningfield and give him the list, he'll contact me for instructions. He'll do everything else.'

'What? You want me to do everything before your release. Don't you want to be involved?'

'No, darling – I trust you implicitly.'

'But... '

'But what?'

Imogen shudders. Healthy humanity forced to enter a plague house of the Middle Ages protected by a bunch of wilted herbs and a crucifix might well have been less daunted.

Geoff grins. 'Don't you worry – I'm not letting you go in there alone. Besides, there's so much to do, it'll take ages. I'll ask Ella to help as well.'

* * *

On an overcast August morning, with Ella taking charge, they hack their way to the house and enter through a protesting front door. Raucous creaking not only spoils the solemnity of the moment, but creates an understandable human reaction of near panic.

They tiptoe cautiously about, scared to disturb the undead; unnecessary caution since all ghosts have fled long before the key finished rattling. Only the spirit of Imogen's childhood remains, unseen, to stare in momentary distain at unwelcome intruders.

Ella, first to regain composure, looks at her white-faced companions. With her own awe dissipating under wet blanket pragmatism, she says, 'Come on, you two – let's get on with it! Geoff, my love, we need that lorry by the front door – and bring in the boxes and newspapers when you come back… there's a lot to wrap I expect. You come with me, Imogen. We'll start you off upstairs, then I'll come down and do the sitting room.'

Amid bustle, Imogen's dreaded chore assumes cathartic hues. No wonder ghosts have fled – saw Ella coming! No place 'ere for any self-respectin' spook! Even the little girl spirit has wandered away in search of its brother.

The work becomes light-hearted – festive even. Having forced herself into her own room, Imogen laughingly calls to Geoff, 'Here's my old teddy bear! He's got no nose! Oh, I must take him with me… '

'Go on then, maybe you can sew him on a new one.'

Later, fastening the gates, they pause for one last look. 'There, that wasn't too bad, was it?'

'Thanks to you, Ella. Don't know what we would have done without you.'

'Nonsense! We made a good team – that's all… ' Ella moves towards the lorry Geoff is already revving.

Imogen turns towards the house again. Unheard by the other two she whispers benediction, blessing and exorcism in one. 'Dear old house… have a happy future.'

It won't take long either – buyers already on the horizon, looking for beauty, bearing vivid imagination before them like battle honours.

Robin has not been told of the excursion. 'No point. It's not as though he's going to help in any way, is it?' Geoff voices unanimous reasoning.

The thought of *her* walking free, light-hearted, away from what blights his existence renews old loathing – driving him evermore urgently to the bottle. It even terrifies Imogen to be near him.

'Oh, my God, Geoff – he's just like a dangerous wild animal!'

'Please stay away from him – just for a while – till he settles down again.'

'I don't think he's going to this time.'

In Robin's warped opinion, salt in his wounds comes from knowing how much his sister is doing for their mother – forgiving her – helping her!

Then, beaten. Oh, what's the point? Briefly renewed hatred melts away, leaving him just plain empty. Without motivation his morning pilgrimage to work becomes progressively infrequent. Soon he doesn't bother at all.

Sixteen

'Here, Boo, what's happened to your friends?' They have pet names for each other – Boo is shorthand for Yogi Bear's friend Boo Boo; his is Goobie or Goobs for short – for no reason whatsoever.

'I dunno – they arrived last month, didn't they?'

'I'm sure they didn't – in fact, I can't remember the last time!'

'Oh?'

Imogen, never very practical about her own physical well-being – always down to Geoff to organise health matters – amid all the hoo-ha of Ada's impending release, has failed to notice certain physiological indications. Looking down at her waist she notices a slight enlargement for the first time. She is five months' pregnant.

'Oh!'

Consternation! 'How are we going to manage?' Joy! 'Oh, how utterly wonderful! You're happy too, aren't you?'

'Course I am – you clever Boo!'

'We'll have to move too – can't have a baby here – too many stairs. Thank God it looks like Mother's sorted. Got to find a house for us now – all three of us! How on earth can we afford it?'

Study the building society bible. Small careless investments of their life together becoming proud achievement. With Imogen's legacy, enough for a deposit!

'I'm not having you overdoing things.' He-man. Reaction

to prospective fatherhood – as universal as resultant alternating solicitude and blindness. Concentrating on the struggle of job, preparing to move house and organising Ada's new home at the same time, exhausted, Imogen sinks into an armchair after the day's graft. Contrition as he makes hot drinks she's too weary to drink. 'That's right, my love – you put your feet up… '

He reasons with himself… home-making is a 'woman thing'. In any case, he's busy too. Working all hours. Need the money. Lots to buy. The urgent desire to protect the mother of his unborn child is lost in reality.

How can either know how much work will be involved? Nest making is hard slog – just ask any care-worn bird! But it's an irresistible compulsion, same as breeding – cause of all the effort.

Brand new it is. Modest. Basic. Three-bed identikit-semi, lost amid acres of new-build Kidlington. They love it with the passion of novel ownership. Furnish it with bare essentials – bed, stove, curtains. No thought of real owners – the building society they must bow down and worship every month – bearing offerings of gold – recurring to infinity and gone.

Let it not be overlooked, our breeding pair must also build for a cuckoo. Thankfully, far from wishing to move in on them, this wily old bird demands independence – resplendent with its own palatial nest.

They'd found the ideal apartment without too much trouble. Lucky they'd called themselves! Bubbling with enthusiasm they described it to Ada. Beautiful, ground-floor apartment; spacious, well-appointed with every modern convenience, in a tree-lined Summertown avenue, which singularly matched estate-agent promise!

Well used to others anticipating her exact specifications,

the mother signs the transfer without anxiety – aware that waiting till her release will involve discomfort and inconvenience. Better trust to her daughter, then supervise alterations later.

Since it is only about half a mile away from Robin's home. Imogen sends him notification of their mother's release and her new address. Just in case...

'Forlorn hope, but you never know, he might see things different now. Anyway, he should know what's happening,' she told Geoff.

* * *

Come the big day of release, Ada simply walks into her ready-made home. She walks in tutting. Everything in the wrong place. Too much sun – 'I'll have to get blinds. Didn't you realise sun will fade my good furniture?' Blameless curtains get a vicious tug to baffle the enemy.

As she watches her daughter's swollen body heaving round on top of a stepladder fixing pelmets to her fastidious requirements, she continues to complain – only now her gripe is with the locality.

'It's too near the main road – the shops are too far away. And there are too many neighbours in close proximity.' Stopping to consider further, she mentions her main concern as though it has just occurred. 'How on earth am I going to employ a cleaner in this area? I never thought of that! It's going to be such a problem. These city women are simply not fastidious enough.' With a sigh of resignation she adds, 'It's all so very unsatisfactory!' 'Don't you remember? There are a couple of women coming round tomorrow to see you about the job. Just decide which one you think will be satisfactory. You can always specify a month's trial.'

Nothing is sufficiently unsatisfactory to warrant moving to another apartment – even in the same block; neither is the furniture ever moved – nor for that matter are window blinds purchased.

Truth is, she's more than pleased with everything – but a carping attitude will banish complacency in her family – keep them on their toes! She likes vigilance in those round her. But Imogen isn't fooled! Knows her mother's endearing little ways of old. Her father's daughter! 'Oh, don't take any notice, Goobs,' she tells a bemused husband. 'She loves it really!'

'Well! You could have fooled me… she had me convinced we were going to have to move her again.'

'No chance of that! She'll stay – you can bet your bottom dollar.'

Meanwhile, our lady of the heavenly visions retreats into her private world. *Elrington is going to love this… it's just how I anticipated!* Clucking with self-importance she settles into her luxurious domain as Geoff, Imogen and bulge move in to their modest new home.

'I wish Mother would talk to me about Baby – it would be nice to get some advice… I wonder just what she thinks about becoming a grandma? Thank goodness I've got your mum!'

In her own inimitable way, Ada has managed to avoid any of those tiresome mother-daughter conferences that mushroom between experience and initiate. She also manages to avoid looking her daughter in the stomach.

How-ev-er. Though declining a discussion on pregnancy or childbirth, she actually finds the idea of grandchildren quite appealing – so long as no one offers to confront her with the more unpleasant aspects of infancy – sleepless nights, crying, smells or anything moistly warm.

In other words, she is shaping up to be a mildly affectionate, hands-off kinda grandma. Pregnancy suits Imogen. Settled, she begins to revel in the experience; fulfilled, content, almost smug. No! *Definitely* smug! Part of that wonderful female world of creativity. Woman. The *first* woman… Eve's mother!

And so, at the end of her seventh month, with the concept of maternity leave or 'child-care facilities' a thing of the remote future, her job becomes a thing of the past. With it goes the salary that has been a bulwark between them and the economic reality of one lowly source of income.

With no suspicion of future financial harassment, she is truly happy. A little time for herself, free of irksome prison visits, no more conflicts between work and personal life. Wonderful!

Before the move she's seen Robin. Softened by her condition, he has been reassuringly approachable. In a mood of optimism she sends him a 'new address' card, leaving messages at work as well, hoping he will visit her. She doesn't realise he isn't working any more – mistaking void for tranquillity.

Seventeen

After one quick glace uphill, a man's huddled form paddles ankle deep through the quagmire of Acre End's entrance. Unmindful of mud and water, still he's careful to push the creaking gate to behind him. Cattle in here – don't want them wandering down the road…

Careless of discomfort, maintaining precarious balance among invisible hazards left by countless submerged wheel tracks, he gains relative dryness on surrounding grass where he pauses for breath. Now there is brief, intense query in his regard of the hill's summit where, clearly visible against a lowering night sky, he sees a massive black frigate breasting a gigantic wave of darkling cloud. Satisfied, he contemplates the path ahead for a few seconds, then starts to climb.

Abandoned to inclement elements in the unholy dark of a rain-soaked November midnight, recumbent beef cattle huddle together for illusive protection under an already leafless oak tree become vaguely conscious of a human shape plodding its way up their field. Reassured as it passes harmlessly by, they gratefully return to oblivion in briefly disturbed slumber.

Nearing his goal, the man smells warm, dry sweetness of straw, redolent of late summer warmth. Responding instinctively to invitation, he scrambles over one further obstacle in a barricade of recently lopped tree branches – makeshift barrier for the cattle. Once through, sheltered at last he flops gratefully down on a loose straw bale, looking about with satisfaction.

One hour later he's still in the same position – immobile, staring intently into the interior as though it holds some great truth. Rain has become even heavier by now; it's increased hammering on metal roofing eventually disturbs his reverie.

Fighting heaviness of an almost overwhelming weariness, he reluctantly stands. Moving as though without volition, he shambles towards a stack of bales and slowly begins to climb – slipping, stumbling, but ever upwards.

Nearing a roof support, he hoists himself onto a three-inch-wide girder, then rises warily till he's standing precariously on its surface. Once there he undergoes transformation – from sluggish instability to tightrope-walker agility.

Confidently upright, he sets off along the metal track to its middle where he finds a substantial piece of rope – about nine feet in length, tied securely by one end to the girder beneath his feet. A sigh of satisfied expectation escapes him as bending down, he catches and pulls it till he can grasp the loose end. This he ties into a loop, placing it jauntily round his neck. Fashion accessory! Standing upright he laughs loud at the thought.

With outraged clatter a barn owl, just finishing its mousy supper nearby, leaps out of darkness in startled fright. Recollecting dignity, its small, pale shape glides to the deepest corner of roof space. Once settled, fixing the intruder with an angry glare it becomes a wee, fist-less, pugilist ghost, bobbing and weaving in impotent threat.

For one heart-stopping moment the man almost loses balance, but steadied, looks around in surprise as though noticing surroundings for the first time. Rain drums the roof in increasing tempo as if to applaud his daring skill. With a flourish he waves to his audience.

His barn, his arena, is suddenly bathed in soft, warm, glowing gold. To his sight it becomes an Eldorado with filamented, shimmering silver circumference illuminating all arcane corners. He can see everything now! Face beautified by a joyful smile, eyes open wide to his magical vision, triumphant he shouts, 'Look at me, Imi!' then steps eagerly into his enchanted world.

Eighteen

Only Britain's Atlantic-informed weather system can produce such a morning! The same climate, seemingly inflicting infinite wind and rain, suddenly relents with breathtaking munificence in a display to uplift depression's deep.

This particular autumn morning boasts sparkling sunshine to reveal kaleidoscopic glory – every shade of green melting into browns ranging from dark chocolate to dirty mustard, whilst palest blue sky, streaked liberally with pink and silver-white, turns purple as it meets the earth in amorous, caressing fusion.

Tom Rhodes has spent much of his life in the English countryside, but never ceases to marvel at Nature's display. Loves every season – all have glory! Mornings like this endorse, but can never deepen his devotion.

This poet and sun-worshipper cheerfully pays the price of sweltering, sweating graft at harvest time – provided his deity keeps rainclouds at bay for the duration.

On a day like today he can and willingly does forgive autumn all its discomfort. He reflects how the sun can sublimate any weather. Just look how it transforms snow or hoar-frost into cake-icing pageantry! Never ceases to thrill him that. 'Lifts yer spirits just when yer needs it most,' his old father-in-law used to say. To a farmer preoccupied with lambing, it's a timely, cheering reminder that spring lurks cosy beneath its blanket.

And here it is goes again… redeeming rainclouds of the

past week, reasserting dominance over a sky that only three hours previous has been dense with incontinent, wind-driven cloud. Behold – the sun!

Despite an appearance of typical, tweed-clad, mud and straw-coated countryman who only removes boots for indoor comfort, he has been born in London's East End – four years before the second world war started.

With the threat of bombs falling, he had been evacuated – and by some wonderful serendipitous chance, landed here at Burton's Farm. He would always remain singularly grateful to fascist Germany for gifting him a wonderful war... a wonderful life!

Armistice brought sorrow to his life, returning him to an uncaring, widowed mother looking for a new life, together with what remained of a London that utterly disorientated – abandoning him to urban grime, bomb sites and hard pavements. Six years later, as a man of fifteen, he'd simply walked away from an alien landscape. Back to his beloved Oxfordshire. Back to Burton's Farm and the welcoming arms of Suzie, the farmer's black-eyed daughter. Back home! In 1956 he and his pretty little black-eyed Suzie married and bit by bit he'd taken over running the farm from old man Burton.

Now he has wife, kids – and this place in heaven.

Braking just before the gateway, he leaps down from the tractor, then picks a path along a fenced bank to reach the catch. Released, the gate swings enthusiastically out above mud and water-filled ruts. Creating a surging tidal wave, tractor and obedient flat hay-trailer churn depths of murky water. Once through, Graham glances uphill to where fifteen head of prime beef cattle casually observe his movements.

Damn, clean forgot! Running 'em here this year. Can't

trust 'em! Soon be off and away given half a chance. With fatalistic sigh, he accepts there's no avoiding cold and wet this time. Having swung open in a pronounced downward arc, the gate will need a good hard shove to catch again.

He wears his wellies with tops turned way down for easy removal (the missus objects to any blurring of division between yard and house); now he stoops to wrestle reluctant flaps up before wading into cold, uneven depths of still-swirling water. *Not a good spot to herd 'em – not much good for anything really. Too much of a hill – too boggy down here! Still, straw's high and dry – that's somethin'...*

On his way up the narrow field he's idly watched by bullocks now unsuccessfully pretending interest they don't feel anyway. Inclemency of last night's weather now forgotten, grass-green stalactites dribbling from slack mouths, they are sublimely unaware of plans for their immediate future.

Momentarily and irrationally irritated by complacent indifference, he yells, 'That's right, my beauties, you just carry on getting nice and plump, then it's market time an' Yorkshire puddings for you lot. Don't go wishing for Sunday whatever you do!' His laughter dances in sunlight as he easily removes the barrier to their night-time comfort.

Eyes reacting to gloom, he advances instinctively towards heaped bales – hook in hand ready to manoeuvre some to the waiting trailer outside.

On a level with his eyes he catches sight of a pair of shoes curiously suspended in mid-air – caked in mud, soles parting company from uppers and resembling two gnarled, wizened faces silently, maliciously cackling at the futility of it all. *Ruined!* His irrelevant verdict.

Held captive in merciless reaction, his sight travels up into gloom – past soiled trousers to long, dark, spattered coat with two white hands, stiff to attention at its sides. On up – up to a head fixed at an odd angle, seemingly just resting on the left shoulder. With most of the face mercifully covered by a fall of dark hair, the complete object gives an incongruous impression of a dozing penguin.

Dropping his bill-hook, ignoring purring tractor and bales, he flees downhill, racing past grass-engrossed cattle, splashing into standing water, vaulting the gate. Landing, he stumbles, then swiftly regains balance before charging onwards up to farmhouse safety – where Su is calmly involved in routine household chores.

'Body hanging in the barn – phone police – ambulance – anybody. Quick!'

Collapsing into a chair he sobs his grief, a small, desolate child again – paradise lost for ever this time.

* * *

After one glance at a malevolently waiting gateway, police, doctor and ambulancemen decide on the advisability of fence climbing, then silently cursing, nervously pick their way up the long, wet hill.

Doesn't take a doctor long. Looking at a waiting ambulance crew he says, 'Nothing here for you boys. You may as well make yourselves scarce.'

When all about them have fled, two hapless men assigned the task of removing a stiff, cut-down body are not so circumspect. Slithering downhill with an incubus constantly threatening to go its own way and followed at a respectful distance by increasingly curious cattle, both swear volubly at each stumbled lurch.

They agree to manoeuvre stretcher over the fence – avoiding the gate altogether. 'Well, who's goin' to know anyway?' Resting his pair of handles on the top bar, Leading Bearer climbs over at its side. Pushed, pulled, Robin's exit from Acre End field is, if anything, even less decorous than his entrance. After joining his mate the second bearer sniggers as he removes remaining handles from the fence. 'More than one way to skin a rabbit, eh? Good job no one's around to see us, though. Not all that dignified for him either, is it?'

The first man, who's idea it has been to avoid an uninviting experience excuses his decision. 'Dignified? Blimey, it's a bit late for dignity! In any case, it's not as though he's going to complain, is he? What a bleedin' place to top yerself anyway. Some folks got no consideration. An' in any case, I didn't fancy wet feet... Did you? Not in this bleedin' weather. Might catch me death!'

As mirth's explosion fades, his mate gazes at the morass. Nodding at it, he observes 'Wet feet? We'd have been up to our armpits in that lot.'

Relaxed now, chatting amiably, they bundle their grievance into a waiting black van.

Having been the cause of so much aggravation, Robin's body now lies in mute acceptance of any decision they might make on its behalf. 'At last! Time for a well-earned fag!'

Bovine residents, now genuinely interested, form a neat semi-circle round their side of the water. Gazing over the gate, they observe procedures with large, soulful eyes like professional mourners.

Nineteen

Pillows on the hospital bed are arranged to support mother as she nurses the new infant. She's crying quietly, trying not to draw attention to tears she's been told are bad for baby.

Birth just over two weeks early; delivery followed by those tears as the immediacy of childbirth subsides and blood-smeared life materialises from a pain-wracked body. Beauty, wonder – all submerged in grief as recollection hits. Motherhood's overwhelming love replacing the urge of childbirth creates a wealth of tenderness. But joy is still-born.

Looking cautiously round, she draws the tiny form ever closer, head bent, shoulders hunched over to protect it from unseen malignant forces. With her fingers she gently wipes downy peach head – where tears have fallen. Cecelia – name she gives in the forlorn exclusivity of this baptism. Patron saint of musicians. Cecilia, for father and brother – both locked away beyond death. For them, she calls her baby Cecelia.

'YUCK!' Geoff's reaction is unequivocal.

In her weakness the battle is already lost – but still she pleads a lost cause. 'Why not? For Dad and Robin… It would be so appropriate, she was born on the right date… '

'Bad omens!'

He tends towards superstition just when you wouldn't expect it. A man who walks without qualm under a paint-ladened ladder, throws out wishbone with chicken carcass, scorning the idea any one bone has special qualities. 'You hit your funny bone – right? What's to laugh at?' Now faced with naming *his* child, he will cast runes with greatest care.

She needs further convincing! He decides on some serious research. What he discovers about the singularly unfortunate saint is the decider. 'Have you any idea how the poor woman died?' he asks a vacillating Imogen. 'In any case, who would choose a name like that nowadays?'

The infant is registered. Donna – gift. Yes, both can be happy with that. But easy victory makes him feel guilty; notices increasingly prolonged periods without tears, but infrequent smiles have an underlying gravity – and are almost exclusively reserved for baby – who takes them as birthright.

Begins to understand he's been robbed. *His* wife gone – this one a stranger! With tears in his eyes, he realises his child will never know the brave-hearted, vivacious mother who, almost single-handed made their house a home. Gone forever, replaced by a subdued, slow-smiling matron, premature mellow-ripe fruit – immediate sequel to falling blossom.

Ada receives the news with silent calm. 'Delayed shock,' they say. Imogen is grateful for calm – remembering childhood's mortified embarrassment as her mother would respond to such occasions with melodramatic over-sentimentality; doesn't realise Ada has long since decided there's no profit in such energetic display. No hypocrisy then, just common-sense practicality – inspiring corresponding strength in her daughter.

Imogen's mind reviews messages left at her brother's office – the reception they received. 'He's not in today. I don't know where he is. I'll leave a note on his desk.'

'I didn't see him for almost a month,' she whispers in

miserable self-reproach. 'I was so busy... but I should have made time...'

Husband tries for a smile. 'Should? Should? Get that stupid word outta here!'

Unknown to her when she'd left messages, Robin was in process of losing his job. As drinking had intensified, work deteriorated noticeably. To make matters worse, there was no sign of him for weeks on end.

Tolerance enjoyed whilst he could do the job departs. Oliver Newson, that fine judge of character, finally admits failure. Admission creates massive spite. 'He's out, and he'll get no reference from me!'

Imogen realises reliance has been misplaced – no one prepared to act as errand boy for *him*. Suddenly! Self-preservation time. Nothing like a sacking to endorse corporate loyalties! Besides, they're not sorry to see the back of that one.

His closest colleague, one-time friend, smirks with virtue. 'It *smells* so much sweeter in here now!' Leering knowingly, he adds, 'Come on in, girls – come say hello to yer old uncle. This is now officially a BO free zone.'

The two passing clerks ignore him. Back-stabbing little runt! Even so, they have to admit...

When Imogen and Geoff clear out her brother's apartment they find her 'new address' letter – unopened, lost among the sordid clutter of home for a chronic inebriate who still has a roof.

He didn't receive her messages! So what? He knew where Ada was – and she knew where they were. Simple! All he had to do was swallow distaste and simply go ask. Imogen can't believe a desperate man would let past differences prevent him finding her. Surely he would have known, no matter how preoccupied, she would have responded to such anguished need? Young, beautiful, intelligent, loving, caring, industrious, considerate – yet she has begun to consider herself deficient.

But Ada hasn't seen or heard from him. Patiently she listens to her daughter's endless debate. 'I know, darling, it makes no sense – but then, he never did make much sense to me – always went his own way.'

Imogen's unanswered questions persist – until perplexity and guilt transmute into anger as Robin's suicide note gets more attention.

A missive subsidiary to the act; mere footnote, overshadowed, waiting. Immediately post mortem, it is simple confirmation, explanation and farewell in one. Mere existence excludes accident or murder. Sufficient at this stage – no one's making a detailed study. Shock ensures inattention.

But as shock fades, so 'the note' gains importance – gets ponderous perusal – every word eloquent with meaning as it expands in power.

Imogen knows every fatal word by heart. 'There is nothing left to live for. I claim my life. I have the right to do what I want with it. I choose the peace of oblivion. TTFN.'

Nothing left to live for? What about a sister? What price *her* peace?

'Donna will never know Uncle Robin. And why? Because Donna is *my* child. That's why! He wants to continue punishing me from beyond the grave – through my child. No! He has no *right* to inflict such agony. And TTFN? Even make a joke of it!'

Geoff gets the awful feeling these are words he will hear again and again. He's right.

Guilt, re-entering the fray, inflicts punishment commensurate with every burst of anger in a refined game of alternating cruelty. Back and forth, creating enough confusion in her unhappy mind to completely obscure injustice in punishment.

Inquest over, his grieving mother merely says, 'Well, we've got us a funeral to arrange – better make it a quiet cremation – we can do without any more fuss.'

So stark! Imogen is chilled. But there is wisdom. 'Yes, I know you're right… '

Geoff is relieved his wife has stopped crying, but fails to gauge her depth of turmoil because she has simply ceased to discuss the issue with him. What he can comprehend of her grief fills him with rage. In secret, his loathing of Robin increases post-mortem. No guilt for him! He's not sorry the bastard's gone – good riddance! He even suspects his late brother-in-law of having done it out of spite. *Be just like him! The shit.*

Imogen knows exactly what he's thinking – doesn't blame him. But now he has come to represent contradiction – the contradiction she can't tolerate.

Time will soften distress – maturity and experience will fade effects to become lasting, poignant regret, but it'll be many years before Imogen can cry again. She's all cried out. Something dries up in her – remaining shrivelled, deep and quiescent – until they demolish the old Dutch barn to build houses all over fields where she and her brother played.

Sobs – retched from the husk of anguish. Cry for pity. Cry for innocence. Cry for a dead brother. Cry for the pointlessness of his death. This time tears will bring healing – catharsis waited for so many long, dry years. As the environmentalist she's become watches the wanton destruction of hedges and trees, tears of relief will flow unfettered. As birds and wildlife flee, so will the mangy cur of guilt-ridden grief.

ACT FOUR

One

Tact, we call it. White lies (neat euphemism that – if a tad uncomfortable in a racial context!) bring mitigation to deceit – and how about that useful, jargon-ese the 'need to know' basis?

Motives for truth-avoiding subterfuge range all the way from impulse to protect individual privacy on to a more rarefied region where it's called diplomacy. All manifestations have the uncanny effect of making a virtue of deception, allowing us to avoid either discourse or other more awkward consequences.

Yes, but ultimately most all our secrets travel – whether or not, blasted by revealing life events or an overwhelming human need to unburden a disquiet conscience. And confidences of others? Tempted beyond endurance by a need to add some tasty morsel to entertaining gossip, away they go, thistledown on the wind – to generate a whole new crop of weeds.

Such luxury was proscribed for Imogen. Her secrets must be lifelong companions. Full realisation was oppressively claustrophobic. As essential compartmentalisation intensified she could do nothing but helplessly witness divisions widening.

Sensing her husband's distaste and faced with Ada's veto, only with sweet Charlie Elrington could she discuss Robin. He alone provided outlet for deprived mourning – tenderly encouraging her talk, listening patiently to thwarted grief.

In its stupid wisdom, life had denied fatherhood to Charlie, so he loved this daughter of chance who graced his lonely world, sharing her grief to the best of his ability.

'My darling, if anyone understands loss, guilt and anger, I certainly do. But I never met Robin – I wish I had, then perhaps I could be more helpful right now.'

'Oh, Charlie – without you I would have no one!'

'But you've always got Geoff… '

'No. He just doesn't understand. Not that I can blame him – I hardly understand myself.'

'But surely you can talk to your mother.'

'If I try, she just changes the subject. She and Robin were never very close you see… '

Considered his comfort incomplete? Better an incomplete comfort than none at all. His death the following year gave her yet another grief – simultaneously depriving her of all consolation.

In a bitter twist of irony, Charlie himself was in another of her compartments.

Geoff unconsciously avoided any discussion about his wife's 'fairy' friend – with her or anyone else – regarding the relationship with amused but embarrassed tolerance and Ada must remain completely unaware of the friendship – that was a given. In desperation, Imogen lied to her husband.

'Be sure never to mention Charlie to my mother – for some reason she hates him.'

'Don't worry – I won't!' Geoff had no intention of entering into a discussion with his mother-in-law that might contain the embarrassing subject of homosexuality!

In any case, Ada, with a head chock-full of delightful fantasy, was never going to recognise her Elrington in Imogen's Charlie.

And it was her mother's delusions that imposed tightest constraint on Imogen. Total silence – with two imperatives. Firstly, the entire business of Ada's grand passion with its awful consequence filled her with a shame so deep, no torture would ever extract intelligence. The second was even more exacting as the imperative to protect her mother now also extended to and engulfed her own family. No indiscretion of hers would ever endanger or hurt ANY of them.

The young Imogen had been correctly described as open, naïve, ingenuous – even unthinking and tactless. Who now would recognise the young woman who had refined a technique of discretion seemingly only achieved within the province of dubious age-given wisdom?

'The truth' silenced her more effectively than personal guilt could have done. Had that guilt been her own, so would the secret of it – with consequent freedom to confess or otherwise. No such immunity here. Candour was buried so deep she forgot it most of the time – on a masochistic whim occasionally digging it up for a quick ghoulish peek, then hastily covering it deep again. Integrity rapidly became luxury as obdurate, hateful secrets kept permanent company – gulls following the plough.

Eventually came the pain of witnessing her children prey to the same imperatives. Despite Grandma's occasionally bizarre actions, they enjoyed her company, loving her just as much as Gran Parsons. However, none of their friends would ever learn of this interesting relation. 'Wish I had a grandpa like your mummy's dad – ours died yonks ago.' But no mention of the granny who accidentally killed Grandpa – and served an unfair prison sentence as a result. Outside the family, veto was total – and who could blame them?

As to this mysterious Uncle Robin, they early learned

to put childish questions exclusively to Mum. Grannie had never heard of him, Dad just pulled a face that made them laugh. Mum would talk as long as they wanted to listen. Sadly, interest was of short duration. This was history! Uncomfortable, morbid shadows. Besides, Mum got upset! Her eyes got sad and her voice wobbled. That was awful!

Two

Land of sexual fantasy – we've all been there (oh, yes we have!) to luxuriate in luscious trance. Go on! You know the place… sanctuary, where hard facts of life are softened as proscribed desires are temporarily sanctioned. Happy, healthy place for occasional, brief visits – recharge rundown batteries – dally awhile when reality isn't being much fun.

Course there are those who want to linger – need to write a book or play, appreciate value in extensive research. Probably write a bestseller with film rights, no less! It's a grey area, but what a way to earn a crust, eh?

The majority lingering indefinitely hereabouts are harmless enough (we'll leave any excess to the criminal justice system) but here also are those social mismatches who eschew reality's introduction at all cost. Masters of self-deception; even the ugliest are desirable. Total privacy is all that's needed for illusion to flourish – with even more waves of intimate, comforting secrecy for sustenance once established.

Nodding at fifty, Ada was just such another happy space-cadet – tourist turned native. If she had been a frequent visitor before Henry's death, prison ensured almost permanent reservation. And our lady knew the route intimately, had wandered its beguiling landscape many and many a time. Here, years previously, she'd fallen in love – and been loved in return. Small wonder fierce reluctance to leave!

At this stage, free from both prison and Henry, she was still an attractive woman. To all external appearances and In spite of Holloway, years had been kind. Once more she dressed with artistic care, regular visits to her hairdresser ensured gleaming blond, whilst manicures and facials maintained other assets.

In a fierce desire to obliterate the past, she'd provided Imogen with plastic sacks and orders to clear her wardrobes.

'What, everything?'

'Yes, everything.'

'You can't just throw them away… it's criminal!'

Irony?

Reassured after a swift searching glance, she'd nodded impatiently as her daughter continued. 'Why don't I take them along to Oxfam for you?'

'Oh, do what you like! Just get rid of them.'

Out damned spot!

For years afterwards women on welfare and under-privileged pensioners were to be seen in the area, dressed in the chic exclusivity of little Bond Street numbers – the kind that never date. Meanwhile, Ada treated herself to a shopping spree or several.

Catharsis on a grand scale? Maybe. But there was another reason for renewal – one that Ada failed to relish!

With passing years she had begun to spread like a chestnut tree. Not even Bond Street could put size twelve where eighteen was more than well established. A sedentary lifestyle of self-indulgent indolence had put its not inconsiderable weight behind the menopause. And, heave-ho, me hearties! Three sizes larger and still expanding!

Ada, desperate to remain desirable and deciding 'fat' had no glamour, faced a daunting quandary. Ah, but our girl hadn't spent so long in her favourite land without picking up a few tips.

Incapable of self-denial prerequisite to a diet, her remedy was to banish full-length mirrors and avoid shop-window reflections. These measures, allied to floaty-flirty dresses and support from sundry heavy-duty corsetry, solved the problem. What problem?

It had become recognised custom to lunch with Imogen and the family most Sundays. The first visit established routine.

Taxi from Summertown. Met by son-in-law at the gate. Escorted through an open front door. Lunch served immediately. Munch through roast 'n' trimmings with gluttonous intensity – not forgetting to question quality of the food… 'My butcher's meat is so much better than the Kidlington ones. You really must see him – be well worth the effort and a little extra expense!' Pudding. Coffee. Burp. 'Pardon me!' Yawn. Best easy chair.

'You know, I've a strong feeling I'll get a visitor this week – now I'm settled.' Her voice floated through to husband and wife busy in the kitchen.

New week – old dream.

That first time, Imogen started nervously and glanced at Geoff, but he'd only heard the last three words. 'No doubt about that!' he whispered. 'She won't be coming out here to help then?' Relaxed conspirator, she smiled.

By the time this scenario had been repeated on several successive Sundays, no one, including Imogen, gave it a thought. Just another Ada-ism! Usual pronouncement, to be savoured – after-dinner mint, predictable as fluidity between table and easy chair preceding it.

Dark secrecy now surrounded her Elrington; mentioned him to no one – not even Imogen. Instead she revelled in enigma, talked a lot about some unidentified caller as though her mystified family shared the secret.

Urge to divulge would lead her thus far, but not a syllable further. Viola, a positive chatterbox by comparison. Ada never told her love – but there was nothing of grief in her smile – or green and yellow melancholy for that matter. *Her* love was unquestionably requited, so she remained "Patience on a monument" – knowing she would soon be reunited with the lover whose quintessence had been a constant companion through years of indissoluble union.[4]

Meanwhile, months following Robin's death witnessed a strange paradox unfolding. Preoccupied with sibling loss and new motherhood, at first Imogen failed to notice anything, till there was no avoiding the issue.

Death of the son whose short life had consistently failed to generate maternal solicitude now triggered rapid mental deterioration.

'Ah… poor soul!'

'Delayed shock… '

'Only to be expected!'

Ada still had her fan club!

Although not one neighbour in the "Brookfields" area had visited during her incarceration – or even given her much thought once excitement subsided, yet they'd deplored her sentence as unnatural and cruel. Now, neglect's uncomfortable guilt was submerged by fervent enthusiasm in over-compensation.

Her wretched, drunken son was utterly condemned.

'I know you shouldn't speak ill of the dead – but let's face it, he was just no good – never was. A surly beggar, even as a child!'

'Yes, and what an unnatural child. When you've suffered

as she has, a mother needs support – not another load of grief. Just another selfish act – nothing more, nothing less!'

'I quite agree!'

'Such a good mother – such a sweet woman – doesn't deserve this – not on top of all that other tragedy.'

Huddled closer together, voices lowered for conclusion, they put the final nail in. 'Y'know, I heard tell he never once went to visit her. Not once in all those years. How's that for a son?'

'How indeed… isn't it terrible? Now this! Enough to unhinge anyone…'

Amid sighs and head shaking, this flurry of concern was predictably short-lived – lasted till words might be expected to translate into action. But sympathy for the mentally challenged is one thing, getting involved and constructive is quite another. Folk prefer emotional exchanges at arm's length – like watching soap opera.

Thus, it came to pass that Ada's acolytes settled back to enjoy the entertainment, and verily, there was quite a show!

Three

'Y'know something? I sometimes wonder which planet your mother lives on – it certainly isn't this one!'

'Well, she doesn't do all that much harm – nothing too serious anyway.'

'Much harm? Let me tell you, some of the stunts she pulls are serious enough! And she's getting worse! You know she's getting worse, don't you?' Geoff's transient disquiet atypically voiced. He would normally spare his wife's feelings, but things had gotten out of hand.

Certainly far more tolerant than most would be, given his situation, over time his attitude to Ada had shifted. Still liked the old girl – after all, you had to admire her spirit, but gradually he'd assumed the perspective of an indulgent parent. Still, there were limits!

Knowing he would soon calm down, she sighed – he merely voiced her own thoughts anyway! 'Yes, you're right. I know she's getting worse… But what can we do?'

'Nothing that I can see. But I honestly don't think she'll get away with this.' Calmer already, he was referring to Ada's latest shoplifting escapade. What had started as an item or two slipped into a dainty handbag, had developed wholesale proportions. 'Poor guy – he'll carry that black eye a while yet. You realise they won't let her get away with that at any rate, the court will probably send her to some psychiatric unit or other!'

'Well, maybe that'll be for the best. This can't go on.'

A whole new dimension to what had previously been regarded, under the circumstances, as excusable misdemeanour, with verbal abuse clearly demonstrating close attention during an earlier cultural exchange and aimed at those foolish enough to object to an unorthodox take on retail therapy, had graduated to physical violence.

Truly amazing, the power of punch those dainty manicured fists were capable of. Shop assistants soon understood need for fleetness of foot. Fly like a butterfly!

When the police arrived, Ada extended her annoyance to them – in a true spirit of democracy. Sting like a bee...[5]

Now, it has to be allowed as reasonable that a constable of the force sorting out a misunderstanding involving a middle-class lady at the local pharmacy, will take a much more liberal attitude than a policeman bearing a black eye and a grudge.

During Ada's first visit to a psychiatric unit she discovered a whole new banquet for an ever-hungry self-absorption. Not since pre-trial assessment had she enjoyed centre stage – this time without threat of portentous legal proceedings too!

In his enthusiasm, newly promoted psychiatrist Dr Edward Green (call me Eddie) burned with ambition. Shine the light of new mental health convictions into murky depths of still-prevailing Victorian attitudes. Transform mental care right here in Oxford, where he'd been given a whole new department to play with. Kindle a blaze, then, modern Mercury, carry enlightenment countrywide – coincidentally, of less importance (he convinced himself) gathering kudos en route.

Psycho-analysis! Joyous voyage of self-discovery and, more important, vindication! Ada discovered deprivation and abuse inherent in an over-privileged childhood, neglect from an over-protective husband.

'How about your children, Ada?'

'Well, Eddie dear, my darling Imogen was difficult as a child, but she's grown into a really caring adult. I couldn't wish for a better daughter. She's been so helpful during and after my incarceration. But the other one… the boy… '

'Yes? Don't stop now, Ada. What was his name?'

'I… well… I can't… it's so painful.'

'Don't give up now. What was his name? Come on, tell me!'

'Rob-in. His name was Rob-in'

'Good. Robin. Now, tell me all about Robin.'

'Well, he was such an uncaring child. I don't recall him ever conversing with me. Not once. I'm sure he influenced Imogen. She was bad enough, but all I ever got from him was surly indifference.'

'What about after your husband's death? Did he visit you?'

'Again, not once… I'm sure he blamed me for what happened to my poor husband – in spite of everyone else knowing I wasn't guilty in that respect. It broke my heart… Even after my release he refused to come near me – and then… Oh, dear God… ' Unable to continue, Ada wiped her eyes.

'Take you own time now, Ada. Slow as you like, tell me what happened next. You'll feel so much better afterwards – I promise you.'

Before long she was convinced of her son's guilt. To blame – for everything! Reinforcement of self-belief – confirmation of delusions.

High on a wave of reforming zeal, convinced of Ada's cure, elucidating Eddie authorised her return to the outside world. A grateful farewell – all smiles and waves.

But. Ah, yes, but! Ada was not to be fobbed off so easily. Felt positively rejected – by Eddie of all people! The hospital – second home, her psychiatrist – the son she'd never had. Hating quotidian anti-climax, she set herself the task of manipulating a return – knew just how to do it too!

Punches levelled on this occasion contained the added outrage of banishment.

On subsequent visits to her private lulu-land she simply turned up in a taxi – even had a small room reluctantly sanctioned by a gradually less cogent Dr Green. Known simply as 'Ada's room', it had to be vacant – she refused to go anywhere other. Staff rapidly learned it was unwise to thwart.

Difficult to decide who's enthusiasm faded first – Ada's or the somewhat more sophisticated Dr Green. Having exhausted every suitable remedy to no avail, both lost interest – he with the intransigence of transmutant symptoms, she with the same old routine.

Pouring out her woes to Imogen, she wailed, 'I might just as well be back in… that place. You can have no idea how boring it gets.'

'Well, I'm quite sure you don't need them any more – there's nothing wrong with you!'

'Thank you, dear. I knew you would agree with me. That's decided it. I shan't be going back.'

With resolution came horrified realisation – Elrington would *never* have visited there!

'You know, I have a strong feeling I'll have a visitor this week. He's so persistent… '

* * *

Attendance, both voluntary and under duress, ceased. Shoplifting was just no fun any more. They saw her coming!

And anyway, drugs had calmed her aggression. Pharmaco-logical straitjacket.

Another success for enlightenment! A weighty bundle of notes landed on her long-suffering GP, almost pulverising the poor sod.

Dr Green (whatever happened to 'Eddie'?) departed for another and larger sphere, his light somewhat dimmed by bitter experience but still capable of illumination. Twinkle, twinkle little star...

Drugs caused hand tremor and a distinct loss of facial control; words refused at the jump and swallowing became unpredictable.

Ada, unaware of diminished charms, still applied make-up in assiduous perseverance – with even a certain residual skill. But her efforts gradually deteriorated, eventually merely achieving a cross between a clown with the DTs and a freshly painted watercolour of a rainbow – abandoned outdoors to the mercy of worsening weather conditions.

Four

At some point towards the end of ten years following release from prison, Ada concluded miser-dom threw a welcome veil of obfuscation over her wealth. Pretending she
was short of cash became a passion. Being Ada's passion, it
became her reality, rapidly reaching the final frontier.

Essential as oxygen to continued well-being, before long
her only extravagance was make-up – only now, she settled
for the cheapest Woolworth's could yield. At the same time,
Harrods lost a good customer as an ever-expanding Ada
began to haunt the same charity shops that had benefited so
opulently from earlier throw-away days.

In this new incarnation, she sought out floral tents to
accommodate her distended shape. An excited child, she
displayed her acquisitions to a bemused Imogen. 'Don't
you just love these loose dresses – beautifully bright and
summery. So comfortable too. You should get some – might
brighten you up a bit.'

'Certainly are lovely colours!'

With a grimace halfway between affected enthusiasm
and painful embarrassment the daughter was thinking...
*Oxford in bloom! Hope she doesn't stay in one place too long
– be in danger of getting watered – maybe even dead-headed!*
Her sense of humour... balm for a battered self-worth –
sanity's saviour.

All summer long Ada waddled the area bedecked in
floral splendour. Winter – just as easy! Oxfam sold their

best customer a huge coffee-coloured overcoat that fell in soft pleats from the yoke covering everything – almost to the ground. Grubby coloured tents, excess weight – all under a huge mobile compost heap. Where have all the flowers gone?

'By the cringe! Just look at that!' Geoff had caught sight of a large brown object clearly visible some 200 yards down a busy street. It was moving purposefully through the crowds.

With impish grin and Goon voice he turned to his family. 'Coo, Eccles, there should be a piece of string holding her down. If we could undo it – off she'd fly. Wheee! We might never see her again… '

His laughter was infectious. The children bent double in teenage mirth, but although she might think it, she baulked at voicing it, so his wife's smile was harassed by a daughter's habitual pitying embarrassment.

Life hadn't finished playing games with Ada yet either. As reluctance to purchase any but dietary essentials took effect, fat melted away. Mighty garments she had paid good money for, so continued to wear, began to resemble slowly closing, festive parasols. Meanwhile, lurking under the folds of gaudy foliage were folds of flesh. Wrinkled folds of flesh that hung like that on an elderly elephant.

Never having experienced the necessity of thrift before, still she determined not to let true facts of her life interfere with a pet enterprise.

'I really have to watch the pennies now – my money has all gone. I knew this place was too expensive, but you would insist I take it! Well, I can't face moving now, so I've no option but to economise where I can.'

Throughout the district she became a byword for parsimony. Hardened cstermongers down from London for the weekly fruit 'n' veg market ('Oh, Christ! 'Ere comes ol' Grannie 'Aggle...') respectfully picked out their best produce. Anything sub-standard was retained during the intervening week, to be loudly brought forth when the returned market was at its busiest. 'If you think I'm parting with good money for this rubbish, you must think again!' Ada loved an audience.

Come to think of it, there was just one more residual extravagance... Imogen would often find her busy arranging flowers – a task to which she still brought considerable artistry – in spite of the shakes. 'Just look at these beautiful freesias... He knows how much I adore them.'

The daughter knew quite well her mother had purchased the blooms, then had them delivered – to be received with rapturous delight. By the time they arrived at her door they'd been transformed into a tribute from 'the beloved'. No card? None needed! 'Who else is going to send me flowers?'

'Sweet smell... ' Imogen's murmur. Later she would catch her mother gazing at the contentious blooms in smiling reverie – made her feel almost envious!

When it came to her family, Ada would give occasional small gifts of cash to the children, but nothing ever ventured towards the parents. Meant what she decided when Imogen first met her future husband! Nothing given. Nothing expected. Even so, they were dumfounded as new economies bit deep. Geoff became her taxi service, 'Sorry about the van!' Whilst Imogen eventually refused to get her mother's shopping unless she was paid up front... 'We just can't afford it!'

'You can't afford it? What do you mean? I always pay my way – always have and *somehow* always will... so don't you get smart with me, my girl!'

Last to be sacrificed to Ada's take on the market economy

was her down-trodden cleaner. Put simply, Madam had no intention of doing housework herself, but still required a pristine environment – for herself and Elrington.

Never satisfied, she had followed the poor woman round, insisting standards were slipping, ignoring the fact that no one else would do the work for the kind of money she was willing to pay.

And so the struggle had continued – with an ever-decreasing supply of scouring powder and polish; would have continued indefinitely had her char (valiant heroine of a bygone age) not headed for another arena of drudgery at the local cake factory where work, although hard, was not reliant on elbow-grease alone.

Ada told all who would listen, 'Let me tell you, a poor workman always blames his tools – she just had to go!' Character assassination that none took seriously. Ada-speak. Ada the frugal. Ada the crafty. Ada the manipulative. Ada triumphant!

Regarding her mother's pathetic figure as the tale of desertion poured out, deep, dreadful foreboding took root.

Five

'Why you, for God's sake?' Thunderstruck, forlorn howl. One look at his wife's face told him discussion was dead in the water. Sometimes she was awesome! His protection? His disapproval? Pointless, simply pointless.

'Because if I don't, no one else will. Besides, this way it'll be easier to keep an eye on her!'

'But it's too much for you!'

'Oh, it's not all that much really – I can manage easily. It's on my way to the office anyway – a bit more work isn't going to make much difference.'

Guilt silenced further objection, adding impotence to frustration's scourge. The firm he had served his apprenticeship with, then continued working for after national service, folded in '68. Armed with a second mortgage on their home and in the face of Imogen's misgivings, he'd started his own plumbing business. He would make her proud!

Excellent plumber – hopeless businessman.

Philip, second and last child, arrived sixteen months after his sister. As soon as both children were old enough for primary school, Imogen had been free (oh, nebulous word!) to find a part-time job. With help from Geoff's family negotiating school holidays and extra-curricular activities, she eventually increased hours to full time.

It shamed him knowing they could never survive financially without her wages as invoice clerk. Now he swallowed righteous indignation, suffering resulting indigestion in miserable silence.

Imogen immediately felt his hurt. Regret coloured her neck. Silently cursing thoughtlessness that had hurt her sweet husband – seeming to suggest a reproach she didn't feel, but knew he thought she must, she carried on with light-hearted chat and laughter about the situation until he seemed placated and cheerful again.

'Nice– that's the best word to describe him,' she'd been told. The remark held no derision, just sincerity – and accuracy.

Resigned, Imogen would smile at some of his 'business' decisions. 'I can't possibly charge the poor old dear the full price – if I do she won't eat for a month… ' Love for him plus a certain sympathy for the customer made her reply inevitable.

'Ah well, just make sure you cover materials then… '

Loved him for his niceness; understood the appeal of self-employment that convinced him he could earn her respect – be like her father.

Father and husband, these two men had more in common than he realised. Both highly intelligent, excessively modest, characterised by pleasant personalities and utterly devoted to wife and family, they only diverged in business acumen. Geoff had none – her father's ability, although a freak of nature – had been undeniable.

Occasionally she wished he would throw in the towel – get employment with another firm – spare himself the stress of staying solvent. Her the nightmare of his paperwork; his contribution to household expenses would then be regular instead of hostage to solvency in his customers. Besides, she suspected he was often chosen as much for his 'niceness' as his plumbing skills.

But none of that mattered anyway. He'd rescued her from a life of misery – and loved her. Total love and loyalty were his reward. Ultimately, she knew she had no real wish to change anything.

Thus did good old reliable Imogen adopt her mother's chores. T'would have been easier to adopt a teenage delinquent. It was an undertaking Ada made as difficult as possible – because, hey, she was that kinda gal!

The daughter's efforts to bring order to her domestic scene were routinely frustrated since she equated order with reality, much preferring the clarity of chaos.

'Mother, have you moved the clean pillowcases? I'm sure I put them in the airing cupboard… '

'Don't ask me! I only live here – I've no control over anything any more. I didn't ask you to take over. Could well have managed without you.'

Contents of newly tidied cupboards and draws were routinely ransacked.

'And what have you moved the sideboard in front of that door for? It means a detour from the kitchen through the bedroom to get to the sitting room. Makes it difficult for both of us.' Furniture moved (by a woman so frail as to be unable to do her own housework) always to the most inconvenient places!

'No, you're right. I don't like it there after all. Move it back for me would you, dear – I'm exhausted!'

As to the bathroom, that was always in process of volcanic eruption – Ada, bemused victim of the fallout. 'I can't find my hair rollers anywhere – have you seen them?'

'Oh, Mother! You don't need them any more – not since you got your wig.'

'I know, I know! There's no need to be smart! I was simply wondering about doing it myself – now I can afford the colour! I wish you wouldn't keep putting everything away. I can never find anything…'

Wig? Oh, yes, the wig. Well, some five months into her miser-dom, the second-hand wig of shimmering, golden nylon had been Ada's inspired solution to expense and mess of the home colouring that had replaced expensive hairdressing appointments.

She never did become particularly adept with it. Often it went on sideways – whimsical version of 'pin the tail on the donkey' from where she peered out angrily through a curtain of blond eartifice at a world conspiring against her.

As the shroud of old age intensified pursuit, Ada became evermore eccentric – like she wanted to give it a good run for its money. On an endless list, activities ranged from laying siege to her favourite vicar (the clergy would be suitable companions for Elrington – let's not forget Elrington!), to wearing two large hats at once. 'I just can't make up my mind… So, I decided on both.'

Donna and Philip referred to her affectionately as their 'parallelogran'. Flamboyant, with grubby flowers and feathers to garland a time-worn wig, together with flowered tents (good value for money these!) she proudly maintained all the allure in a heap of jumble-sale rejects.

* * *

Some time towards the end of the 1970s, Ada decided she should be independently mobile. Imogen shuddered. Truly amazing, the mischief her mother was capable of on foot – awful to imagine wither a set of wheels would carry her.

So urgent the desire for independence, in a fit of

extravagance, Ada bought a second-hand moped – aptly called the 'Phillips Gad-about'. Geoff was all assurance (would he never learn?) 'Don't worry, she'll never master it – in any case, she hasn't got a licence.'

No licence? No problem! Her expertise was amazing. Born to burn! Headscarf tied wig, skirts a-billow, foot skimming road surfaces, cornering at break-neck speed, she roared up and down hills in a paroxysm of joyous freedom to halt in an agony of vulcanised liberality.

'You've got to stop her! She's terrifying!' Fear for the old lady overcame envy-tinged admiration in her fourteen-year-old grandson. His parents stood immobile with shock at his side.

Ada's career as Hell's Angel was mercifully short-lived, brought to an abrupt, dusty halt by her natural enemy, 'the law'.

Dragged from the seat of an engine that had chosen *this* moment to run out of petrol, floral flurry of billowing skirts and knickers, untethered wig askew, rage in every movement, Ada was escorted to the police station.

The desk sergeant was afterwards heard describing her arrival. 'You couldn't tell where she began or the constables left off. Like as explosion at the municipal gardens it was – flowers and helmets everywhere. I've seen a lot in my time but that really took the biscuit! My old dad remembers when she was lady of the manor. Bet she didn't make such an impact in those days!'

It ended in another spell in the mental hospital. It wasn't pleasant this time. Eddie's regime had been superseded by a return to something a lot less comforting. One session of electric shock treatment accomplished complete cure – well, it certainly subdued her desire for life in the fast lane.

'Whilst she's in the hospital, I reckon we should

rid ourselves of that blasted machine.' Hospitalisation represented breathing space – opportunity to assess the situation. 'It's certainly given us all enough excitement.'

Imogen agreed with her husband – only the children had reservations.

'Didn't we ought to wait till she gets home? It doesn't seem fair somehow.' Donna's half-hearted reluctance was shared by her brother. Both were secretly impressed by Ada's skill.

'Perhaps we could persuade her to get a licence and a crash helmet… '

'Better wait till the pigs have had their wings clipped! No, it's better it goes now. She's probably forgotten all about it anyway.' Imogen nodded reluctant agreement with her husband. Conference over.

Fortunately, Geoff had recently obtained an enduring power of attorney which he used for his wife's delinquent mother's day-to-day needs – it had become obvious the old girl's mental faculties were receding rapidly. When he'd proposed it, true to form she acquiesced without demure. Neither of them had much of a clue what was involved, there was an awful lot he didn't understand – so avoided – but his mother-in-law understood it was business and business was man's work.

Ada never enquired after the offending machine – which was curious since thrift was still life's driving force. It's certain she figured exactly what had happened – even why – but ultimately deferring to her son-in-law's will was habit. He was the only person with whom she avoided confrontation. Canny Imogen had long since prefaced all difficult suggestions with a 'Geoff says' clause. Saved a lot of agro.

So, as far as Ada was concerned, the moped vanished

of its own volition, without trace. When a buyer was found, there was another conference.

'Y'know something? I propose we use the cash towards the price of a new violin for Donna.' Warming to his theme, Geoff added, 'The child's got talent – she should be encouraged!' It was the only occasion he ever considered abusing his authority; he also felt fully justified.

Imogen was uneasy but wistful. 'I'm not sure… doesn't seem right using her money without her say so. Mind you, it'll take ages to save up…'

'Ah, come on, love… after all we've been through. She's got plenty in her Post Office account – she can afford it – wouldn't even miss it.'

'Oh, go on then. Let's do it! She'll never know.'

All the time Donna had the contentious instrument, Ada lavished looks of sorrowful regret on it whenever it caught her attention… She knew all right! But never a word did she utter.

Ada's parsimony had early become rich family joke. Christmas presents for grandchildren were cheap as she could find – usually inappropriate for that reason. She'd have preferred to avoid effort and expense altogether, but continued to punish herself year on year in order to bask in fulsome gratitude – as of right.

In early years there had been brief rebellion. 'Why should we say thank you? There's never anything much in all that old paper!' (Ada recycled last year's wrapping).

Eventually the saga became part of traditional Christmas fun, with Ada accepting flowery speeches of thanks with gracious nobility. Narrow largesse with 'It's the thought that counts!' was her maxim – and her presents did materialise after long and poignant consideration.

However, generosity only extended as far as the children.

Adults were there to spoil her – adults always had; she saw no reason to alter the dynamics. Fact she was all grown up herself never registered in her reasoning. Dissipated eleven-year-old grandmother eagerly anticipating yearly unwrapping of gift paper in search of treasure hidden amongst crackle.

Six

'Twas one of those April days that hide behind skirts of a chilly mist-oppressed early morning, only to bustle proudly out in the form of a mini heatwave come eleven o'clock.

To augment unexpected warmth's pleasure, Imogen had a whole afternoon free. No work, no mother, nothing much to do at home either. Strolling towards the bus stop, discarded jacket resting a-top her shopping bag, savouring noon's heat on her back, anticipating a pleasing prospect of lounging in the garden – book and cool drink for company, her unaccustomed mood of happy anticipation was vaguely unsettled by a disturbance on the crowded pavement some distance ahead.

Drawing nearer, mild apprehension assumed alarm, then became total devastation as a sea of ogling pedestrians parted to confront her with the approaching vision of her seventy-five-year-old mother – a vision designed to crush all joy in unsurpassed humiliation.

There, like the manifestation of some bad hallucinogenic trip, was a bikini-clad Ada, drenched in enough sun-tan oil to lubricate the engine room of an ocean liner.

'Have you seen the man with the deckchairs?' she enquired in simpering naivety of passers-by who, with eyes averted, hurried on in embarrassed haste. Undeterred by this unaccountable attitude, she sauntered on. *She* at any rate was in a goood mood! Could afford to ignore ignorance in others!

And why not? Hadn't she been so shrewd? Found this gorgeous bikini only yesterday in her favourite charity shop! In the chill of spring it had been at giveaway price – absolute bargain! Now – lo and behold – she'd been tickled awake by the fingertips of a brazen sun. Come and join the fun, it said. Yes, they would definitely have put up the price today!

Bright orange it was, in a pleasing iridescent material – just right to bring an extra glow to sun-kissed flesh. It had also been designed for the fuller, more Rubenesque figure – a standard from which Ada's body fell far short, hers being a poor, pallid object, permanently confused by dietary contradictions. Hanging in folds where fullness should have been, bulges flourished in areas where they had no business. On it, day-glow triangles merely achieved the forlorn appearance of having been abandoned on a pale beach of cascading cellulite.

Once hirsute nipple, purple-brown and wrinkled, peered out from the area that might once have been waist. It had the aspect of a startled mole, having surfaced in quite the wrong place, unsuccessfully seeking to regain subterranean safety.

Over the years Ada's bizarre dress sense had become part of local colour; almost an institution – good for a laugh. Twenty years younger and she might have been deemed a 'game old girl', the world gaining as much enjoyment from the episode as ingenious ickle Ada. At this time of life, the best reaction to be anticipated was pity – at worst, just plain old-fashioned revulsion.

Imogen's initial reaction fell into the last category. *Her* mother! Her mother's disgusting body – on public view!

Work of a second to cover strategic amounts of offence with her cardigan, then roughly steer a loudly protesting

Ada down quiet side streets in the direction of her apartment block.

Later, she poured out the full horror to a secretly amused husband. Subduing a slight tremor in his voice, he tried amelioration. 'Might have been worse – she might have been in the complete buff!'

'You weren't there – it wasn't funny! Oh, God, I was so rough with her – could have hit her I was that angry – but she hasn't got a long mirror, couldn't have known what she looked like.'

Forgiving pity had drowned angry humiliation. The intensity of her initial reaction now amazed. Her rage? Her humiliation?

'I suppose I should be used to *anything* by now… but I'm not.' Her face assumed pensive reverie. 'She used to be so beautiful… always made me feel so clumsy – a great cart horse lumbering along in her wake. These days… well, I just wish I knew what stunts she's likely to pull – wouldn't be such a shock then…'

'That crafty madam could outwit any of us – she never ceases to amaze me!'

'Don't be like that – she can't help it.'

'No, I know she can't.'

Obvious there was no joking it away this time! All earlier amusement had faded away like the mist that morning, to be replaced by the usual baffled desire to protect. Their quiet murmuring voices continued long into the night, blindly seeking the usual inconclusive conclusion.

'All those different treatments she's had – and none of any lasting good.'

'I don't think anyone has done any good at all – makes you wonder what they're being paid for. Complete waste of time and money…'

Again and again they questioned efficacy of her mother's many treatments. None had been of lasting value. True, there were long periods of relative sanity, but the price was a terrible, ugly travesty of an Ada who grimaced and gurned at a world that brought no real joy. Cured? What a joke. What a bitter joke!

'She was *so* lovely... ' Sobbing quietly, her head on his chest, Imogen drifted into a troubled sleep. He stroked her hair, whispering, 'Not as lovely as my darling Boo.'

Seven

All down the years, not one professional ever assumed lasting responsibility for Ada – her chaotic mental state never considered serious enough to warrant intervention beyond medication. Further concern went no further than a disinterested 'Leave it to the family... She has family, doesn't she? Ah, yes, a daughter – we've met her, haven't we? Steady sort. That's all right then.' But damn it, it wasn't all right at all!

And like all concerned, it never occurred to Imogen she really could do with some help. Regardless, she just battled on, lost in incomprehension's dark, with bitter experience her only mentor.

After that last shocking visit, Ada never again received psychiatric treatment, or anything remotely similar. Her GP issued prescriptions – both the hospital's and his own. That was it!

Ada had never once lost faith in her Dr Chapman, boldly overstepping parameters of dependency with unfailing enthusiasm. Never a week passed without at least two appointments to gaze on her medical guru, drink in his every word.

Over time she'd been prescribed every suitable drug and in the strictest honesty, some, although safe, perhaps not quite so suitable – anything to get the old girl gone. Ada would carry home her new prescription like battle honours, convinced of rapid results.

With religious fervour, following instructions to the

letter, she would take her latest medication for all of two days. Then, 'It's no good, Imogen. Doing me no good at all. I'll have to see him again.'

'Don't you think you should wait a day or two longer? They've hardly had time to work yet.'

'What do you know about it? You qualified as a doctor without me being aware, I presume! You don't mind if I stay with my own physician do you?'

Faith in the product was always brief; faith in her GP never wavered. Sometimes in consequent visits she forgot what condition was being treated, but a ready imagination could always produce any number of substitutes – and there was always insomnia for a good old standby in case ingenuity overslept. 'Oh, those endless nights! You can have no idea… '

Rising from her bed just before noon after eight hours of customary catch-up repose, her plaintive rationale to her daughter was, 'If I could sleep at night I wouldn't be tired out in the morning, would I?'

Since her surgery appointments were never morning ones (suspicious in itself) her doctor could never confidently question her mode of living. 'Are you sure you get up early enough, Mrs Phillips?' his tentative enquiry.

'I can assure you, Dr Chapman, I'm up every morning by seven – really look forward to that first cup of tea after a sleepless night.' Ever a firm believer in a touch of pathos to reinforce a fragile argument, she would conclude with, 'So would any poor soul!'

Her medicine cupboard was commodious enough to hold a month's groceries for the average family. Magnificent shrine to generosity endemic within the British health service of the day, over time it had contained every low-level painkiller, every assistance for the digestive system (top to bottom) and, most important of all, every type of sleeping draught known to medical science – none of which had ever had any lasting efficacious result.

Arriving unexpectedly at Ada's apartment one evening during a 1970's power cut, Imogen once surprised her mother, candle in hand, gazing into its cavernous interior. The religious parallel wasn't lost on the daughter as, embarrassed, she looked away, pretending not to notice the only light in pitch darkness.

With defensive belligerence Ada had snapped, 'What are you doing here? Where are the aspirin? I need something for this dreadful headache.'

'Oh, hello, Mother – didn't see you there. Aren't they in your handbag? They usually are.'

'Of course they're not. That's the first place I looked. Must you always talk to me as though I were slow witted?'

'Sorry, don't mean to. I just called in to make sure you're all right. Aren't the power cuts dreadful?'

Used to hearing Ada's constant gripe, Imogen usually turned a selectively deaf ear, whilst ensuring that medication for the angina her mother had begun to suffer was regularly taken. Fortunately, Ada paid this real ailment no heed, much preferring imaginary ones. Consequently, prescribed medication, which Imogen controlled, was taken without demure.

The beleaguered Dr Chapman, knowing this trustworthy daughter dispensed his patient's drugs, prudently decided against further enquiry.

But it was that cupboard with its dangerous, prescribed contents available at Ada's whim that gave our 'steady sort' her most serious misgivings. Concealing anxiety from Ada only made the predicament additionally perilous. Ada, blind to her mental shortcomings, would have been outraged by any reference to them. Imogen wasn't that brave!

Pondering every angle, she eventually hit on what she considered the perfect ploy! With assumed facial expression of slightly bored indifference she asked, 'Have you never thought of having a lock fitted on your medicine cupboard? What if someone managed to break in while you were out, they could just help themselves.'

'No one's going to break in – I'll get a better lock fitted to the front door.' Ada was all assumed nonchalance but Imogen could tell attention was alerted…

'Just as you think, only there're so many drug addicts around these days. They're desperate, you realise – get in anywhere.'

Now an increasingly alarmed, Mother stared at her, eyes clearly betraying concern she refused to admit. Time for the rubber mallet…

'Only last week some druggie climbed through old Mrs Wetherall's window and helped themselves to her tablets. Fancy that – a new prescription too! The poor old dear hadn't even had time to put it away.'

'Well, you'd better arrange it then if it'll make you feel better. I'm not worried either way.'

An additional key materialised as the contentious deterrent was fitted.

'Why have you got to have a key? You don't need it – why on earth would you?' Ada was outraged – very idea of shared access, anathema!

'Geoff feels it'll be safer that way.'

'Why?'

Affecting deafness, knowing Ada would soon forget to question, Imogen exited the apartment, new key a-jingle with other's on her key ring, calling, 'Got to go now – see you tomorrow.'

Now the difficult bit! Older prescriptions to dispose of – those bottles with one or two tablets used, lurking in the gloom of cupboard depths. Quick! Into the bathroom. Locked door. Flush 'em down the lav!

Have you ever noticed how tablets given this treatment sit grinning from the depths? Look like once valued, brightly clad party guests. Obstinate bastards – welcome long outstayed – lingering indefinitely in an increasingly chilly hall – flirting with the exit, only to be drawn back towards an apparently irresistible magnet of mangled vol-au-vents and stale dregs of a once-tempting bouquet you now feel was as pearls before swine.

Getting rid of either manifestation is no task for impatience. Armed with lavatory brush, hand poised on the handle – awaiting that moment as a tedious cistern gains sufficient capacity for a more efficient flush – only to discover it hasn't quite filled yet!

'What on earth are you up to in there? Imogen, unbolt this door at once! Do – you – hear – me?'

'Sorry, Mum. I've got *such* an upset tum... Shan't be long...'

Later, 'What on earth am I going to do, Goobs?'

'Oh, that's easy! Legerdemain.'

'What d'you mean by that? This isn't the moment to get clever!'

'It's just the moment! Listen, you get a bag from the chemist every time you collect her prescription, don't you? Well, put the new medication into the cupboard, quickly shift some of the old stuff into it, then screw the whole lot up ready to go in the bin. Mission accomplished – without loss of life or even collateral damage!'

'Genius! Why didn't I think of that?'

'Because you're too involved. It needs the distant view.'

'I guess. Mind you, I'll have to be very careful till the bag's in the garbage. Don't want 'em rattling and giving the game away!'

'Ha! That's your job. Thank God… Good luck!'

Eight

Advancing age slowly curtailed Ada's obsessive pilgrimages to her doctor, a factor that failed to make life easier for the poor, harassed guy who now found himself cursing a national medical service that expected him to pay regular visits to his patient's home for free instead.

Eventually, as her mother's short-term memory became evermore faulty, Imogen was at least able to modify demands for unnecessary medical attention.

'I must see him again. Ring for a visit.'

'He was here this morning – don't you remember?'

Ada, who hated to admit any failure of recall, would snarl, 'Of course I remember – what do you take me for? I'M NOBODY'S FOOL!'

To which her daughter would respond, 'Oh, Mother, I didn't say you were… '

'But don't you think I need him again, dear? I feel so poorly… '

'I haven't had a chance to change the prescription he left. Just going now.'

'Well, hurry up then. No wonder I'm ill. No one seems to care… '

Latterly, she was frequently stricken with chest pains and palpitations symptomatic of the heart condition only medical aid could alleviate. Since Imogen would never permit her to become genuinely distressed, Dr Chapman remained enthralled to Ada's sad world of utter dependence.

About this time the daughter assumed full control of *the* cupboard as Ada's key mysteriously disappeared. Something seemed to tell her she'd been cheated, but for the life of her, she just couldn't recall of what, or how.

* * *

During the next couple of years, floundering in confusion Ada the outrageous became Ada the in-rageous. Never again did she overrun her bikini line, but that temper continued unabated – juuuust below the surface. Bubbling, toiling, troubling – a constant seething.

The relationship between these two women continued much the same as always, one giving, one taking – in bizarre mutual need.

For Imogen it consisted of a spiral of love alloyed with heavily muted resentment that amplified with the passing years along with corresponding pity. However, contemplation of escape always ended with a rueful shrug of fatalism. She could never forget her mother must be protected – for all their sakes.

And Ada's feelings for this one surviving child? Was there *any* love at all?

As trauma of incarceration had receded, her emotions in this respect achieved a kind of neutral plateau. No real warmth, but equally the chill of Imogen's childhood memory gave no sign of recrudescence. Beneath fluffy, overdone femininity and flamboyance that had mutated to become an aura of loud confusion, Ada was still a canny old dear.

Always capable of shrewd assessment, she acknowledged reliance on her daughter, realising with painful clarity her inability to manage alone. Knew without doubt she benefited from the stability Imogen brought to life – even though it cramped her style. Yes, the girl was undeniably useful. A price worth paying – until Elrington could move in permanently. And even then?

Well, since that wretched wig had disintegrated, Imogen had been bleaching her hair for her. That would have to continue – she could hardly expect Elrington to assume such a chore. Well, a girl owes it to herself to preserve the mystery of her allure.

In spite of such considerations, though, she never restricted herself when it came to the pleasure of inflicting damage on Imogen's fragile self-worth; did it as a matter of course – unthinking. To Ada's cannibal ego, that of her daughter was easy meat.

'What a pity you didn't get my skin. Your father's side of the family were all so sallow. Maybe it's that dress of yours – that shade of green is so ageing. And I wish you would consider lightening your hair – blonde would look so much better. At least you really should do something about that grey – so very ageing! Don't ignore me when I'm talking to you… I'm only saying it for your own good.'

Nine

Meanwhile, on a more healthy note, granddaughter Donna was receiving bounty of her own as beauty and talent increased year on year.

Hands up all parents acquainted with suffering that accompanies the career of a child violinist! There should be a medal struck! Should the little darling progress past the introductory phase, pain mellows as demonic shifts gratefully into harmonic. From the hazard of this shifting perspective (there's improvement!) a real pleasure can blossom.

Even close neighbours almost enjoy ever-lengthening hours of practice. 'Could be worse – could be a wannabe drummer in a rock band, for instance... ' So it was with Donna. 'She's such a sweet child anyway.'

From first tentative fingering on a classroom hostage that seemed to sense freedom to fly in her touch, she nurtured a burning ambition for a musical career. Noting dedication and talent, her mentors considered this an eminently achievable prospect.

And brother Philip was developing other attributes in equal measure. Phil the practical, with enough intelligence to gain a 'first' in engineering and enough idealism to send him to Ethiopia with VSO after graduation to become involved in clean-water projects.

Both children had their dreams. Golden dreams with an

indestructible thread of silver pragmatism, both destined to achieve distinction.

But whilst their parents glowed with pride, Ada was completely mystified. Why all the fuss? Her grandchildren had developed into what might just as well have come from another planet. Self-imposed silence shattered in spite of respect for their father as she began to exhibit an obsessively critical attitude to Imogen.

'That boy's just wasting himself! Working for nothing! Never mind Africa... I watch the television, don't I? Always starving... always got the begging bowl out. He should be concentrating on his career... And as for Donna, well, she's just plain unfeminine. Why does a pretty young woman want to look such a fright? Stomping about in a pair of working-men's boots, clothes in tatters and *everything* pierced through with metal – nose, lips, ears – everywhere you look there's more of it winking at you... It's beyond me!'

'Well, that's how they all are now.'

Privately, Imogen could find common ground with Ada where her daughter's dress sense was concerned, but she refused to utter criticism of either child. Ada naturally had more to say.

'And another thing – why Manchester? Couldn't she go somewhere a little more refined?'

'Oh, Mother. Have you never heard of the Hallé Orchestra?'

'Of course I've heard of the Hallé. Who hasn't? But what's that got to do with it?

'Well, that's what she's aiming for – and that's Manchester-based too. Besides it's a wonderful music school. She was very lucky to get a place there.'

'Well, all I can say is, it was different when I was a young woman. It's a pity it's not a bit more like that now. They're both such a disappointment.'

'Not to *us* they're not!'

'Well, some people are more easily satisfied than others!'

Ten

Thankfully, gratefully, bouts of irrationality that have plagued Ada's earlier life fade in conjunction with her physical strength. The family maintains her independence and their own sanity with able assistance from Emmy.

Easygoing, efficient, Ada's home help reminds Imogen of Ella (now enjoying the privileges of matriarch to a growing brood of great-grandchildren).

In a happy state of complaining self-indulgence, Ada wallows in all the extra attention, then just as Emmy is about to make a bid for freedom, utters a low, plaintive moan, 'I haven't had a cup of tea all day.'

Pure invention overlooking the phalanx of cups that have passed her way already. Ah, but, she hasn't had her money's worth – not yet she hasn't! And therein lies grit in the ointment – Ada is expected to make a financial contribution!

In these glory days, when a briefly progressive British state acknowledges and even acts on a duty of care for the elderly, it isn't that much – just enough for her to regard Emmy as personal drudge. Emmy doesn't mind – she's used to it – all her old dears are the same.

'I don't know why we have to have her!' Ada's habitual complaint comes from a position of safety in assured permanence in the arrangement. 'I'm quite sure we could manage without her... After all, I'm no trouble, am I?'

Under this regime Ada's inherent laziness increases;

often she doesn't bother getting out of bed at all, save for irksome trips to the bathroom. Eventually she becomes too indolent to get anything to eat or drink either – preferring to wait for the assistance that is never far away. She never refuses any meal prepared for her either, however large, never leaving a scrap!

'My appetite's so very tiny, dear... needs to be coaxed... That was very nice... thank you... '

'Hmm, your appetite seems all right – don't think we're in any danger of you fading away,' Imogen, muttering, removing Ada's sparkling plate.

'What's that you said?' Sharp as a razor!

'Glad to see your appetite's all right – don't want you fading away. Got to keep your strength up, you know!'

Unconvinced, lazy Ada lets it pass.

Imogen welcomes the idea of her mother staying in bed, even though she knows ultimately the procedure isn't in Ada's best interest. 'I can't see the harm, so long as she gets up to go to the toilet,' she tells Emmy during one of their whispered conferences. An Ada in bed all day is one thing – an Ada in bed and incontinent is something else.

Ada's last grand passion (apart from the ever-faithful Elrington) has been her state pension. Age and widowhood have brought it – without her having to lift a finger!

Every week for around fifteen years there has been a pilgrimage to the Post Office – always late in the afternoon to accommodate sleeping arrangements and avoid other oldsters (with whom she naturally has nothing in common). It is her dream ticket – something for nothing in the form of cash!

At first she extracts just sufficient for existence then deposits the remainder in a newly opened Post Office account – with an account book containing details of deposits and (let joy be unconfined!) *interest*. That book becomes Ada's bible – with a glorious new message every week.

Interest wanes with the advent of a home help. Indolence wins as she loses the faith – her Bible is discarded among other papers in a drawer she thinks private.

Now comes new delight: CASH.

Having a "servant" means she doesn't even need to collect it herself – can barely conceal impatience for a new hoard to arrive and the wretched woman to go. No last-minute cups of tea on a Tuesday! Out of bed, eyes aglow, greedy fingers a-tremble, she crackles her progress through banknotes, counting like a child in a favourite game... One – two – three...

Loose change is discarded into jam jars – no interest there. But the lovely musty-smelling crispness of notes become elastic band-wrapped bundles – bundles that now need a place of safety.

Coming – ready or not!

'Found a lump under the large rug in the hall when I was vacuuming this morning. Right in the middle it was – £70. It's on the hall table.'

'Good grief! How'd she manage that? And her so infirm – where does she get the strength?'

'God knows. Last week it was in the oven – wonder where next week.'

'What's going on out there?' Ada dislikes conspiracy.

Emmy grins rueful understanding at Imogen. She always finds the new hoard the day after it's hidden. It's a matter of pride to her.

'I have to take my hat off to her. She's as honest as the day is long.' Imogen tells her husband that evening. 'The bundles always correspond with Mother's pension – never a note missing.'

These days she settles her mother's bills, then deposits the remainder in the now-neglected Post Office account.

Ada's increasing confusion ensures that once excitement of camouflage is over, cash out of sight, it ceases to exist for her. But she always knows which day is pension day.

Eleven

'Oh, no! No chance! She's not coming here!'

Geoff's tolerant attitude towards his mother-in-law falls dismally short of sharing a home with her. Glaring at his wife with uncharacteristic belligerence, he continues, 'I've had to stand by, year on year, and watch you being a drudge for her. I'm looking for an end to it – not for things to get worse!'

His attitude softens as he watches Imogen's face assume its now habitual, haunted aspect when the subject of her mother is up for discussion. 'I tell you, Boo, if she comes here she'll chew you up and spit out the bones.'

He loves this beautiful woman. God how he loves her! Convinced she can never equal his love because somehow he's inferior, now, with perceived threat looming, his latent insecurity becomes painfully obvious.

Unwittingly he hurts both of them. 'She'd split us up – I just know she would!'

In sudden, angry irritation she snaps, 'Don't be so daft – you know perfectly well, no one could do that!' Then pensive, she adds, 'But she'll have to leave that apartment – she's in danger and I just can't take the worry much longer.'

Maybe his assessment isn't so outlandish. He's grown to understand Ada's ruthlessly demanding, manipulative nature far better than his wife. Clouded by pitying love, her judgment also contains overwhelming personal need; together they unerringly achieve sufficient emotional confusion to ensure the depths of her mother's perfidy are, for the most part, obscured. It is no different now.

Her anxiety has caused them to blunder into one of those 'what are we going to do about Mother?' discussions – the kind that occur when dark clouds can no longer be ignored, when years of growing apprehensions are forced to confront themselves.

She's annoyed with herself. Idiot! Badly managed it – and then some! A few ill-chosen remarks borne of desperation have precipitated them into altercation – where constructive dialogue should be.

Smiling softly, she ameliorates. 'Well then, if the idea upsets you, looks like we'll just have to find a care home for her.'

Ada's opinion of the scheme lacks that quality of placid acquiescence essential to crown the project with anything like success. Her predictable reaction is explosively damning.

'Definitely not! Don't even think of it! Are you trying to suggest I'm senile? I'd rather be *dead* than enter one of those places!'

No equivocation then? No room for compromise?

'I tell you, I WOULD RATHER BE DEAD!'

As debris settles, so does Ada, but her mood remains ominously adamant. Her preferred method of dealing with the situation is stony silence, but Imogen's unusual persistence provokes the occasional belligerent response.

'I'm staying here… This is my home… No one's going to make me leave it!'

'But that's the whole point, Mother. Social Services say you're not safe on your own. It's them that won't allow you to stay here.'

She offers up a silent heartfelt 'thank you' to this obliging authority for assuming the mantle of scapegoat. Even more efficacious than 'Geoff says' – there's real authority here!

The mere mention of them alters the tone of her mother's truculence to accommodate peevishness.

'What a nerve! They don't know me from a bar of soap. Coming in here, telling me what to do… Well, they can say what they like – I'm telling you once again – I'm not moving…'

Constant drip, drip, drip. Wear down the hardest Adamantine! Eventually, even she has to admit there's a problem. A fall onto the hard unkindness of her kitchen floor one Tuesday afternoon as she seeks out a home for the weekly hoard, shakes both old bones and confidence. Unable to get up unaided, she lays for two hours waiting for help surrounded by the notes of her pension – realisation rudely dawning.

'I know! Why don't I come to live with you? That would be lovely, wouldn't it? You've got enough room now the children have left – I could fit in easily.'

Silence. Obviously something more is needed.

The ickle girly-whirley surfaces - smiling, coy, wheedling, artless. Simpering and lisping, she adds, 'Oh, g'won. You know I'd be no twubble! You'd hardly know I wus dere.'

'Well, I'll talk it over with Geoff, but I'm sure he'll say it won't work – I'd have to give up my job, and we need my salary.'

'Oh, we could manage. I jus' know dat we could.'

By this stage in her life, Ada has obscured her wealth so completely, even she believes the fabrication and is now firmly convinced of her own poverty. However, she's not about to let mere details spoil a grand plan. Sinking back into her pillows with undaunted confidence, she simply reiterates, 'I'm sure we'd manage.'

Imogen's stress levels now take off for heights uncharted. Again she starts a discussion with Geoff on her return to a home under siege, but falters in the fatigue of despair.

'Let's drop the subject for tonight. We're both too tired.' She hides her weary face in her hands for a few minutes as he just stares bleakly at her. Looking up, she smiles weakly. 'It's no good. I just don't know what to think any more. I'm really defeated this time.'

A cloud of depression envelopes both, and circumstances aren't improved by the social worker who descends from it to "help".

Designed in some diabolical drawing office specifically to exacerbate the Ada situation, she has a peculiar rotund shape – girth and height in almost exact unison. Literally bouncing into their world, she rapidly assumes the character of a baleful barrage balloon intent on blocking out all sunshine of hope. Empire State Building ego, bungalow ability – body to match – she sails into Ada's home intent on quashing all resistance with the force of her authority.

Present 'em with a juggernaut – unstoppable momentum to brook no opposition. Always works with the old dears. *Soon have this one zipped up!* Strategy never varies – listen with kindly interest – dismiss objections with world-weary, amused tolerance then with withering superiority allied with patronising inflexibility, *tell it like it is. Never fails! Especially with these genteel ones.* Complete demoralisation – success assured!

Wearing a sweet smile, Ada listens to the barrage balloon's well-worn spiel with assumed polite interest.

It's in the bag!

Exactly thirty seconds of total silence. Then thunder roars – the earth shakes in terror. Oxford's dreaming spires wake in befuddled fright from centuries of slumber. Far away a couple of rocky mountains edge nervously towards safety nearer the Pacific coast, atop the San Andreas Fault.

'Really! I've never been so insulted in all my life!'

'Well, you fat bag of shit you. Unless you want more of the same, you fuck off out of here – and stay out!' Ada's voice, loud and liberally spiced with Holloway's finest, follows the deflating balloon as it farts on its way out of her life… never to return.

Imogen weeps. 'All those months pussy-footing – just blown out of the water. Damn the woman!'

Geoff knows which woman… In a forlorn effort to comfort, he says, 'It'll be all right. You'll see – things are bound to get better soon.' Her answer is a sigh of utter defeat.

As she plods into the kitchen to begin mindlessly moving things around he's alarmed to note her shoulders have developed a definite stoop and her hair has more silver than mahogany. It cuts him to the quick. 'Damn the woman… ' he mutters. We know which woman.

He's right, of course – improvement *is* just out of sight, in the form of Irene Stokes. What a social worker should be all about. Determination, softened by compassion, bringing a wealth of understanding to her work. Could immediately sense it was going to take its time – no rushing this one.

Reversing the barrage balloon's methods, she oh-so-gradually becomes Ada's friend – then persuades her to a kind of acceptance of the project. By the end of three months, Ada makes a visit to the chosen home and is waiting for a place to become ominously vacant.

Cheers everyone… Things are mending now!

Collectively, they fail to perceive that Ada's placid acceptance belies all-consuming depression. No escape this time. Even *her* imagination buckles in contemplation of the future. A life sentence – without hope of parole!

For the first time ever, certainty's cruelty hits a life that has always brimmed with possibility. Now she realises Elrington will never find her again. The dream shrivels in the cold blast of a reality she has always been able to avoid.

Surveying the beauty of her elegant apartment, furnished with such care especially for her lover, she realises she will be saying goodbye to both when she leaves. Fantasy has always allowed her to be positive, bestowing boundless enthusiastic optimism – but that fantasy relies totally on the ambience of her home. No home – no dream.

Filled with a compound of misery and dread that only death can end, she acquiesces quietly to plans for her immediate future.

Twelve

Providentially, that reliable old bulldog Reality holds some valuable compensation for Ada in softened jaws.

As misery increases, so does a clutching affection for none other than her down-trodden daughter – growing to a degree to establish real love for another human for the first time in her history.

Since, in an act of unwilling generosity, she has given life to Imogen, the obvious conjecture is that of a right to be repaid indefinitely for the effort – get good value! Now at last there is doubt about such hypotheses.

With that growing doubt comes feeling that most would recognise as gratitude – arriving after a lifetime of exploitation. Unprecedented therefore strange, it simply makes her genuinely sentimental – a little pleasantly weepy. Then comes recognition of all her child has done for her – without complaint or hesitation. All those years – how much she has been loved – without realising as much! Is still loved! She's blessed – and so grateful. At long, long last, gratitude – and real love!

After Irene Stokes' gentle cruelty has shattered dream existence, she accepts what she privately regards as her doom. With unprecedented resignation, she never again mentions moving in with Imogen and Geoff – recognises the plan as unworkable and accepts it.

Nevertheless, concurrent with dread certainty of her destiny is growing conviction that her darling Imogen will be able to do *something* to make everything all right. Her new faith grows as days pass.

She abandons bed during the day now, preferring to sit in her chair waiting for the first sign of her daughter's approach.

Wants to know all about Imogen's day and sometimes, as she prepares to leave, will shyly beg her to stay a little longer – for a chat… 'If it's not going to delay you too much – I know how busy you are… '

'Of course I'll stay. Let's put the kettle on, shall we?'

For the very first time, Imogen relaxes in the warmth of a mother's genuine love. They chat cosily about little incidents in her day, laughing at office staff in perpetual fear of an over-bearing boss. 'They're all delighted when she has a day off – her annual leave is holiday for all!'

'Surely she doesn't worry you though… you mustn't let her worry you… '

'No chance! I do my job well. She can't find any fault with me. Don't give her the opportunity to carp, say I!'

'That's my girl!'

Asked to stay – Imogen stays. Simple as that. No matter there's so much to do at home.

'Watch out! She's still after coming here. When she turns on the charm, that's when she's most dangerous!'

Tentatively Geoff is starting to anticipate a whole lot more of his wife's company. Signs of weakening resolve? For so long, the 'Ada problem' has hung over him – a huge, dark cloud of dread – he's ultra-sensitive to any darkening in his sky.

'D'you know, I don't think she is any more – she never mentions it anyway. I think she's just terribly depressed.'

Imogen is increasingly alarmed by the changes she notices in Ada. Charmed by novel sweetness, flattered by the older woman's obvious delight in her company, she is also painfully aware that confusion of old age has recently accelerated significantly.

'I suppose it's natural,' Geoff reasons. 'What with all the upheaval and uncertainty in her life... She'll be all right after the move.'

'Mmm, there's some truth in that – but there's more. She's really altered – fundamental, if you see what I mean... Can't quite put my finger on it yet, but yes, I'm sure she's terribly unhappy.'

As the obfuscation of Ada's fantasy world vanishes, there were long spells of lucidity when conversations no longer go off at a tangent. The effect gradually reveals the true depths of her depression. Imogen realises both Ada's new-found mother love and concurrent depression have genesis in lost illusions – and weeps. She knows all about the pain of loss.

Thirteen

Ada spends her final evening luxuriating in warm, foaming-bath comfort. These days she waits till Imogen is the other side of a closed but unlocked bathroom door – just in case of difficulties!

Both women are apprehensive for her safety as frailty of age takes its toll. An impatient funeral bell.

Ritual of bath time – she loves it! Temperature just so. Pink, scented bath salts and soap, matching of course, good quality too – presents. And afterwards? Large, warm, fluffy, thick towelling sheet to sweetly envelope her dry followed by a cloud of talcum – again matching – thence into cosy-clean blue bathrobe. Sensual mix of snug and sacred to promote the sweetest of slumber.

A rainbow blending now!

In previous years she's shared this sacrament with the intimacy of dreams. Since dreams have fled leaving a world with no future, residual bath-time opulence creates one small haven of reassurance during a day filled with old-aged insecurity.

This evening she's additionally comforted by a now-firm conviction that Imogen will soon affect a rescue. It has become an *idée fixé* – giving cocooning assurance to add to her *après-bain* tranquillity. For the first time since her dream has been demolished, she feels something of hopeful optimism.

Imogen is a-bustle in the kitchen. She's preparing Ada's

supper. 'I really will have to get away early this evening… *so much to do!*… Now then, cheese on toast… not really a good idea before bed, but you love it. Touch of Worcestershire sauce. Kettle on for tea. Breakfast things set. You make sure you eat some breakfast – it's not good to go without… don't know if I can get here in the morning.'

During the past week, Dr Chapman has been called twice. Ada's already-manifest frailty has significantly increased. In this state, should Imogen fail to appear in the morning, she tends to stay in bed once more, waiting for safety of the late afternoon visit.

The daughter frets. *Tomorrow's Emmy's day off. Don't like the idea of her without a visit to the bathroom, or even a cup of tea all day. Mmm. Yes, I'll definitely have to call in on my way to work. Trouble is, she hates it when I rush off – but if I don't, I'll be late for work…*

Thus preoccupied, she cuts toast into dainty bite-sized pieces before scurrying with it into the sitting room where Ada sits in an armchair beside her bed. Placing the plate of melted cheese fragrance on a side table, she says hurriedly, 'Right. You can help yourself from there, can't you? I've cut them nice and small for you. Kettle's on. Sorry I'm in such a rush – so much to do yet.'

Happening to glace at her mother's face as she turns to go, she's transfixed by the triumphant cunning there. In sudden dread she quietly asks, 'What is it, Mum?'

No confusion now – completely lucid, Ada glances at her food, then back to her daughter's face. The triumphant expression never wavers.

'Thank you, darling… always so good to me. Mind you, I've done my bit to help where I could over the years!'

Intrigued, unaccountably apprehensive, Imogen, forgetting her need for haste, stands at her mother's side. Waiting.

315

'You remember when you moved to Kidlington?' Imogen nods, puzzled. She hasn't expected to be taken this far back!

Ada, enjoying her moment of glory, continues, 'That Robin was round here… '

Imogen starts violently. That name? On her mother's lips after so many years of silence?

'Wanted to know your new address. All dirty he was, unshaven – and smell? Phew, I tell you, he stank! And so wild… quite scared me.'

Now incapable of action, Imogen remains immobile – like in a party game waiting for the signal to move – riveted by the older woman's words. 'And as though you didn't have enough on your plate… expecting Donna at any moment… trying to get everything organised – and looking after us all at the same time… You were marvellous, darling – like you always are.'

Imogen is trembling, eyes wavering as she tries to focus on her mother's face. She must be making it up! He was never here!

'No! You had your hands full – and I told him so in no uncertain terms – gave him a piece of my mind! Told him you hadn't got a phone – said I hadn't got your new address yet. Fibs I know, but I couldn't have him pestering you. What a cheek, eh? I soon sent him packing! You see what I mean, darling? I've always done my best for you – in my little way.'

Self-righteous triumph fades, replaced by the vacant expression Ada habitually retreats behind when the subject ceases to be of interest. Within seconds, conversation is forgotten. Fumble. Ah, the remote. Switch on. Evening news. Munch scrunch toast – noisy relish. 'The cheese has got a bit cold, my love… still, never mind – it's lovely. Mmm. My favourite!'

Leaving her mother to a mixture of uncomprehended world events and simple gastronomic delight, a numb, trembling Imogen stumbles to sanctuary in the kitchen as though escaping horrific, adrenaline-pumping danger. Blinded by terror, she instinctively shuts the door quietly behind her. Legs buckling, she sinks to the floor, back tight against the door – shut out evil forces behind it.

It's an action so reminiscent of the night her father died, that fighting a mounting nausea she concentrates her mind on the horror of that time.

Murdered!

Illumination is sudden, unforeseen, dazzling – but as the glare fades Imogen is seeing clearly – for the first time since childhood. The vision leads her to hell's gates – and laughing, pushes her through.

Inebriate, her mind reels – back to the dreary confines of a prison visiting room where Ada's angling skills stranded her on the bank of mainstream life, to gasp for an existence of her own.

Typically her own sacrifices are dismissed, but thought of family joys this woman's all-devouring needs have despoiled fills her with cold rage.

It had been the work of just one small minute for Ada to make her claim to gratitude. Beyond any shadow of comforting doubt, reconstruction of events on that wild night so long ago have been authentic.

She always maintained she'd never seen him! Liar. Liar. Liar...

Sobbing quietly, she recalls rejection's misery, believing Robin had avoided her. Blamed herself! All those guilt-ridden years she'd blamed herself! Been doing life-long penance for sins uncommitted! Surging, white-hot rage brings her to her feet.

Ages that have passed since a kitchen door closed on her have been but minutes. What kitchen door? This kitchen? Now as trembling vanishes, she quietly opens it again, amazed at calm clarity in her voice answering Ada's request for tea. 'Right-ho, be there in a sec.'

As she milks and sugars the cup she hears Ada yawn. 'Think I'll go to bed now. Be much more comfy. There's nothing on the telly.'

Television off. In ensuing quiet the shuffle of slippers, then tortured squeal of bedsprings registering the old lady's movements.

'Mind you,' she continues once settled, 'I'm sure I'll never be able to sleep. Bring me those new tablets he gave me, would you? De-jocks-in they're called.' Fearless of any medical word, Ada still approaches them with a mixture of awed respect – using an awkward, staccato, phonetic form of delivery until she becomes accustomed.

'Will do.' Imogen appears bearing a tray with tea and requested medication. 'There you are. Thought you'd want them.'

'Thank you, dear. You think of everything.'

She watches as Imogen removes the child-proof cap with an ease that always fills her with envy. Philosophically shrugging off thoughts of physical loss she sinks into luxury on her pillows with a sigh of contentment. It's been a long day; she feels quite exhausted!

'There, I've taken the top off. You can help yourself can't you? I've still got a few things to do.' Imogen puts the opened bottle beside the tea on the bedside table within easy reach of her mother.

As she goes from the room a gratified Ada takes a tablet. Risking a scalded mouth, impatient, she swallows it with a sip of tea.

Within less than a minute, previous actions forgotten, she repeats the procedure. Five more tablets later, tea finished, she allows her mind to wander long-accustomed routes. Recent events have excluded the comfort of Elrington's arms, but somehow it seems appropriate tonight. She hardly notices Imogen appear once more at her bedside.

Drowsily she says, 'Bring me a glass of that nice orange squash I like – just in case I get thirsty later.'

'Okay, but don't drink too much – you'll need to get out in the night else.'

A minute or so later Imogen returns with the drink. 'There you go then. I'll clean up the rest tomorrow. Must dash – I've got a mountain of ironing to climb. See you in the morning.'

'Mmm?' Rousing slightly, Ada heaves herself up against crisp pillows. 'Yes, dear. You pop off now. You've thought of everything. See you tomorrow.'

In an empty apartment she sighs contentedly. Several tablets and sips of orange later she snuggles up to the ever-faithful Elrington.

Outside the door, clamour ceases in Imogen's head. It's raining as she walks out into the street. Her smile is reminiscent. Ah, sweet rain! Makes her think iced buns, fizzy lemonade and sweet, sweet, reassuring smell of straw. Looking up with wide-open eyes, she lets drops trickle down her face. Nearing the bus stop she turns, sees transport slowing as it approaches, hesitates for a second, shrugs, then continues walking. Snubbed – gears angrily snarl upwards again as the bus continues its route.

* * *

FINALE

Isn't memory lane a funny old place? You think you know the way, but, well, nearly got lost a few times there, I can tell you. What an afternoon! More stones and thorns than soft resting places – and so much pain – so, so much pain... Ah, but lots of happiness too – let's not forget the happy times!

Feel so tired – like I've been on the longest of hikes. Totally drained. No anger, not even too much regret and certainly no guilt. That's all over now. No more worry, no more subterfuge. I'm free of all that! Whatever free means. Huh, not as though I'm used to it, is it?

This will never do! Got to get my mind in gear – I've waffled long enough. Let me think now, there's a lot to do when someone dies, isn't there?

A funeral! Oh, my God, a funeral. How we going to pay for that? How on earth... Keep calm, girl – think, think!

We can do without the hassle of a bank loan – that's if they would consider us anyway. Wonder if there's any money in her bag. We didn't find anything these past weeks – all her usual hidey-holes stayed empty. Ah, here's her bag – let's have a dekko.

Good God! Must be hundreds in here – with 'lackey bands round 'em. Yes, bundles of £100. At least twenty bundles... £2,000!

I don't understand. What on earth was she playing at? I reckon that's enough for a funeral! Oh... I get it... The old devil! The. Old. Devil...

Oh, don't go and lose it again. Concentrate! I'm sure the registrar's office closes around four-thirty – it's nearly half-past three already. Then the funeral directors – I'm sure they can contact Dr Curtis for me. They were ever so helpful when Geoff's mum died. I shall have to make an appointment to see her lawyer too. I've no idea how thing's stand. Wonder if she made a will. Probably left it all to a cats' home! She can't have left much anyway – never seemed to have two dry sticks to rub together. Just this place.

Later, later. Concentrate on the present! Keep practical... Enough cash for the funeral directors. Everything in order here. Nothing else to do. So, where did I put my coat? Ah, yes, got it. Right, ready to go. But... trouble is, I keep seeing those little, laughing kids again in my mind's eye – flying through the air they are – wisps of straw on the breeze. Poor little souls! Never stood a chance – not against her! My beautiful brother dead, and me turned into a purblind plodder – just following the rut ahead. And what about Dad? Poor Dad. And all for a sick, empty dream!

Solace. That's what I shall be getting now – after all those years! And I've got to enjoy it for all three of us. Naa – come on! Four of us... yes, four. Knowing me, pity will include her before long – as always. Just as much a victim in a way... then there was a baby brother... Blimey, that makes five!

Oh, now I'm crying. Idiot! Come on – just one last look. Won't be seeing her again. I'll drop off the key with the funeral people. They can sort it all out – they won't need me. Won't come back till she's gone.

'Well, Mother. You've got your happy ending after all – and we've got us another funeral to arrange – for you and your wretched secret. Better make it a quiet cremation, eh? Less fuss...

NOTES

1. *"Alone, alone, all all alone." The Rime of the Ancient Mariner, Samuel Taylor Coleridge*

2. *Oh blow that thing. Paraphrase King Oliver's Creole Jazz Band 1923 recording of "Dipper-mouth Blues" on Parlaphone "Oh play that thing!"*

3. *"dancing, chancing, glancing, backing and advancing" Tarantella Hilaire Belloc*

4. *Viola", "grief in her smile", "green and yellow melancholy", "Patience on a monument" Shakespeare, Twelfth Night Act 2 Scene 4*

5. *Fly like a butterfly, sting like a bee.' Muhammad Ali*